I0561029

Henry D. Waller

History of the Town of Flushing

Long Island, New York

Henry D. Waller

History of the Town of Flushing
Long Island, New York

ISBN/EAN: 9783337369187

Printed in Europe, USA, Canada, Australia, Japan

Cover: Foto ©Andreas Hilbeck / pixelio.de

More available books at **www.hansebooks.com**

HISTORY

OF THE

TOWN OF FLUSHING

LONG ISLAND, NEW YORK

By

HENRY D. WALLER

FLUSHING

J. H. RIDENOUR

1899

PREFACE

In this age of many books one feels inclined to apologize for adding to the number. A history of Flushing has never been published. This fact has seemed to the author a sufficient excuse for the present undertaking. Mandeville's *Flushing Past and Present* contains some valuable material; but that material has not been digested, and has not been arranged in chronological order. The book cannot be called a history.

The plan pursued by the author of the following pages has been, to tell the story of our town as simply and briefly as possible, avoiding the introduction of long quotations from old documents, and in foot notes referring the reader to the authority for every statement. Only so much of the history of the Province has been introduced as was deemed necessary to explain events in the town. Without this occasional broader vision, our history would in many places be but a series of disconnected and meaningless entries.

The author is indebted to many persons for kind assistance. The files of local newspapers have frequently been referred to, in preparing the chapter on modern Flushing. To his friend, Mr. E. A. Fairchild, the author again acknowledges his indebtedness for valuable assistance and suggestions in the correction of proofs.

CONTENTS

Part III—The English Colonial Period

Part IV—The Revolutionary Period

Part V—The American Period

Appendix

THE

HISTORY OF FLUSHING

PART I—New Netherland

CHAPTER I

DISCOVERIES AND DISPUTES

To tell our story properly, we must begin at the beginning. Without a clear idea of the conflicting claims to jurisdiction in New York, advanced by the English and the Dutch, or without a general knowledge of Colonial history prior to the settlement of Flushing, many of the references to our town, that may be found in the Colonial Documents, would not be understood.

Jean and Sebastian Cabot, sailing under a commission 1498
from Henry VII of England, claimed the whole of North America for their sovereign. They passed the coast of Long Island, and were the first Europeans to do so. There is, however, no evidence that they saw the New York coast. They certainly did not land on its shore.

1524 Early in the next century, Jean de Verrazzano, a Florentine in the service of Francis I of France, entered the "most beautiful bay" of New York. In his report to Francis, he says: "After proceeding one hundred leagues, we found a very pleasant situation among some steep hills, through which a very large river, deep at its mouth, forced its way to the sea. . . We would not venture up in our vessel, without a knowledge of the mouth; therefore we took the boat, and, entering the river [i. e. the Narrows], we found the country on its banks well-peopled, the inhabitants . . . being dressed out with feathers of birds of various colours. . . . We passed up this river about half a league, when we found it formed a most beautiful lake, three leagues in circuit. . . A violent, contrary wind . . forced us to return to our ships, greatly regretting to leave this region which seemed so commodious and delightful."[1]

Thus the French were the first Europeans that visited New York. Plans for colonization were frequently discussed by these first discoverers, but nothing was done. Nearly two

1606 centuries later, James I of England granted a charter for the colonization of "that part of America, commonly called Virginia, and other parts and territories in America either ap-

1 Letter to Francis I, dated July 8, 1524. *N. Y. H. S. Coll.*, *I* (*second series*), *45, 46*. *Brodhead's New York*, *I*, *2*.

pertaining to us, or which are not actually possessed by any Christian prince or people." The country described in this charter, extended from Cape Fear to Nova Scotia. None of the colonies organized under this charter, came to New York.

In the meantime, a rival in exploration and colonization appeared. After a long and bitter struggle, Spain was compelled to acknowledge the independence of the United Provinces of the Netherlands. The energy and dauntless courage of these, now independent, Netherlanders soon caused them to push their enterprising commerce into many lands. The legend on their earliest coinage (1562), borrowed from Holy Scripture, "Thy way is in the sea and Thy paths in many waters," was not only a description of their Fatherland: it was, as well, a prophecy of their achievements abroad.

It had long been a favorite theory in Europe, that a passage to the East Indies could be found by sailing to the northwest. Henry Hudson, an Englishman, had already, in 1607 and in 1608, made two unsuccessful attempts to find this northwest passage. The London Company, under whose patronage he had sailed, declined to make further attempts. Not discouraged by his failures, Hudson sought, in Holland, assistance for another expedition. In response to his appeals, the East India Company fitted out the Half-Moon, and placed him in command. The Half-Moon is described as a Vlei-boat of eighty tons burden. It was a two-masted vessel and was a fast sailer. It was manned by a crew of twenty, Dutch and English, sailors. The commander, Hudson, was an Englishman; the "under-skipper" was a Dutchman. To Hudson's clerk, Robert Juet, we are indebted for an account of the expedition. After an eventful voyage, Hudson entered the Narrows, Sept. 3, 1609. He had first attempted to enter the Rockaway inlet to Jamaica Bay. As he sailed up the majestic river that now bears his name, he felt confident that he had at last discovered the long-sought northwest passage to the Indies. When he reached the head of navigation, he was compelled to change his mind. But he had discovered a country rich in fur, and "the finest land for cultivation that ever in my life I have trod."[2]

The Dutch were not slow to avail themselves of the opportunity offered for trade in this new country. For a time, this trade was carried on by private enterprise.
1611 Hendrick Christiaensen and Adrian Block made a voyage to the Mauritius River, as the Hudson was then called, two
1612 years after Hudson's visit. During the following year, some

2 Hudson's Journal, quoted by De Leat. *Flint's Early Long Island*, p. 5.

influential merchants of Amsterdam equipped two vessels, the Fortune and the Tiger, and dispatched them, under the command of Christiaensen and Block, to trade with the natives at the Island of Manhattan. One of their vessels was burned at Manhattan. The Onrust[3] was built to take 1614
its place. In this, the first vessel built by a European at Manhattan, Block passed through the dangerous strait of "the Hell Gate," and sailed up Long Island Sound, exploring the bays on either side. It is probable, therefore, that he was the first European to enter Flushing Bay. Block returned to Holland, during the same year. To the Amsterdam merchants, who had inaugurated this trade with the Indians, a charter was granted, securing to them the exclusive right to trade in the regions they had explored. In this charter, granted by the States General, Oct. 11, 1614, the name New Amsterdam appears for the first time. The charter gave the grantees no power of government. It 1615
was to be in force for three years from June 1, 1615. At the expiration of that time, the States General refused to renew the charter.

During the summer of the following year, an English 1619
vessel, commanded by Captain Thomas Dermer and owned by Sir Ferdinando Gorges, sailed through Long Island

3 Restless.

Sound. Dermer, in his description of Long Island, said that the island had been "hitherto taken for main." This was five years after Block's voyage in the Onrust. Dermer passed through Hell Gate—"a most dangerous cataract, among small, rocky islands"—and sailed as far south as Virginia. On his return, he met some Dutch traders at Manhattan, and warned them to quit the place, as it was English territory. This, it will be noticed, was ten years after Hudson's exploration, and eight years after the Dutch had established trade with the Indians at Manhattan.

CHAPTER II

ESTABLISHING THE COLONY OF NEW NETHERLAND

The Dutch soon realized the value of Manhattan, and 1621
the necessity of making definite arrangements for defending and governing this new-world possession. A charter was granted to the West India Company, empowering it to colonize, defend and govern New Netherland. This was the beginning of a new era. The charter provided that, for the next twenty years—from July 1, 1621—no inhabitant of the United Netherlands should sail to any part of America, without the consent of the West India Company. The Company was empowered to build forts, to appoint and discharge governors and civil and military officers, to administer justice and to promote trade. The appointment of governors and the instructions issued to them, were subject to the approval of the States General. All superior officers were required to take an oath of allegiance to the States General, and to the Company. The States General promised to protect the Company in the enjoyment of its rights, and to assist it with a grant of a million guilders—about $500,000.

Sir Dudley Carleton, the British ambassador at the Hague, protested against the West India Company's occupation of territory granted by James, to Englishmen. No attention was paid to this protest. England, in her controversies with Spain concerning papal grants, had always maintained that occupation conferred title, and that "prescription without possession is of no avail."

The Company was not fully organized, until two years
1623 after the date of the charter. Cornelius Jacobson May was
the first Director-General. To assist him, in the govern-
1626 ment of the colony, a Council was appointed, in which was vested all local authority—legislative, judicial and executive—subject to revision by the Amsterdam Chamber. The Council could fine and imprison. It could not inflict capital punishment. Persons convicted of capital offences were to be sent to Holland. Next in authority to the Director-General and his Council, was the Koopman, or Book-keeper of the Company, who acted as Secretary of the Province. Then came the Schout, whose office combined the duties of Public Prosecutor and of Sheriff. He was not a member of the Council, but was the Council's executive officer.

The Company reserved Manhattan Island for its own possession. To immigrants the Company offered as much and as they were able to improve. To any member of the

Company who would plant a colony of fifty adults, would be granted the title and authorities of a Patroon—or feudal chief. A Patroon had civil and judicial authority, within his colony. In cases involving more than fifty guilders, an appeal might be made from the Patroon's court to the Council of New Netherland.

It is somewhat strange, to say the least, that the New 1627
England Puritans protested strongly against the Hollanders' right to settle in New Netherland. It is well known that the Puritans had been treated with great kindness by the Dutch, in Holland. It may not be so well known that, when the Puritans first thought of coming to America, they asked the Prince of Orange and the States General to allow them to come as Dutch subjects—"All under the order and the command of your Princely Highness and of the High and Mighty Lords States General." They sought protection especially against the English, who were—the Puritans asserted—'inclined to deprive this state of its rights to these lands."[1] The States General were not able to grant this petition for armed protection, but it seems strange that these Puritans should deny the right of the Dutch to settle in unoccupied territory, after they had asked the Dutch to protect them in their right to do so, and had even desired to

---

1 *Historical Documents I*, 22 *et sq.*

come as subjects of these same Dutch. The friction between the New Englanders and the New Netherlanders, so early begun, never entirely ceased. The Cavalier colonists of Virginia were always more friendly to the Hollanders in
1633 New Netherland, than were their more austere neighbors at the north. There is land enough;"—said Sir John Harvey, Governor of Virginia, to De Vries—"we should be good neighbors. You will have no trouble from us—if only those of New England do not approach too near you."[2]

The English never relinquished their asserted right to dispose of the whole of North America, from Nova Scotia to Cape Fear.[3] One of the last acts of the Plymouth Com-
1635 pany was, to convey to William, Earl of Sterling, "part of New England, and an island adjacent, called Long Island."[4] This act gave the Director-General and the Council of New
1638 Netherland, no little trouble. Lord Sterling gave to James Farret, a power of attorney, to dispose of any of his prop-

---

2 *De Vries, p. 110. Brodhead I, 227.*

3 To complicate matters still further, Charles I granted to Sir Edmund Plowden and eight other petitioners (June 21, 1634), the whole of Long Island and forty leagues square of the adjoining continent, to form a county Palatine, to be known as New Albion. Plowden was created Earl Palatine of New Albion. He spent the remainder of his life in trying to make his title good. He died in 1659. His descendants claimed the title until the close of the eighteenth century.

4 *Documents III, 42. Brodhead I, 259.*

erty on Long Island or in its neighborhood. Farret selected 1639
for his own use Shelter Island and Robins Island, in Peconic
Bay, confirmed Lion Gardiner's title to the island that still
bears his name, and induced a colony from Lynn, Mass., to 1640
settle on Cow Bay. He next appeared at Manhattan and, in
the name of Lord Sterling, claimed the whole of Long Island. "His pretention was not much regarded, and so he
departed, without accomplishing anything, having influenced only a few people." [5] The colony at Cow Bay was
broken up. Thus ended the first attempt to plant an English colony within the present limits of Queens County.

Governor Kieft had already, at the beginning of the 1639
previous year, (Jan. 15, 1639), secured, from the Indians, a title to what is now Queens County. The land was sold "for, and in consideration of, a party of merchandise, which they acknowledge to have received into their hands and power, to their full satisfaction and content." The chief sachem reserved the right, "with his people and friends, to remain upon the aforesaid land, plant corn, fish, hunt, and make a living there as well as they can, while he himself and his people place themselves under the protection of the said Lords." [6]

---

5 *Thompson's Long Island I*, *117*, *305*. *Brodhead I*, *298*.
6 *Historical Documents XIV*, *15*.

1643 Kieft had, since 1640, been carrying on an unjust war against the Indians on the main land, but the Long Island Indians remained friendly to the Dutch. The Colonists, on the west end of the Island, desired to extend this war to the friendly tribes about them. The Council prevailed on Kieft to withhold his consent. This he did for two reasons; viz., the Marechkawieks had always been friendly, and they would be "hard to conquer." Nevertheless, he added, after this commingling of gratitude and prudence, that every colonist was authorized to defend himself, should the Indians show signs of hostility. It was not difficult to induce the Indians to exhibit the desired signs of hostility. A foraging expedition was set on foot and the unsuspecting Indians were robbed of two wagon-loads of grain. In the attempt to protect their property, three Indians were killed.[7] A general uprising and a cruel war followed. One of the sufferers, in this war, was the Rev. Francis Doughty, who had settled at Mespat. We shall refer to him again.

Having begun the war, the Dutch found it difficult to make peace with the Indians. "Are you our friends?" said the Indians to Kieft, when he sought peace. "You are corn thieves."

---

7 *Historical Documents I, 184.*

Peace was, however, at last secured. The ways of the strangers seemed inexplicable to the Indians. A number of them attended a religious meeting, held by the pious Domine Magapolensis. They stood about, with pipes in their mouths, regarding this strange procedure. They asked the good Domine what he wanted, standing there alone, making so many words, and not allowing the others to speak. He replied: "I admonish the Christians that they must not steal, nor drink, nor commit lewdness and murder." The Indians solemnly gave their approval of such instruction, and wonderingly added: "Why do so many Christians do these things?"[8] 1644

8 *N. Y. H. S. Coll.*, *(second series) III*, *149-160*. *Broadhead I*, *375*, *et sq.*

PART II—The Dutch Colonial Period

CHAPTER III

1645 THE SETTLEMENT OF FLUSHING

The spring of 1645 saw an end of the Indian wars that, for five years, had harassed the colonists. During these five years, they had enjoyed scarcely five months of peace. A day of Thanksgiving was proclaimed, and was observed, with great joy, on the sixth of September.

The restoration of peace, encouraged the planting of new colonies in New Netherland. The liberal policy of the Government caused many colonists in New England to look to New Netherland for the freedom of conscience which they had failed to find among the Puritans. Francis Doughty was, by no means, the only person who found that he "had got from the pan into the fire," [1] when he went from England to New England. "In Massachusetts," says Judge Story, "the arm of the civil government was constantly

---

1 *The Representation of New Netherland*, p. 51.

employed in support of denunciations of the Church: and, without its forms, the Inquisition existed in substance, with a full share of its terrors and its violence." [2] The Hollanders, in New Netherland, were not always so tolerant in fact, as their laws required: still they offered a brilliant contrast to their Puritan neighbors.

Among the many other English colonists, who sought the protection of the Dutch colony of New Netherland, were the incorporators of the town of Vlissigen. The name appears in many different forms: we shall hereafter use the modern spelling, except when quoting from old documents. There appears to be no authority for the tradition, that the incorporators chose the name, because they had at one time found refuge in the Holland town of the same name. The creek was evidently called Flushing Creek, before the arrival of the English settlers, for the charter describes the boundary in these words: "To begin at ye westward part thereof, at the Mouth of a Creeke upon the East River, now commonly called and knowne by the name of fflushing Creeke" etc. [3] The patentees, or incorporators, were: Thomas Farington, John Townsend, Thomas Stiles, Thomas Saull,

---

2 Miscellanies, *p. 66*.

3 The date of the Charter is Oct. 10, 1645. See Appendix I.

John Marston, Robert Field, Thomas Applegate, Thomas Beddard, Laurence Dutch, John Laurence, William Laurence, William Thorne, Henry Sautell, William Pigeon, Micheall Milliard, Robert Firman, John Hicks, Edward Hart. The original draft of the charter conveyed to these men all the land between the east and west limits of Flushing, from the sound to the ocean. A memorandum affixed to the charter before it was signed and sealed, placed the southern limits of the town "as far as the Hills." This rather indefinite boundary was, in later years, the cause of much dispute with Jamaica. William Thorne had come to Flushing or rather to the region that now became Flushing three years before, and had settled at Thorne's Neck. John Lawrence was one of the incorporators of Hempstead, in 1644. He now joined his brother William, as an incorporator of Flushing. John Lawrence repeatedly held important offices under both the Dutch and the English. He was several times Mayor of New Amsterdam, and, at the time of his death, in 1699, was Judge of the Supreme Court. William Lawrence was a magistrate of Flushing, under both the Dutch and the English, and held other offices of importance=civil and military. He died in 1680.[4]

The original inhabitants of the region, now incorporated

---

4 *Thompson's Long Island II*, 362.

as Flushing, were the Matinecock Indians. They sold the land to the Dutch, at the rate of fifty acres for an axe. The Long Island Indians "were a seafaring race, mild in temperament, diligent in the pursuits determined by their environment, skilled in the management of canoe, of seine, or spear, and dextrous in the making of seawan, or wampum."[5] The shores of the Island supplied abundance of shells, from which this Indian currency was made. This fact gave the Island its earliest name—Sewan-hacky, i. e. the Land of Shells. Sewan, or wampum, was the common currency among the Indians and was extensively used by the colonists.[6] The black wampum was made from the purple part of the quohang shell.[7] One bead of this black wampum was equivalent to an English farthing, and had twice the value of the white wampum, which was made

5 *Flint's Early Long Island, p. 45 et sq.*

6 The following tradition, concerning the scarcity of silver money, is taken from a note on a fly-leaf of an old vestry book of St. George's parish. The date of the writing is about 1797. "Even as late as 1670, an English shilling being found in the road, a mile east of the landing, it was immediately concluded to belong to one Lawrence, who kept a few articles to sell, as they could not think of any other person in the town who had such a thing as a silver shilling."

7 "The Quohang, or whelk, was the *Buccinum Undulatum.* As that became rare, the common clam, *Venus Mercenaria*, was used.". *Flint.*

of the periwinkle shell.[8] Long Island became the colonial mint; and the manufacture and exportation of wampum became the source of considerable profit. But even at this early date, the problem of a depreciated currency, circulating side by side with one of standard value, troubled the Dutch. In 1641, an ordinance was passed setting forth the fact that "bad wampum is at present circulated here, and payment is made in nothing but rough, unpolished stuff . . . and the good, polished wampum is wholly put out of sight or exported." The ordinance, therefore, provided that the inferior wampum should be accepted for only three-fourths of the value of good wampum.[9]

The government, provided by the Charter, was very simple. The pantentees were to "enjoy the liberty of conscience according to the custom and manner of Holland, without molestation or disturbance from any magistrate, or magistrates, or any other ecclesiastical minister." They were to elect a Schout, or Sheriff, whose duty it should be to preserve order and arrest offenders. The offenders were to be taken before the Director-General for trial. At the end of ten years, the inhabitants of the town were to pay to the

---

8 *Turbo Littoreus.*

9 *Laws and Ordinances of New Netherland*, p. 26.

general government a tax of one tenth of their product for that year.

The colony at Flushing appears to have prospered from the beginning.[10] Director-General Stuyvesant said that when he took charge of New Netherland, one year after the settlement of Flushing: "The Flatland [was] stripped of inhabitants to such a degree that, with the exception of the three English villages of Heempstede, New Flushing and Gravesend, there were not fifty bouweries or plantations on it [i. e. on Long Island] and the whole Province could not muster two hundred and fifty, at the most three hundred, men capable of bearing arms."[11] 1646

The little village was only two years old, when it was drawn into the dispute, between England and Holland, concerning the ownership of Long Island. Lord Stirling, to whom the Plymouth Company had deeded the Island, died, leaving his title to his wife. She appointed a Scotch- 1647

---

10 From contemporary documents we may learn the prices current, about the time of the settlement of Flushing. The prices are given in florins and stivers. There were twenty stivers in a florin; a florin was equivalent to forty cents. An ax was worth about 2 fl.; a scythe or spade, 2 fl. 10 st.; a plough, 28 fl. 16st.; a ploughshare, 25 fl.; wheat brought 2 fl. 10 st. per schepel (3 pecks); Indian corn, 1 fl. 10st.: oats, 1 fl.; a horse, 160 fl.; a cow, from 50 fl to 120 fl.—*Account Books of Rensselaerswyck. O'Callaghan's New Netherland I, 477.*

11 *Documents, II, 365.*

man, named Andrew Forrester,[12] to be Governor of Long Island, and gave to him a power of attorney. Forrester appeared in Flushing, in Sept., 1647, and proclaimed himself, Governor of Long Island. He exhibited his commision, to which was attached an old broken seal, but which bore no signature. He was also armed with a power of attorney, signed by "Mary Steerling." The Schout notified Stuyvesant of Forrester's arrival and of his claims, and asked for instructions. Forrester was arrested, and sent as a prisoner to Holland, that he might plead his cause before their High Mightinesses, the States General. The vessel, on which he sailed, put in at an English port, on its way to Holland, and Forrester made his escape.[13]

During the same year, the Rev. Francis Doughty came to Flushing, as its first minister of the Gospel. He had been a Church of England clergyman, and was silenced for non-conformity.[14] In 1637, he emigrated to Massachusetts, and settled at Cohannet, now Taunton. Here he gave utterance to what was considered heretical doctrine. In a

---

12 Some historians speak of Forrester and Farret, who came as Lord Stirling's agent in 1639, as one and the same person. I can find no reason for this. The surnames are similar, but one is called James and the other Andrew.

13 *Documents, I, 286.*

14 *Flints's Early Long Island, p. 163.*

public address, he said he thought Abraham's children should have been baptized. This statement greatly scandalized Mr. Hook, the Pastor of the town, and his assistant, Mr. Street. They reported the matter to the magistrates, who ordered Doughty's arrest. He was brought for trial before Wilson, Mather, and other ministers, and "was forced to go away from thence, with his wife and children." [15] This was in 1642. He went first to Rhode Island, and then, with a company of friends, came to Long Island, "in order to enjoy freedom of conscience." [16] New Netherland granted to Doughty and his company a patent for 13,332 acres of land at Mespat, now Newtown. Here they settled, Doughty acting as their minister. But the Indian war, already referred to, broke out. The colonists were scattered and their property was destroyed. For two years, Doughty preached to the English residents at New Amsterdam. At the restoration of peace, about 1645, Doughty and his companions returned to their land in Newtown, but not to the harmonious possession of it. Doughty desired to play the Patroon, whereas his companions regarded him as one of a number of equal pantentees. The case was referred to the

15 *Plain Dealings or News from New England, Thomas Lechford, London 1642, p. 41. Mass. Hist. Coll. Third Series, III, 96.*

16 *Riker's Annals of Newtown, p. 17.*

Director-General and Council, at Manhattan. It was decided that Doughty had control over no land but his own farm. He refused to recognize the jurisdiction of the court, saying he would appeal to Holland. For this he was arrested, imprisoned, and fined twenty-five guilders. The matter was happily settled, for Newtown and for the Director-General, by Doughty's receiving a call to Flushing. It came out later, that Flushing's representatives had not acted from their own free will in this matter, but under intimidation by Stuyvesant. The Director-General took them, one by one, into a room, and, by threat, compelled them to sign the articles of agreement with Doughty. What arguments or threats were used, we are not told. The Director-General seemed to be very desirous to provide for Doughty—whether in order to relieve himself of a troublesome person, or because he had exceeded his authority in punishing Doughty, it is hard to say. The agreement, however, was signed: and Doughty was settled in Flushing, at a salary of 600 guilders a year.[17]

17 Doughty was apparently not popular, as witnesses the following record: "June 10, 1647, Wm. Garretse sings libelous songs against the Rev. Francis Doughty, for which he is sentenced to be tied to the May-pole." On the first of Feb., 1648, "William Harck, sheriff and associates, appear in council, and request that the Hon. Director-General and Council would favor them with a pious, learned and reformed minister, and then order that each inhabitant

Flushing's only legal official, thus far, had been a Schout.[18] In the third year after the settlement of the town, the Director-General and Council consented to make certain improvements in the form of the local government (April 27, 1648). Hereafter a Schout, three Schaepens and a Clerk were to be elected by the freeholders, and confirmed by the Director-General and Council. These officials were to take an oath of allegiance to the colonial government and pledge themselves to obey and enforce "rules and articles" issued by that authority. The people were commanded "to respect said persons, each in his quality, and to lend them a helping hand, in the execution of their office." [19] The first officials, chosen under this enlargement of the Charter, were: John Underhill, Schout: John Townsend, John Hicks, William Thorne, Schaepens: John Lawrence, Clerk. 1648

---

should contribute to such godly work, according to his ability, and that an end be put to the present differences in a manner that shall promote peace, quietness and unanimity in said town."—*Historical Documents XIV, 82.*

It is difficult to say whether this was during Doughty's incumbency or after his expulsion. We take it to be the former for it was when Harck was Sheriff. Underhill was evidently Sheriff when Doughty was expelled, for he it was who closed his church.

18 He was sometimes spoken of as Sheriff. On April 8, 1648, Thomas Hall, of Flushing, was fined twenty-five guilders for preventing the Sheriff from arresting Thomas Heyes. *Mandeville, p. 42.*

19 *Laws of New Netherland, p. 96.*

These officials were to constitute a court, before which were to be tried all suits not involving more than fifty guilders.[20] The first recorded official act of Flushing's new Schout--Capt. John Underhill—was ecclesiastical in its nature. He did not approve of the Rev. Mr. Doughty's preaching. The minister was probably still sore from his treatment at the hands of the Director-General, and was not so guarded as he should have been, in his references to that official. Captain Underhill ordered the church closed, because the minister "did preach against the present rulers, who were his masters."[21] Doughty now gained permission to leave the colony and to go to Virginia. We find him again in Flushing, five years later, and after that, in Maryland. What finally became of him, is not known. Before leaving Flushing, he authorized his son, Francis Doughty Jr., to collect from the town his year's salary. Another son, Elias Doughty, later became a magistrate of Flushing. His daughter, Mary, married Adrian Von der Donck, a prominent man in the affairs of New Netherland. Van der Donck

20 *Laws of New Netherland.* The functions of a Schout were those of a Sheriff and a Public Prosecutor. The Shaepens were magistrates. Together, they constituted a court of civil and criminal jurisdiction; and also formed an assembly with legislative powers, for municipal purposes. *O'Callaghan's New Netherland II, 211 et sq,*

21 *Riker's Annals of Newtown, p. 23.*

was Patroon of a colony above the "Spyt den Duyvel." The colony was commonly called "de Jonkheer's Landt," i. e., the nobleman's estate. This name survives in the corrupted form of Yonkers.

We cannot pass over this appearance of Underhill as an official of Flushing, without some allusion to that remarkable person. Captain John Underhill has been called "one of the most romantic persons in our early history." We first hear of him, as an officer in the British forces in Holland. He emigrated to Massachusetts in 1630, with Winthrop, and became the Captain and Instructor of the military force of the colony.[22] The colony frequently employed him as a leader in expeditions against the Indians. He was a man of energy, determination and great bravery. He was also a religious enthusiast, much given to sanctimonious expressions in his writings, but a man of vile impurity of life. About 1637, he got into difficulty with the theologians of Massachusetts; was cashiered and disfranchised, because of his association with Anne Hutchinson and the Rev. Mr. Wheelwright—the leaders of the antinomian enthusiasts. In 1638, we find him in England again, where he published an account of his Indian wars, under the title of "Newes

22 *Mass. Hist. Coll Fourth Series, VII, 170.*

from America."[23] The next year he returned to Massachusetts, only to fall again into trouble with the Church. One witness testified, that Underhill had been heard to say: "He had lain under a spirit of bondage and a legal way five years, and could get no assurance, till, at length, as he was taking a pipe of tobacco, the Spirit set home an absolute promise of free grace with such assurance and joy, as he never since doubted of his good estate, neither should he, though he should fall into sin." "The Lord's day following, he made a speech in the assembly, showing that, as the Lord was pleased to convert St. Paul, as he was a persecuting, so He might manifest Himself to him as he was taking the moderate use of the creature tobacco."[24] Underhill was banished from the colony and went to New Hampshire, where he became Governor of Exeter and Dover. But he had not gone beyond the reach of the Church. Friction with the ecclesiastical authorities still continued. In 1640,

---

23 In this account, Underhill relates how his life was saved on Block Island, by a helmet turning aside an arrow which otherwise must have pierced his forehead. His wife had pursuaded him to wear the helmet. "Therefore," he said, "let no man despise the advise and counsel of his wife, though she be a woman. It were strange to nature to think a man should be bound to fulfil the humour of a woman, what arms he should carry, but you know God will have it so, that a woman should overcome a man."

24 *History of New England, J. G. Palfrey, I,578. Mass. Hist. Coll. Second Series. VI, 351.*

the Church at Boston, of which he was still a member, sent for him to answer charges of gross immorality—which, it was alleged, he had committed before leaving for Exeter and Dover.[25] He admitted his guilt, and confessed that he had perpetrated his base immorality under the guise of religion. He appeared "before a great assembly in Boston, upon a lecture day, and, in the court house, sat upon the stool of repentance, with a white cap on his head, and with a great many deep sighs, a rueful countenance, and abundance of tears, owned his wicked way of life, his adultery and hypocrisy, with many expressions of sincere remorse, and besought the Church to have compassion on him and deliver him out of the hands of satan."[26] The sentence of excommunication and banishment, which had been passed against him, was removed after this act of humiliation. But he left Massachusetts and for a time settled at Stamford. While here, in 1641 and 1642, he was employed by the Dutch on

---

25 Underhill's manuscripts show that he was an illiterate man. Here is an extract from a letter, written at this time, to Governor Winthrop: "I am trobeld that chuch hard reportes should gooe out agaynst me, and my slfe not thorroli vnderstand mense displesure, tel this morning: I came simpli to satisfi the choch, not thincking to haf herd reportes agaynst me, thogh som smale ingling I had before." *Mass. Hist. Coll. Fourth. Series, VII, 181.*

26 *Thompson's Long Island. II, 357. Mass. Hist. Coll., Second Series VI, 358 et sq.*

Long Island in their Indian wars. In 1648, he appears as the Schout of Flushing, acting as censor of the pulpit. We shall hear of him again. He married, in Flushing, Elizabeth, daughter of Robert Field—one of the original patentees of the town. She was his second wife. His first wife was a Dutch woman.[27]

The appeal for "a pious, learned, and reformed minister", already referred to in a note, was not answered. Flushing had still to pass through many religious commotions.

1649 The village, however, continued to prosper, in a material sense. An official document, sent to Holland, speaks of "Flushing, which is an handsome village, and tolerably stocked with cattle."[28] The only tavern on the Island, except the one at the ferrry, was at Flushing. This we learn from the excise report.[29]

---

27 *Mass. Hist. Coll., Second Series, VI, 365.*

28 *Documents I, 285.*

29 *Documents I, 425.*

CHAPTER IV

TROUBLE WITH NEW ENGLAND—CAPTAIN UNDERHILL BANISHED

The political disturbances in Europe were always, to some extent, naturally reflected in the colonies. William II, Prince of Orange, had married the daughter of Charles I, of England. When Charles was put to death, in 1649, his son, Charles II, fled to Holland, where he was received with many expressions of sympathy. The popular sentiment, in Holland, following that of the beloved and heroic Prince of Orange, was always against Cromwell and the English Parliament. The States General made repeated attempts to conclude a treaty with the English Commonwealth, but all efforts seemed to miscarry. The Trade and Navigation Act, passed by the English Parliament in 1651, struck, with great severity, at the Dutch, who were the common carriers of Europe. The strained relations and the constant friction resulted in an open engagement, between the Dutch and the English fleets, in the straits of Dover. This was in May, 1652. The States General, thereupon, wrote to Director-

1651

1652

General Stuyvesant, to warn him of possible trouble with the English, in these words: "Although we flattered ourselves with the hope that some arrangement would have been made, between our government and the commonwealth of England, we have been disappointed . . . This unexpected rupture, which we have not courted, induced many merchants, trading to New Netherland, to solicit us to send an express to your Honor, so that you and the colonists might be informed of this state of things." After expressing the hope that the boundary disputes with New England had already been settled, "so that we have nothing to fear from New England," the letter adds: "We consider it, nevertheless, an imperious duty to recommend you to arm and discipline all freemen, soldiers and sailors . . . We warn you not to place an unbounded confidence in our English inhabitants, but to keep a watchful eye on them, so that you may not be deceived by a show of service, through their sinister machinations, as we have been before deceived. If it happen, which we will not suppose, that those New Englanders did incline to take a part in these broils, and injure our good inhabitants, then we should advise your Honor to engage the Indians in your cause, who, we are informed, are not partial to the English."[1]

---

1 *O'Callagan's New Netherland, II, 204 et sq. Documents, XIV, 186.*

The recommendation concerning the employment of Indians, in case of an attack, was unfortunate. But the authorities in Holland regarded the Indians as subjects, and they had the example of the New Englanders, who had used Indians as soldiers in the Pequot war. Besides, it was to be done only in case of an attack. The vessel, bearing these instructions, was captured by the English, who thus learned the plans of the Dutch.

On the feast of Candlemas, Feb. 2, of the following 1653
year, a more popular form of government was inaugurated at New Amsterdam, modeled after the government of the parent city, in Holland. One of the first acts of the new government, was to send letters to Virginia and New England, expressive of esteem and of hopes for continued friendly intercourse.[2] But rumors had become current, in New England, that Stuyvesant was inciting the Indians to an attack on the English. A meeting was held, in Boston, to consider the subject. Indians were interrogated, but they denied all knowledge of such a plot. Stuyvesant wrote letters, denying the charges and courting an investigation. The Commissioners of the United Colonies of New England appointed Francis Newman, Capt. John Leverett and Lieut. William Davis, to go to New Amsterdam and investigate.

2 *O'Callagan's New Netherland, II, 214.*

At the same time, five hundred troops were ordered to take the field, 'if God called the colonies to make war against the Dutch." Capt. Leverett was appointed Commander of this force, because "of the opportunity he now hath to view and observe the situation and fortifications at the Manhattoes." Thus Leverett was to act as spy, as well as ambassador. The three delegates reached New Amsterdam, on the twenty-second of May. Stuyvesant offered every opportunity for an impartial investigation, but all his proposals were rejected. It was plain that the New England committee came as inquisitors and not to make an impartial investigation. They came to demand satisfaction for wrongs which they claimed had been committed, not to ascertain, by impartial investigation, whether these charges were true. They concluded the conference, by demanding satisfaction for affronts offered "in former and later times."[3]

As might have been expected, Capt. John Underhill was found to be in the thick of the trouble. By him, Flushing was made the headquarters of sedition. He had been in correspondence with the Commissioners of New England. When the three delegates left New Amsterdam, they came directly to his house, in Flushing. Here they met the Rev. Francis Doughty and his daughter, Mrs. Van der Donck.

---

3 *O'Callagan's New Netherland, II*, 222 *et sq.*

Doughty said, "he knew more than he durst speak." Mrs. Van der Donck said, she knew that the Maquaas were "ready to assist the Dutch, if the English fell upon them."[4]

"Underhill openly charged the Fiscal, Van Tienhoven, with plotting against the English. He was therefore, arrested at Flushing, and conveyed to New Amsterdam under guard."[5] He was not long detained, and was dismissed without trial. Returning to Flushing, he committed open treason, by raising the Parliament's colors, and by issuing a seditious address. In this address, he states what had caused the insurgents "to abjure the iniquitous government of Peter Stuyvesant over the inhabitants living and residing on Long Island." He declared, that the wrongs endured were "too grievous for any brave Englishman and good Christian to tolerate any longer," and called upon "all honest hearts, that seek the glory of God and their own peace and prosperity, to throw off this tyrannical yoke." "Accept and submit ye then to the Parliament of England"—he adds—"and beware ye of becoming traitors to one another, for the sake of your quiet and welfare."[6]

---

4 *Brodhead's New York, I, 555.*

5 *Brodhead's New York, I, 556.*

6 *Brodhead's New York, I, 556.* This address, though inspired by Underhill, was evidently not written by him. His manuscript letters prove that he was incapable of such a composition, crude as it is.

This much may be said in justification of Underhill's address: Stuyvesant was tyrannical; he was greatly disliked by both the Dutch and the English inhabitants. He would, in all probability, have been removed from office before this, had not the unexpected war with England come on. Underhill's appeal met with no response. He was ordered to quit the Province. He went to Rhode Island, and appealed to that colony for assistance to save the English. The Colony of Providence Plantations gave, under seal, "full power and authority to Mr. William Dyer and Captain John Underhill to take all Dutch ships and vessels, as shall come into their power, and to defend themselves against the Dutch and all enemies of the Commonwealth of England."[7] Underhill afterwards settled at Oyster Bay, where he died in 1672.

In November, of this year, 1653, Director-General Stuyvesant received instruction from Holland, directing him, because the English inhabitants of Hempstead and Flushing had allowed the English flag to be raised "by some freebooters," "not to trust to any of that nation residing under our jurisdiction." Immigration was to be restricted, "that we may not nourish serpents in our bosom, who finally might devour our hearts."[8]

7 *Hazard II, 249. Broadhead I, 557.*

8 *Documents, XIV, 216.*

In those days of small vessels, Flushing was not an unimportant seaport. News was received, at New Amsterdam, about the middle of December, that several English privateers had been seen hovering about, near Flushing. The Hon. Jean de La Montagne was sent to pursue and attack them.[9] With what success the expedition met, we are unable to state. Thus closed an eventful year.

Flushing's Charter provided that, at the expiration of 1655 ten years, one tenth of the revenue, that should "arise by the ground, manured by the plough or hoe," should be paid to the government of New Netherland.[10] The Council, therefore, issued instructions to the tithe-commissioners, concerning the manner of collecting the tithes. The town was "either to make an agreement regarding the tithes to be this year, or to leave the crops, mowed, sheaved, and in shocks, upon the fields," that the commissioners might "count off the tenth, as it is done in the Fatherland." The town authorities wrote to the Council, by their Clerk, Edward Heart, that they were "willing to do that which

---

9 *Document, XIV, 237.*

10 During the summer of this year, Aug. 6, 1655, the first cargo of slaves came, directly from Africa, to New Netherland, on the ship Witte paert. An ordinance was passed, levying a tax of ten per cent. on all negroes exported to other places beyond New Netherland. *Laws of New Netherland, p. 191.*

is reasonable and honest," although "the insufferable insolence of the Indians" prevented them from enjoying the "land in peace, according to the pattent." They agreed to pay, "fiftie scipple of peas and twentie-five of wheat."[11]

---

11 *Documents*, *XIV*, *361*, *et sq*.

CHAPTER V

ANABAPTISTS AND QUAKERS

Flushing's religious experience, thus far, had not been altogether satisfactory. Since the Rev. Mr. Doughty's forced resignation, the village had been without the regular services of a minister. When, therefore, William Wickendam, a cobbler from Rhode Island—who did not stick to his last — essayed to minister to the religious wants of the people, he was by many kindly received. The Sheriff, William Hallet, offered his house as a place of meeting. Wickendam was not content with exhorting his neighbors and leading them in prayer. He undertook to administer the Sacraments. He "went with the people into the river and dipped them." The Dutch ministers, the Rev. John Megapolensis and the Rev. Samuel Drisius, sent to the classis of Amsterdam an account of Flushing's religious condition: "At Flushing, they heretofore had a Presbyterian preacher[1] who conformed to our Church, but many of them became imbued with divers opinions, and it was with 1656

1 The Rev. Francis Doughty.

them *quot homines tot sententiae.* They absented themselves from preaching, nor would they pay the preacher his promised stipend. The said preacher was obliged to leave the place, and to repair to the English Virginias. Now they have been some years without a minister. Last year a fomenter of error came there. He was a cobbler from Rhode Island, in New England, and stated that he was commissioned by Christ. He began to preach at Flushing and then went, with the people, into the river and dipped them. This becoming known here, the Fiscaal proceeded thither and brought him along. He was banished the Province."[2]

We have, also, an official account of the trial. It states that William Hallet, born in Dorsetshire, age about forty, "has had the audacity to call and allow to be called conventicles and gatherings at his house, and to permit there in contemptuous disobedience of published, and several times renewed, placats of the Director-General and Council, an exegesis and interpretation of God's Holy Word, as he confesses, the administration and service of the Sacraments by one William Wickendam, while the latter, as he ought to have known, had, neither by ecclesiastical nor secular authority, been called thereto."[3]

---

2 *Documentary History of New York, III, 71.*

3 *Documents XIV, 369.*

As the result of the trial, Hallet was degraded from office, fined £50 Flemish, and banished from the Province; Wickendam was fined £100 and banished. When it was discovered that Wickendam was a poor man, with a family, and was a cobbler by trade, "to which he does not properly attend," his fine was remitted. He was, however, banished, and so passes beyond our field of view. Hallet pleaded for mercy. His sentence of banishment was remitted, and he was allowed to remain in the Province as a private citizen, if he should pay his fine at sight.

In the summer of the following year (Aug. 6, 1657), 1657
the ship Woodhouse brought to New Netherland, several members of the Society of Friends.[4] Many of them went to Rhode Island, "where all kinds of scum dwell" said Domine Magapolensis. Some, however, came to Long Island, under the leadership of Robert Hodgson, and settled in Jamaica and Flushing. The Friends of Jamaica and Flushing, for a time, held their meetings in Jamaica, at the house of Henry Townsend. Townsend was arrested, fined £8 Flemish, and ordered to leave the Province within six weeks. A proclamation was issued, imposing a fine of £50 on any one who sheltered a Quaker for one night, one half

---

4 *Flin's Early Long Island, p. 175. Brodhead's New York, I, 636.*

of the fine to go to the informer. "Any vessel, bringing Quakers to the Province, was to be confiscated."[5] This cruel law called out the famous and noble remonstrance of Flushing, which was signed by twenty-eight freeholders of Flushing, and two from Jamaica.[6] The Remonstrance said: "Ye have been pleased to send up unto us a certain prohibition, or command, that we should not retaine or entertaine any of those people called Quakers. . . We cannot condemn them. . . neither stretch out our hands against them, to punish, banish or persecute them. . . We are commanded by the Law to do good to all men . . . That which is of God will stand, and that which is of man will come to nothing . . . Our only desire is not to offend one of these little ones, in whatsoever form, name or title he appears, whether Presbyterian, Independent, Baptist or Quaker, but shall be glad to see any thing of God in any of them, desiring to do unto all men, as we desire that all men should do unto us, which is the true Law both of Church and State . . . Therefore if any of these said persons come in love unto us, we cannot in conscience lay violent hands upon them, but give them free egresse or regresse into our town and houses . . . This is according to the Patent and Charter of our

5 *Laws of New Netherland.*
6 Appendix II.

town . . . which we are not willing to infringe or violate."[7] This Remonstrance, dated Dec. 27th., was written by Edward Heart, the town Clerk, and carried to New Amsterdam, early in January, by Tobias Feake, the Sheriff, who 1658
had succeeded William Hallet in that office. Feake and Heart, together with Edward Farrington and William Noble, Magistrates and signers of the Remonstrance, were arrested and imprisoned. Noble and Farrington humbly craved pardon "for acting so inconsiderately," and, promising to offend no more, were pardoned on the tenth of January. About two weeks later, January 23rd., Heart also weakened and pleaded for mercy. He said: "My humble request is for your mercy, not your judgment: and that you would be pleased to consider my poor estate and condition, and relieve me from my bonds and imprisonment, and I shall endeavor hereafter to walk inoffensively unto your Lordships." He was pardoned, on condition that he paid the costs. On Sheriff Feake, fell the weight of Stuyvesant's wrath. The Sheriff had given lodging to "that heretical and abominable sect called Quakers," and had been foremost in securing signatures to "a seditious and detestable chartabel." For this he was degraded from office, and sentenced to pay a fine of two hundred guilders, or to be banished.

---

7 *Documents XIV, 402.*

As the result of this disturbance, an ordinance was passed, March 26th., which stated that for this "seditious and mutinous" remonstrance, the town richly deserved "to be corrected and punished by the annulment of the privileges and exemptions granted . . . by patent and by the enlargement thereof." Therefore, "in order to prevent in future the disorder which commonly arises from general town-meetings, or village assemblies," no such meetings should be held, without the consent of the Director-General and the Council. Instead of town-meetings, seven persons should "be chosen and appointed out of the best, most reasonable and most respectable inhabitants, who shall be called Tribunes or Town'smen, to be employed by the Schout and Magistrates as counselors on and about any Town matters." Whatever was decided by the Schout, Magistrates and Tribunes, the inhabitants should obey, "on pain of arbitrary correction." The ordinance further stated, that, "for the want of a good, pious and orthodox minister, . . . the inhabitants had fallen into disregard of Divine worship, and profanation of the Sabbath . . . into heresy and indecent licentiousness." The town was, therefore, ordered, "to look out and inquire for a good, honest and orthodox minister." Each landholder was to be required to apply for a special patent and henceforth to pay an annual tax of twelve stivers for each Dutch morgan of land, for the support of the minister—the deficit to be made up, by the Director-General, from the tithes. All persons who were unwilling to submit to these requirements, were ordered to dispose of their goods and, within six weeks, to quit the Province. All others, and all new comers, were to sign a pledge of obedience.[8]

In the midst of this attempt to stamp out Quakerism, 1660
there came to Flushing a number of French Huguenots, who introduced the industry of horticulture, for which the town has ever since been famous.[9]

Among the influential inhabitants of Flushing, at this 1661
period, was John Bowne, who is described as "a plain, strong-minded, English farmer."[10] He was born at Matlock, Derbyshire, England, in 1627. In 1649, he emigrated to Boston. Two years later, he visited Flushing, with his brother-in-law, Edward Farrington. Later, we find him settled in Flushing. Here, in 1656, he married Hannah, daughter of Robert Field[11] (or Feke, as the name sometimes

8 *Laws of New Netherland*, p. 338-42.
9 *Flint's Early Long Island*, p. 183.
10 *Brodhead's New York*, *I*, 705.
11 Underhill writes to John Winthrop, Jr., April 12, 1656: "Sir, I wase latli at Flushing. Hanna Feke is to be married to verri jentiele young man, of gud abilliti, of a louli fetture, and gud behafior." *Mass. Hist. Coll. Fourth Series*, *VII*, *183*.

appears), and sister to Captain John Underhill's second wife. Bowne's house, built in 1661, still stands on the avenue that bears his name, and presents a quaint and beautiful picture of early Flushing. Bowne's wife was a member of the society of Friends. Meetings at this time were held secretly in the woods. Bowne attended these meetings with his wife, at first out of curiosity, but he soon became interested, and invited the Quakers to meet at his house. Later, he became a member of the society. The magistrates of Jamaica notified the Director-General, that Bowne's house had become a "conventicle" for the Quakers of all the neighboring villages. Bowne was arrested, fined £25 Flemish, and threatened with banishment.[12] He refused to pay the fine. After three months imprisonment, "for the welfare of the community," he was told that he would be transported "in the first ship ready to sail," should he continue obstinate. Bowne remained firm. On

12 An ordinance was passed, in September of this year, ordering, that "beside the Reformed worship and service, no conventicles or meetings shall be kept in this Province, whether it be in houses, barnes, ships, barkes, nor in the woods, nor fields, under forfeiture of fifty guldens, for the first time, for every person present, and twice as much for every person who exhorted or taught, or who shall have lent his house, barn or other place." "Seditious and erroneous books, writings and letters" were to be confiscated, and the importer and distributer of such writings was to be fined 100 guldens. *Laws of New Netherland, p. 428*

the ninth of January, of the following year, he was sent to Holland, on the Guilded Fox. He stated his case to the Directors of the West India Company, who set him at liberty, and rebuked Stuyvesant. They wrote to the latter: "Although it is our cordial desire that similar and other sectarians may not be found there, yet as the contrary seems to be the fact, we doubt very much whether vigorous proceedings against them ought not to be discontinued: unless, indeed, you intend to check and destroy your population, which, in the youth of your existence, ought rather to be encouraged by all possible means . . . The conscience of men ought to remain free and unshackled. Let every one remain free, as long as he is modest, moderate, his political conduct irreproachable, and as long as he does not offend others or oppose the government.[13] Bowne returned to Flushing after two years' absence. At this early period, Quaker meeting was held at different houses: viz., those of John Bowne, John Farrington, Hugh Cowperthwaite, Benjamin Field and Dr. John Rodman.[14]

1663

1665

It must not be supposed that the Dutch were exceptional in their treatment of the Quakers. The Church of England colony in Virginia had similar laws: Puritan New England

---

13 *Brodhead's New York I, 705 et sq.*

14 *Onderdonk's Friends on Long Island, p. 94.*

had worse ones. In Massachusetts, Quakers were not only fined and imprisoned: they were whipped, their ears were cut off, their tongues were bored with hot irons, and some of them were put to death.[15] Nothing can be said in justification of persecution for religious belief: but, in this cruel treatment of the Quakers, something may be said by way of explanation. The early Quakers were not all the quiet, orderly persons whom we to-day are apt to associate with the name. Many of them were the wildest fanatics. To read, for instance, that certain persons were arrested, fined and imprisoned for "bearing testimony," gives one the impression that the civil authorities were altogether cruel and unreasonable: but the action of the authorities does not appear so unreasonable, when we know that "to bear testimony" frequently meant that women went through the streets, stark naked, crying: "Woe! Woe!" and called down curses on all who differed with them. If persons, of any name, should, to-day, thus destroy the peace and shock the sense of modesty of any community, they would, without doubt, be punished. The Quakers' disregard of titles and offices, we are inclined to consider a harmless idiosyncrasy, but in those days it not infrequently amounted to contempt of court, and open insult to officials. In New England,

15 *Elliott's History of New England I, 289 et sq.*

Quakers had been guilty of many excesses.[16] Some of the first Quakers that arrived in New Netherland, came from New England. The sect, therefore, had a bad name, before any of its members appeared among the Dutch. As stated above, all this is said by way of explanation, and not in justification of religious persecution. The injustice committed was, in punishing a whole sect for the misconduct of some of its members. The more reasonable Quakers, themselves, condemned the excesses of these fanatics. It is not generally remembered, that it was Charles II who compelled the Puritans to cease persecuting the Quakers. For the excessively religious New Englanders to be taught toleration by such a master, is one of the strange things in history.

16 *Elliot's New England II*, 299.

CHAPTER VI

TROUBLE WITH CONNECTICUT—CAPTAIN JOHN SCOTT.

1650 The line of division, between New Netherland and the colonies of New Haven and Connecticut, had, from the beginning, been the subject of much dispute. As early as 1650, a treaty, known as the Hartford treaty, was signed, which gave all of Long Island east of Oyster Bay, and that part of the main land east of Greenwich Bay, to the "United Colonies of the English," "until a full and final determination be agreed upon in Europe, by the mutual consent of the two states of England and Holland." This treaty was ratified by the States General, but not by England. Six years after the treaty had been signed, the English encroached upon Long Island, west of the line that had been agreed upon, and extended their settlements far into West Chester.[1]

1 The inhabitants of Flushing were also troubled by Indians. On April 13, 1662, Messrs. Lawrence, Noble and Hallet were sent to notify the Director-General that the Indians were demanding pay for the land in Flushing. They asked that the Indians' "mouthes may bee stopped and our selves preserved from any danger." *Documents, XIV, 512.*

Advice was finally received from Holland that all hope 1663
of settling the dispute in Europe must be abandoned.[2] Encroachment on the land of West Chester continued. Agents were sent from Connecticut to the English towns on Long Island, to stir up discontent. The Director-General, therefore, went to Boston, with the hope of settling the dispute. Nothing, however, was accomplished. The New Englanders denied that the Dutch had any right to lands in the new world. It was all the King's land: the Dutch were intruders. Stuyvesant was compelled to return empty-handed to New Amsterdam.

In the meantime, the English towns on Long Island became restless. A petition, signed by certain inhabitants of Jamaica, Middleburgh and Hempstead, was sent to Hartford, praying that colony, "to cast over us the scurts of your government and protecktion."

In October, Stuyvesant sent a delegation to Hartford, to make one more attempt to settle the boundary question. In vain an appeal was made to the treaty of 1650: the Hartford men declared it void. After much debate, the

---

2 Edward Fisher was Clerk of Flushing during this year. Richard Cornell was sent to New Amsterdam to make arrangements for the tithes, being authorized to offer 100 schepel of grain—half of pease and half of wheat. *Documents XIV, 531.*

Hartford deputies announced, as their ultimatum, that West Chester must be given up to Connecticut, and that the English towns on Long Island be allowed to occupy a position of quasi-independence Connecticut agreeing to exercise no authority over them, if the Dutch would refrain from coercing them.

New disturbances, which arose among the inhabitants of the English towns on Long Island, in November, compelled Stuyvesant to agree to these terms. Anthony Waters, of Hempstead, and John Coe, a "miller of Middleburgh," with a force of nearly a hundred men, went to Flushing and the other English towns, declared that the country belonged to the King, removed the magistrates, and appointed others. To make the revolution complete, new names were given to several towns. Jamaica (or, as it was then written, Gemego) became Crafford: Flushing became Newarke; Newtown (or Middleburgh) became Hastings. Stuyvesant realized that he was powerless, and hastened to accept the terms offered by the Hartford convention.

1664 The villages were now in the anomalous position of quasi-independence. They proceeded, therefore, to form a "Combination." Prominent in this agitation was Captain John Scott.[3] Scott was one of the many restless English

3 *O'Callaghan's New Netherland II, 497 et sq.*

adventurers to whom the unsettled state of affairs in America offered an attractive field of operation. He had been an officer in the army of Charles I, and was banished to New England by the Commonwealth. Thence he came to Long Island, and, according to his own statement, purchased about one third of the island. On receiving news of the Restoration, he returned to England. He asked the King to appoint him Governor of Long Island, or to authorize the people to elect a Governor and an assistant. Charles II was disposed to grant Scott's request, and referred the matter to the Committee on Foreign Plantations. Scott laid his claims, and his complaints against the Dutch, before this Committee. He then departed for America, armed with a royal letter, recommending him to the protection of the New England governors. Connecticut invested him with magisterial powers, granted him a stipend for his services, and sent him to Long Island to bring the western towns under Connecticut's control. But many of the inhabitants of the Long Island towns had left New England because of persecution, and were not anxious to return to that affiliation. They preferred independence, and invited Scott to assist them in maintaining it. The towns of "Heempstede, Newwarke, Crafford, Hastings, Folestone and Gravesend," therefore, formed a "Combination." Scott was elected to act as their President. "until his Royal Highness the Duke of York, or his Majesty, should establish a government among them." The towns further agreed to elect deputies to make laws for this new "Combination." Efforts were made to induce the Dutch towns to join them, but without success. The action of Scott, in taking part in this combination, soon brought down upon him the hostility of both New Netherland and Connecticut. Stuyvesant sent delegates to Jamaica (or Crafford, as it was then called) to confer with Scott. He was at the time in Newwarke[4] (Flushing). On his return to Jamaica, it was agreed to allow the old order to prevail for the time being. This was in January. Scott said he would return in the spring. He warned the Dutch delegates that the king had granted the whole of New Netherland to the Duke of York, who would certainly take possession of it—by force, if necessary. In March, Stuyvesant went, with a military escort, to Hempstead, to meet President Scott and the delegates from the English towns. It was agreed that the English towns should remain under the King for twelve months, or until the whole question should be settled in Europe, and that the Dutch towns should remain under the States General, for the same time.

Scott's action on Long Island, naturally, did not please

---

4 *Documents, II, 399.*

the Connecticut authorities. They considered him a traitor to their interests. In the disturbance that followed, Flushing was visited by two distinguished men. John Winthrop Jr., Governor of Connecticut, accompanied by deputies from Hartford, came in June. He removed the magistrates appointed by Scott, and put others in their places. Help was promised the magistrates and inhabitants, against all who might disturb them. Next came Director-General Stuyvesant. A contemporary document tells us: "The General, accompanied by Secretary Van Ruyven, Burgomaster Cortlandt and some other principal Burghers, as an escort, went thither himself in person, to protest against such irregularity."[5] The Dutch declared that they would be guiltless of the mischief and bloodshed that would certainly follow. The protest was, however, in vain.[6]

---

5 *Documents, II, 407, et sq.*

6 During these troubles, the inhabitants of Flushing endeavored to secure the support of the Indians by again paying them for the land. Tapansagh, Chief of the Long Island Indians, and Rompsicka, appeared before the Director-General and Council, and stated that they had been summoned to Flushing by William Lawrence. There they met Noble, Robert Terry, Doughty and a houseful of others. They told the Indians that the land was really theirs and offered to buy it of the Indians. They also told the Indians that three ships were coming from England and would drive out the Dutch. The Indians replied that they had already, in 1635, sold the land to the Dutch and hence could not sell it again. *Documents, XIV, 540. Calendar of Historical Manuscripts, I, 258.*

The General Assembly of Connecticut then drew up charges against Captain Scott,[7] and called on all civil officers to arrest him. This document declared that Scott was guilty of "sundry hainous crimes and practices," "seditions," "the disturbance of the peace of his Majesty's subjects," "gross and notorious profanation of God's word," "forgery and violation of solemn oath," and treachery to Connecticut. Scott was arrested, at Setauket, and taken to Hartford. Flushing stood by him in his trouble. A remonstrance, signed by one hundred and forty-four inhabitants of Flushing, was sent to Hartford, stating that Scott had acted in accordance with the will of the people, and that, "in their silence, the very stones might justly rise to proclaim his innocence."[8] Scott addressed "A humbell petition to the Court at Hartford," in which he confessed his wrong-doings, and begged for mercy. He was released, and afterwards lived at Ashford, now Brookhaven, where he was the proprietor of the "Manor of Hope." Later, he had trouble with the English colonial officials, and emigrated to the Barbadoes.

In taking leave of the Dutch Colonial period, it may be

---

7 *Thompson's Long Island, II, 321.*

8 *O'Callaghan's New Netherland, II, 552.*

well to say something about the general condition of society at that time, and of the influence which society received from the Hollanders.[9]

In the absence of shops, every farmer was, to a great extent, his own mechanic—carpenter, mason, wheelwright, blacksmith. His home was simple, but comfortable. White sand, sprinkled on the floor, took the place of carpets. High-backed chairs, ornamented with brass-headed nails around the cushioned seats and leather backs, were conspicuous articles of furniture. Plates and dishes of pewter and wood furnished the table. In the more wealthy families, silver plate, in the form of large trays, bowls and tankards, was not uncommon.

Both Negro and Indian slavery prevailed. A species of white slavery was also common. Indigent immigrants, in return for the payment of their passage money, sold their service for definite periods, during which time they could be bought and sold like any other slaves.[10] A public official

---

9 *Furman's Antiquities of Long Island.* Below is given a list of Flushing officials, during the Dutch period, and for a short time after:

SCHOUT-FISCALS (OR SHERIFFS)

1647, William Hark	1657, Tobias Feake
1648, John Underhill	1658, John Mastine. (Town constable)
1655, John Hicks	1673, William Lawrence
1656, William Hallet	1674, Francis Bloodgood.

known as "the negro whipper," or "the town whipper," was appointed for each town. The slaves, in Flushing, generally received very kind treatment from their masters.

Nearly all the marriages were performed under the Governor's license.[11] There was a special officer in New York, whose jurisdiction extended to Long Island, known as: "The First Commissary of Marriage Affairs." It was his duty to determine all matrimonial disputes.

MAGISTRATES

1648, John Tousend
John Hicks
William Toorn
1651, John Underhill
Thomas Saul
Robert Terri
1652, John Hicks
(other two not recorded)
1655, Thomas Saul
William Lawrence
Edward Farrington
1656, William Lawrence
Edward Farrington
William Noble
(same names until 1662)

1662, William Lawrence
William Noble
William Hallet
1664, William Hallet
William Noble
(appointed by Connecticut)

1673, John Hinchman
Francis Bloetgoet
Richard Wildie

TOWN CLERKS

1648, John Lawrence
1657, Edward Heart
1662, Edward Fisher

Register of New Netherland, p. 44, 88, 105.

10 Aug. 13, 1678. Indenture. Katharine Jeffreys to serve Chas. Bridges and Sarah his wife, of Flushing, Long Island, for five years, in payment for her passage from England. *Calendar of Historical Manuscripts, II, 73.*

11 William Harck, Sheriff of Flushing, was fined 600 Carulus guilders and deprived of his office, April 3, 1648,

At funerals, a cold collation, with wines and liquor, was provided for the guests, and linen-scarfs and gloves were often distributed among them. Funerals became very expensive affairs, and often very nearly resembled joyous feasts.

Where the Dutch influence prevailed, Sunday-afternoon visiting was a common custom. To the Dutch we are indebted for Santa Klaas, and for the custom of hanging up stockings at Christmas. New Year's day was celebrated with noise and hospitality. A group of men would assemble before the door of a neighbor and salute him with the discharge of guns. The person thus saluted would invite his friends into his house, to partake of refreshments, and would then join them in saluting others. The company would thus go from house to house, until all the men of a neighborhood were collected together, when they would proceed to some rendezvous, and pass the day in athletic sports and shooting at a target. St. Valentine's day was also celebrated with great hilarity. The whole of Easter week was a time of merry making, and was marked by the custom of presenting colored eggs to one's friends.

---

for solemnizing the marriage of Thos. Nuton, widower, and Joan, the daughter of Richard Smith, without the consent of the bride's parents and contrary to the law of the Province. The parties were legally married on the 16th of the same month. *Calendar of Historical Manuscripts, I,115.*

Money was very scarce. Trade was carried on by the exchange of different kinds of produce, at prices fixed by law, or the Indian wampum was used as a circulating medium.

Punishment for different misdemeanors was inflicted by whipping, branding, putting in stocks, banishing from the Province, or hanging.[12]

12 "September 15th., 1733, Edward King, a tinker, was hanged for killing William Smith on the road near Flushing." *History of Queen's County, p. 51.*

PART III—The English Colonial Period

CHAPTER VII

THE DUKE'S LAWS SEDITION AMONG FLUSHING'S MILITIAMEN– GEORGE FOX'S VISIT.

While Flushing was thus torn by three contending factions, things were hastening to an end in Europe. On the twenty-second of March, Charles II gave to his brother James, the Duke of York, a patent for Long Island and that part of the main-land lying between the Connecticut river and the Delaware Bay. Lord Sterling's heirs surrendered their claims for a stipulated amount, though it does not appear that the price was ever paid. Colonel Richard Nicolls, a devoted Royalist, was appointed Governor of the Province, and Commander of the fleet that was sent against New Netherland. New Amsterdam was surrendered to the English, on the eighth of September.[1] New Amsterdam became New York: and Fort Amsterdam became Fort 1664

---

1. *Brodhead's New York. I, 742. O'Callaghan's New Netherland, II, 536.*

James. Director-General Stuyvesant surrendered, because compelled to do so by his own people, the burghers of New Amsterdam.

Peter Stuyvesant, though arbitrary and quick-tempered, was a brave and patriotic man. After the surrender, he went to Holland to give an account of his action, and then returned to New York. There he lived, for a few years, on his farm. He was buried beneath a chapel which he had built on his estate. This chapel—St. Mark's in the Fields—has since been replaced by the present St. Mark's Church.[2] Beneath this church, no longer in the fields, rest the bones of the most illustrious Governor of New Netherland.

Under the rule of Governor Nicolls, Long Island, Staten Island, and West Chester were united to form the district, or county, of Yorkshire. The present Suffolk county became the East Riding: Staten Island, Kings County, and Newtown constituted the West Riding: West Chester and Queens County, except Newtown, made the North Riding. Thus Flushing (the name Newwarke was dropped, without
1665 official action) was in the North Riding of Yorkshire. An assembly of delegates from the various towns met in Hempstead, early in the next year, and adopted the Code of laws

---

2. *Flint's Long Island*, p. 297,

that are known as the "Duke's Laws."[3] The Duke's Laws were intended, ultimately, for the whole Province, but many of the provisions were evidently applicable to Yorkshire alone. A high-sheriff over Yorkshire was to be appointed, annually, by the Governor and Council. An under-sheriff was to be appointed for each riding. Justices of the peace were to be appointed, in each riding, and were to continue in office during the Governor's pleasure. These justices of the peace were to hold a "Court of Sessions," three times a year, in each riding. The "Court of Assizes" was to be held, once a year, in New York. Each town was to elect, annually, a constable and eight overseers. The constable and six of the overseers were to constitute a local court, for the trial of cases not involving more than £5. From this court of the constable and overseers, an appeal might be made to the Court of Sessions. The jurors of the Court of Assizes were to be chosen from the town overseers.

The Church of England was not established in the Province by the Duke's Laws. Those laws required that every town was to build and maintain a church. No minister was to be allowed to officiate, who "had not received ordination either from some Protestant Bishop or minister,"

---

3. The delegates from Flushing, were Elias Doughty and Richard Cornhill. *Brodhead, II, 68.*

within his Majesty's dominion, or within the dominion of some foreign prince of the Reformed Religion. The overseers in each town were to act as assessors. Two of them were to be chosen to "make the rate," for the support of the Church and clergyman.[4]

William Wells, of Southold, was the first High Sheriff of Yorkshire. Captain John Underhill appears again, as the Deputy-Sheriff of the North Riding. Elias Doughty, son of the Rev. Francis Doughty, was appointed Constable of Flushing. Doughty now brought suit against John Hicks, Captain William Lawrence and Captain John Underhill, for the year's salary due his father. Why this matter had been allowed to rest for eighteen years, we are unable to say. The contract between the town and the Rev. Mr. Doughty could not be found. It had been destroyed a year before. Captain Lawrence's wife confessed that she had "put it under a pie in an oven." Doughty recovered six hundred guilders. Each party was to pay its own costs. It came out in the trial that the sum now awarded to Mr. Doughty had already been offered to him, and that he had declined to accept it as the full amount due him.

1666 There was much dissatisfaction on Long Island, because the new laws made no provision for a representative form of

4. *Brodhead's New York, II, 70, 71.*

government. Several persons were arrested and fined for seditious utterances. Among them, was William Lawrence, of Flushing, who was fined £5, and required to make public acknowledgment of his fault.[5]

Governor Nicolls came to Flushing, July 3, 1667, accompanied by Captain Betts, to inspect the militia and put it into an effective condition. The militiamen were assembled and were addressed by the Governor and Captain Betts. Then occurred the following scene, according to the deposition of Captain Betts: "After the Governor, among other matters, had told the people met together, that he would furnish them with powder for their present occasions, and would be content to receive fire-wood for it: he heard William Bishop speak these words aloud, (vizt.) 'That there was another cunning trick!' Upon which, the said Capt. Betts told the said Bishop, that if he had anything to say in answer to what had been proposed by the Governor, he was best to speak it to the Governor himselfe who was hard by, and not to mutter such words among the people—to which he made answer: 'It is very like that he hath sett ye here to hearken to what we say, that you may tell him? Whereunto Capt. Betts replied, 'It was not so, but since he thought so, he should take further notice of what he said.'

1667

5. *Brodhead's New York II, 108.*

Then Bishop returned answer, 'What have I said? I said nothing, but there is another cunning trick.' "[6]

For these "seditious words spoken at Flushing," Bishop was sentenced "to be made fast to the whipping-post, [in New York] there to stand, with rods fastened to his back, during the sitting of the Court of Mayor and Aldermen, and from thence to be conveyed unto the Common Goale till further order."[7]

There must have been other evidence of disloyalty on that memorable third of July. The Governor sent orders that a town meeting be summoned, and that, at the meeting, an accompanying letter be publicly opened and read. This was done. The letter, which was addressed to the inhabitants of the town, stated that the Governor had, on the third of July, spoken, at the head of the militia company, of the necessity of cheerful and ready support. " I did very much wonder,"—he proceeds—"and am not lesse troubled at your absurd returns which have given me just cause to

6. Mandeville, page 44, cites this as an instance of the persecution of Quakers. There is no evidence that Bishop was a Quaker. That he was a militiaman and, after his punishment, volunteered to serve again, is evidence that he was not a Quaker. The occurrence had nothing to do with Quakerism. It was apparently part of the general discontent with what was regarded as an arbitrary form of government.

7. *Mandeville, p. 45. Brodhead, II, 124.*

call back my former favours to you and not to qualify you hereafter to receive from mee the civilityes truly intended. Now, because you have given me just reason to suspect your fidelities and your courage, at a season when a true Englishman is most zealous, and seeks the first occasion to serve the king and country . . . You are to expect all the scorne and disdaine that lyes in my power against such meane spirited fellowes." After these bitter words, follow the orders which the local authorities were to enforce. The commissioned and non-commissioned officers are to be suspended: the colors, presented to the company by the Governor, are to be returned; twelve matchlocks are to be returned to his Majesty's store, at the fort; none of the company is to presume to appear in arms, without a special warrant: "none of that company which I saw stand in arms, under his Majesty's colors (whose names are enclosed) shall presume, upon any private occasion, to resort to New York for three months, under penalty of being arrested as a spy, unless he first report to the officer of the guard in the fort, state his business, and the length of time he desires to stay."[8]

The offence must have been grave that caused the Governor thus to humiliate the inhabitants of Flushing.

8. *Documents XIV*, 597.

His action, however, seems to have put an end to all sedition, during his administration. That some of the militia repented is evident from the fact that, on the twelfth of August, fourteen men sent their names to the Governor, stating that they were "ready to serve him on all occasions." In the list was the name of William Bishop. The others were: John Elee, Aaron Foreman, Edw. Griffin, Jos. Hedger, Richard Long, William Noble, Nich. Parcell, Thos. Sadler, George Tippetts, Jos. Thorn, Jno. Thorne, Geo. Wright, Jonathan Wright.[9] The Governor directed Mr. Cornhill to form them, and others "sensible of their late error," into a company, and forward the list to him. Later in October, a town-meeting was called, to elect two men each for the positions of captain, lieutenant, and ensign. From these, the Governor appointed the officers of the company.[10]

Some time during the next year, Elias Doughty and William Noble, overseers of the town of Flushing, were summoned before the Court of Sessions, at the Sessions House in Jamaica, for neglecting to pay the public rates of the town, and for failing to make an assessment for building a Sessions House.[11]

---

9 *Documents XIV, 598.*
10 *Documents, XIV, 609.*
11 *Documents, XIV, 605*

About the middle of August, Governor Nicolls, who had for some time desired to be relieved of his duties in New York, surrendered the government of the Province to Colonel Francis Lovelace, who was a brother of John, Lord Lovelace, and a favorite of the king. Nicolls embarked, August 17th., amid many demonstrations of respect and regret on the part of those whom he had governed. It was said of him, at the time, that he had "kept persons of different judgments and diverse nations, in peace and quietness, during a time when a great part of the world was in wars."[12]

The agitation for a representative form of government, which had met with no success during Nicolls's term of office, was resumed shortly after the arrival of Governor Lovelace. At the November Assizes, a petition was presented from Flushing, asking for privileges similar to those enjoyed by his Majesty's other subjects in America—"which privileges," said the petition, "consist in advising about and approving of all such laws, with the Governor and his Council, as may be for the good and benefit of the commonwealth . . . by such deputies as shall be yearly chosen by the freeholders of every town or parish."[13] Similar petitions

12 Maverick's letter to Lord Arlington. *Brodhead, II, 142.*
13 *Brodhead, II, 160.*

were sent in from the other Long Island towns, but Lovelace had no authority to grant such requests.

1670 We have still preserved for us, a description of this part of the Island, as it appeared to a writer of that period which we have now reached in our history. Daniel Denton, the son of the Rev. Richard Denton, of Hempstead, was at one time Clerk of Hempstead, and later held the same office in Jamaica. He published, in London, in 1670, "A Brief Description of New York," in which much space is given to Long Island. Hell Gate, he says, at flood tide, "continually sends forth a hideous roaring, enough to affright any stranger from passing any further." "The fruits natural to the Island are Mulberries, Posimons, Grapes, great and small, Huckleberries, Cramberries, Plums of several sorts, Roseberries and Strawberries, of which last is such abundance in June, that the Fields and Woods are dyed red: Which the Countrey-people perceiving instantly arm themselves with bottles of Wine, Cream and Sugar, and instead of a Coat of Male, every one takes a Female upon his Horse behind him, and so rushing violently into the fields, never leave till they have disrobed them of their red colour, and turned them into the old habit . . . In May you shall see the Woods and Fields so curiously bedecke with Roses, and an innumerable multitude of Flowers, not only pleasing the eye, but smell, that you may behold Nature contending with Art, and striving to equal if not excel many Gardens in England." Denton reported the "Indians few and harmless," in his day. "It hath been generally observed," he says, "that where the English come to settle, a Divine Hand makes way for them, by removing or cutting off the Indians, either by Wars one with the other, or by some raging mortal Disease."[14]

An examination of the palisades around Fort James, revealed the fact that they were in a bad state of decay. The Court of Assizes, therefore, ordered that a tax be levied on the towns of Long Island, to furnish means for the necessary repairs. This met with such violent opposition 1672
that the order was never enforced. Two years later, the Governor asked for a voluntary contribution, or "benevolence," from each of the towns. To this request Flushing promptly responded and forwarded a contribution of £20 15 s. 6 d. The Council, thereupon, ordered that thanks be given to the inhabitants, for their "forwardness."[15]

It was in June of this same year, that George Fox, the founder of the Society of Friends, visited Flushing. He describes his visit, in these words: "From Oyster Bay, we

---

14 *A Brief Description of New York, etc.*, p. 2, 4, 7.

15 *Documents, XIV.*

passed about thirty miles to Flushing, where we had a very large meeting, many hundreds of people being there; some of whom came about thirty miles to it. A glorious and heavenly meeting it was (praised be the Lord God!) and the people were much satisfied."[16] This "glorious and heavenly meeting" was held in the open air, the speaker standing under the great oaks that ever afterwards bore his name. The Fox Oaks were two in number and stood near each other. One of them fell on the twenty-fifth of October, 1841, and the other, in the year 1863. A stone, near the sidewalk, on the west side of Bowne avenue, opposite the Bowne house, marks their site. Gabriel Furman describes the oaks, as they appeared in 1825. "Among other ancient remains," he says, "may be reckoned the two venerable oak trees at Flushing, under the shade of which the famous George Fox preached, in 1672. I visited these trees, Aug. 4, 1825, in company with Messrs. Spooner and Bruce, and assisted Bruce in measuring them, which we did around the trunk, six feet from the ground. We found one to be thirteen feet in circumference, and the other twelve feet, four inches, in circumference."[17]

---

16 *Fox's Journal, p. 453.*

17 *Long Island Antiquities, p. 78.*

During Fox's visit in Flushing, he was the guest of John Bowne. The couch on which Fox rested, after his exhausting labors, is still to be seen in the Bowne house, together with many other quaint articles of furniture belonging to those olden days.

CHAPTER VIII

ANOTHER YEAR OF DUTCH RULE

The war which broke out between England and Holland in 1672, had its effect on the American colony of New
1673 York. The Governor, Francis Lovelace, had gone to Hartford, to confer with Governor Winthrop about a post-office scheme which had for some time claimed much of Lovelace's thought. On his way home, he heard, at Mamaroneck, that the Dutch had taken New York. He at once crossed to Long Island to raise troops. At Justice Cornwell's, near Flushing, he met Secretary Matthias Nicolls. It was agreed that Nicolls should go on to the fort and that the Governor should keep out of the way of the enemy, and attempt to raise troops for the recapture of New York. Lovelace was, however, induced, by one of the Dutch ministers, to revisit his old quarters in New York. On his arrival he found that his house had been plundered, and he was arrested for debt. He was told that he could leave the country, if he would pay his debts. The Orange flag again waved over Manhattan: New York Province again became New Nether-

land, and the city became New Orange. Flushing and the other English towns were compelled to submit to the Dutch. These towns were ordered by the Council "holden in Fort William Hendrick," Aug. 13th., "to send hither immediately their Deputies, together with their Constables' staves and English flags, when they would, as circumstances permit, be furnished with Prince's flags instead of those of the English."[1] The deputies of Flushing appeared, on Aug. 22nd., and surrendered "one English flag and one Constable's staff." They expressed a willingness to submit to the Dutch. The inhabitants of the town were, therefore, pardoned, and to them were promised "the same privileges and rights which are given to the inhabitants and subjects of the Dutch nation." The deputies were, however, warned that any further acts of disloyalty would certainly result in the ruin of the town.

William Lawrence was appointed Schout, and Carel Van Brugge,[2] Secretary, for the five towns of Flushing, Jamaica, Middleburgh, Oyster Bay and Hempstead. Captain William Knyff and Lieutenant Jeronymous de Hubert, accompanied by Ephraim Hermann, were sent to these

---

1 *Mandeville, p. 30.*

2 Van Brugge died at Flushing in 1682. *New Netherland Register, p. 27.*

towns to administer the oath of allegiance.[3] They reported, on the first of September, that there were sixty-seven men in Flushing. Fifty-one of these had taken the oath of allegiance: the others were not at home. Of these sixty-seven, twenty were Dutch. Before the middle of September, all the men in Flushing had taken the oath of allegiance to the States General. The magistrates were instructed to "take care that the Reformed Christian Religion be maintained, in conformity to the Synod of Dordrecht, without permitting any other sects attempting anything contrary thereto."[4] Thus the Dutch Reformed Church was established in Flushing, but the village was not provided with a resident minister. "Cases relating to security of peace and justice, between man and man," were to be settled by the magistrates, without the right of appeal, when the amount involved did not exceed sixty florins. The Schout and Schepens were to settle such matters as laying out roads, disposing of lands, enforcing the observance of the Sabbath, and erecting churches and school houses. Francis Bloodgood was appointed a special officer, to guard the interests of the Dutch inhabitants of Flushing and the neighboring towns. He was to instruct them to be always ready, on the

---

3 *Documents, II, 589.*

4 *Laws of New Netherland, p. 476.*

receipt of notice of the arrival of an English ship, to repair, with arms, to New Orange. The magistrates were compelled to give up all arms furnished by former Governors of the Province.[5]

Thus Flushing again became a Dutch town. But the Dutch government, and Dutch customs, did not long continue. Before the close of the following year, the Province 1674
passed finally into the hands of the English. The record of an official act, during this second period of Dutch supremacy, helps to give us a picture of the times. On the twenty-second of February, 1674, James N., of Flushing, was brought to trial for "divers evil deeds and actions, using force in breaking doors open, beating women and children, burning houses and threatening further acts of arson." The court decided that the prisoner was "not in possession of his right reason." He was, therefore, pardoned and sent to Staten Island, where he was to be put to work by the magistrates, who were "empowered to punish him if he behave badly."[6]

5 *Documents, II.*
6 *Documents, II, 689.*

CHAPTER IX

REVOLUTIONS AND NEW LAWS

1674 Peace between England and Holland, was declared. The treaty of Westminster restored the Province of New York to England. The English quietly took possession, on the tenth of November. New Orange again became New York. A day of thanksgiving was proclaimed. But it was not observed by all of the inhabitants of Flushing, as witnesses the following record: "On the twenty-first of November, Daniel Patrick and Francis Coley were arrested, for "contemptuously working on Thanksgiving Day and giving reproachful language to the magistrates that questioned them." They were sent to the New York Court of Sessions, by Justice Cornell and Mr. Hinchman.

Major Edmund Andros was appointed Governor of New
1675 York, by the Duke of York. He was not a popular Governor, and had much trouble with the rather contentious population at the east end of Long Island. Andros visited Flushing, on September 15, 1675. There were indications that the Indians were becoming restless: and the white inhabitants

began to fear a general uprising. The Governor, to quiet the Indians and to reassure his white subjects, sent an armed sloop to cruise in the Sound, and went, himself, in his pinnacle, "as farre as Mr. Pell's, to the Indyans there, and from thence to fflushing, and home by land, the better to settle the People's mindes."[1]

During the first thirty years of its existence, Flushing passed through many and great changes. The English were now secure in their possession of the province. Public and private affairs moved along in a quiet and orderly manner and left few marks in history.[2]

Colonel Thomas Dongan, succeeded to the governorship of New York, in August, 1683. The instructions given to 1683

---

1. *Documents, XIV.*

2. The taxes collected in Flushing, in October of this year, 1675, amounted to £18.3.10. The taxable property, of the town, consisted of "Negeres, Landes, Madoes, Horses, three yer olds, to yere olds, yerlinges, oxen and boles, cowes, thre yer oldes, yerlinges, swine and shepe." The collector of taxes, appends this note at the close of his report: "Cap. Thoms hikes hath not yet prought in a list of his estate." The tax returns for 1683 amounted to £26.15.10. *Documentary History of New York, II, 263, 300.*

In 1680 Henry Willis and John Bowne protested to the Governor and Council against the action of the Court of Sessions in fining them £10 for allowing marriages contrary to the laws. When Willis and Bowne refused to pay the fines, Joseph Lee, Under-sheriff, seized a barn of corn from Willis and took from Bowne five milch cows. *Documents, V. 753.*

him, by the Duke of York, provided for a General Assembly to consist of eighteen representatives of the freeholders of the Province. Laws passed by this body were to be subject to the approval of the Governor. Even after receiving his approval, they might be rejected by the Duke. Yet they were to be "good and binding," pending his action. The first meeting of this first representative body in New York, under English rule, was held in New York, October 17, 1683. Among the other laws passed, was one which divided the Province into counties. This abolished Yorkshire, with its three ridings, and established the county lines on Long Island as they exist to-day. All towns were required to renew their patents. Flushing and Hempstead made large grants of Land to Governor Dongan and thereby obtained advantageous patents. Flushing conveyed to him four hundred acres of land, extending south of Success Pond to the edge of Hempstead Plains. Hempstead gave him two hundred acres. This splendid property constituted the Manor of Queens Village.[3]

1684 The last Indian deed for land in Flushing, is dated April 14, 1684. The deed is made by Sackapowsha and other Indians, who are described as "the true owners and propri-

3 When Dongan resigned the governorship, he retired to his farm on Long Island. On the usurpation of office by Leisler, Dongan was compelled to leave the country. He afterwards became Earl of Limerick.

etors of all the land." These Indians "sell, for good reasons," this land, "unto Elias Doughty, Thomas Willett, John Bowne, Matthyas Harvey, Thomas Hickes, Richard Cornell, John Hinchman, Jonathan Wright and Samuel Hoyt—who were the agents of the freeholders of the town. The Indians reserved "the priviledge of cutting bulrushes forever, within said tract."[4]

The Duke of York became King James II. New York, 1685
therefore, became a royal province, under the supervision of the Committee on Foreign Plantations. The General Assembly was abolished. On the twenty-third of April, James was proclaimed sovereign of the Province. New instructions were issued to Governor Dungan. These instructions gave the Church of England the same position in New York, that
it had always occupied in the mother country. "Ye shall 1686
take special care,"—said the Governor's instructions—"that God Almighty be devoutly and duly served throughout your Government: the Book of Common Prayer, as it is now established, read each Sunday and holiday; and the Blessed Sacrament administered according to the rites of the Church of England; . . . that no minister be preferred by you to any ecclesiastical benefice, in that our Province, without a certificate from the most Reverend, the Lord Archbishop of

4 *Mandeville*, p. 29.

Canterbury, of his being conformable to the doctrine and discipline of the Church of England, and of good life and conversation."[5] While the Church of England thus became the established Church of the Province, liberty of conscience was secured to persons of all creeds. The Governor was directed, to "permit all persons, of what religion soever, quietly to inhabit within your government, without giving them any disturbance or disquiet whatever, for or by reason of their differing opinions in matters of religion; Provided they give noe disturbance to the public peace, nor doe disquiet others in the exercise of their religion."[6]

The new militia law made all men, who refused to train, liable to a fine. A refusal to pay this fine was punishable by a seizure of goods. The Quakers refused to train, re-
1687 fused to pay the fine. When their goods were seized to satisfy the fines, they complained that they were deprived of the liberty of conscience that had been promised them, by the Royal Instructions.[7] This explains the many cases of Quakers' being mulcted of their property. They were not cases of unreasonable cruelty, but of enforced payment of fines. A militia was necessary for the protection of life and

---

5 *Documents, III, 36, 372.*

6 *Documents, III, 218, 359, 373.*

7 *Documentary History, III, 607 et sq.*

property. The authorities thought all the colonists should contribute to its maintenance.

James II. had already united all the New England colonies under one Governor Sir Edmond Andros, New York's former Governor. This policy of consolidation was now 1688 extended to New York, New Jersey and all the territory between Passamaquoddy Bay and Delaware Bay, except Pennsylvania. These united colonies became the "Territory and Dominion of New England in America." Andros was now appointed Governor of this enlarged New England.[8] He was assisted in the government by a Council of forty-two, appointed by the King from the several colonies. No seat of government was named: the Governor and seven members of the Council could, at any time and at any place, make laws.[9] In these new instructions, nothing was said about the ecclesiastical supremacy of the Archbishop of Canterbury or the Bishop of London.

But the reign of James was short. William, Prince of Orange, invaded England, in the autumn of the year 1688. On the twenty-third of February, 1689, William and Mary 1689 were formally proclaimed King and Queen of England. This revolution in England threw the American colonies

8 *Brodhead II*, 501.
9 *Brodhead II*, 505.

into confusion. An insurrection broke out in Boston, which resulted in the imprisonment of Andros. In New York Lieutenant Governor Nicholson and other officials appointed by James were accused of being Papists. Nicholson declined to proclaim the new king, until he should receive orders to do so. The people became impatient and mutinous.

Jacob Leisler, a native of Germany, had come to New Netherland, as a soldier, about thirty years before this date. He was now a rich merchant, and Captain of the militia. In him was found a ready leader of the insurrection against Nicholson. Fort James was seized and its name was changed to Fort William. Nicholson, deprived of power, sailed for England. William and Mary were proclaimed King and Queen, in New York, on June twenty-second. Six days later, Leisler summoned a convention. Flushing sent two representatives, though the majority of the inhabitants of Queens County appear to have opposed his usurpation. This convention appointed Leisler "Captain at the Fort at New York" and thus started him on his short but despotic reign.[10]

1690 The inhabitants of the towns of Flushing, Hempstead, Jamaica, and Newtown directed Capt. John Clapp to write

10 *Brodhead II, 564-591.*

to the King's secretary an account of their miserable condition, stating that Leisler and his officials had been seizing and selling their property because they declined to obey him; that these same officials had stripped their wives and daughters of their apparel, had shot and wounded Englishmen, and then sequestered and sold their estates.[11]

Colonel Henry Sloughter was appointed Governor of New York. He arrived in New York, March 19, 1691. Leisler 1691
was arrested, convicted of treason and murder, and was executed on May sixteenth.[12]

11 *Brodhead II*, 626.

12 Gov. Sloughter, died June 16. 1691, and was succeeded by Colonel Benjamin Fletcher, in August, 1692. Fletcher was recalled in 1695, and Richard Earl of Bellomont was appointed to succeed him, in 1698. Among the Council of Bellomont we find the names of Thomas Willett and John Lawrence—presumably from Flushing. Bellomont died March 5, 1701.

Governor Bellomont wrote to the Lords of Trade, in 1699, that "a great many men in that county (Queens) pretend themselves Quakers to avoid taking the oaths," but that these same pretended Quakers "got very drunk and swore and fought bloodily."

CHAPTER X

QUAKERS IN FLUSHING.

1692 Peace being once more restored, the inhabitants of Flushing had an opportunity to turn their attention to religious affairs. Up to this date, there had been no building in Flushing devoted to public worship. The Friends were the only people who held regular services, and they met in private houses. The society had now become large enough to justify it in building a public meeting-house. Three
1694 acres of land, together with a dwelling-house, were purchased for £40; and the Meeting-House was built.[1]

---

1 Following are the principal dates and facts connected with the Friends' meeting-house: 1692, the ground was purchased; 1694, the meeting-house built; 1696, the first yearly meeting was held in the new meeting-house; 1704, the meeting-house was shingled, plastered and repaired; 1707, a complaint was recorded that the monthly meetings were "cumbered with people having no business there," and that "children and young people disturbed the meeting by frequently running in and out;" 1716, orders were given for a new meeting-house; 1719, the new meeting house was completed; 1707, Samuel Haight made the remainder of the

The census, which was taken toward the close of the seventeenth century, reveals the fact that the town of Flushing had, at that time, five hundred and thirty white inhabitants and one hundred and thirty negroes.[2] Among the inhabitants, at that early date, may be found names of families that are to-day represented by many descendants in Flushing. 1698

In the journals of Roger Gill and Thomas Story travelling Quaker preachers we find frequent mention of visits to Flushing, where they were hospitably entertained and where they held satisfactory meetings. Thus Roger Gill 1699 to 1703

---

front fence, hung the gate and provided a lock for it; during the same year John Farrington was engaged, at £2 a year, to make fires; 1748, Samuel Bowne and John May sat in the gallery, during the yearly meeting, to keep order; 1752, complaint was recorded that the yearly meeting was much disturbed by "the rude and unchristian practice" of many who attended; 1760, "Thomas Franklin got an iron stove for the meeting-house;" 1763, the gallery was taken down, the second story was built and divided into two rooms; school was kept in one of these upper rooms; 1773, Rebecca Walsh was engaged to build fires, at £1.10 per annum, and John Eagles was paid three shillings for mending the bellows; 1776, the meeting-house was occupied by the Royal army as prison, barracks, hospital, store-house; the fence was used for fire wood; 1783, the meeting-house was repaired and restored to its original use; the ground was rented for £3 a year, the grass being reserved for the horses of Friends who attended yearly meeting; 1794, yearly meeting was transferred to Westbury. *Onderdonk's Friends on Long Island and in New York*, pp. 94, 95.

2 Appendix, *III*.

writes: "June 24, 1699. Lodged at John Rodman's.[3] Next day we went down the sound, in a sloop of John Rodman's, to Flushing . . . We lodged that night at Thomas Steven son's. Aug. 25, we lodged at Samuel Bound's. So Friends received us very joyfully, and were glad that we were come. . . . Aug. 31. From thence to Flushing (5th day) to Samuel Bown's. This day we held a meeting at Flushing. A good and large and lively meeting it was."

From the journal of Thomas Story, we cull the following: "Aug. 30, 1699. After this we went with Samuel Bowne and his wife to Flushing, where we had a glorious meeting next day . . . Jan. 28, 1700. We went by water to Flushing, where the Lord gave us a good and comfortable meeting: and then rested at Samuel Bown's until the 30th . . . Feb. 1, 1700. I was at the monthly meeting at Flushing, where several marriages were presented, and the countenance of the Lord was over us for good . . . July 29, 1702. Returned to Flushing; the next day I was at their week-day meeting, which was hard and shut up, at first, but ended comfortably: and on the 31st, I visited several families and returned in the evening to Samuel Bowne's

3 John Rodman was a physician and Quaker preacher in Flushing for about forty years. He died October 7, 1713, aged 78 years, "He did abundance of good . . . A man beloved by all sorts of people." *Record of Men's Meeting.*

where, next day, I wrote divers letters. Thence crossed the Sound . . . March 16, 1703. I was at Flushing week-day meeting, to which came some strangers. The meeting was very open and bright, and many truths of the Gospel were declared in the authority of it, to their satisfaction."[4]

Edward Hyde, Lord Cornbury, was appointed Governor of New York in 1702.[5] Cornbury was probably the most thoroughly disliked of all the Governors of New York. He was conspicuous for his zeal for the Church of England; but was more conspicuous for his unjust extortion and reckless expenditure of the colonists' money.[6] It was sometimes doubted whether he was entirely sane. He was fond of masquerading in women's clothes, and "was frequently seen in the evening in this costume, strolling about on the ramparts of the fort, with a fan in his hand." A portrait of him, which represents him in this dress, is still preserved in England.[7] 1702

The first year of Lord Cornbury's term of office was marked by the first appearance in Flushing of a Church of

---

4 *Onderdonk's Quakers of Hempstead. Onderdonk's Quakers on Long Island and in New York.*

5 King William died in 1702. His queen, Mary, was already dead. Mary's sister, Anne, succeeded to the throne of England. She appointed Cornbury, who was her uncle.

6 *Roberts' New York, I, 228-231.*

7 *Men, Women and Manners of Colonial Times, II, 104, 105.*

England clergyman. He was the Rev. George Keith, a missionary sent out by the "Society for the Propagation of the Gospel in Foreign Parts." Keith had formerly been a Friend and, as a travelling minister, had visited the yearly meetings of the Friends in Flushing. He, however, became dissatisfied with the doctrines of the Friends and took orders in the Church of England. The recently organized Society for the Propagation of the Gospel, sent him as a missionary to the American colonies. The Rev. John Talbot, chaplain of the war-ship which brought him to America, became his travelling companion and assistant.[8]

Keith's journal, published four years later, gives us an account of his visit to Flushing, on September 24, 1702. Arriving in the village, he proceeded to the Quaker meeting which was in session. "After some time of silence," he stood up "in the gallery, where their speakers use to stand when they speak," and began his address. He was recognized, and his presence was resented. He says: "I was so much interrupted by the clamour and noise that several Quakers made, forbidding me to speak, that I could not preceed." One of the Quakers spoke for an hour. His discourse, in the judgment of Keith, "was a ramble of nonsense and perversion of Scripture, with gross reflections both

8 *History of St. George's Parish*, p. 5, 6.

on the Church and the Government." Keith was accused of violating the Act of Toleration and was ordered out of the house. He maintained that it was a house for public religious meetings, and that all had a common right to it: if the Quakers should put him out, he could prosecute them. Moreover, since they appealed to the Act of Toleration, he inquired whether they had fulfilled the requirements of that act, by having their meeting-house licensed. The Act further required their preachers to sign thirty-four of the Thirty-nine Articles. Had they done this? They changed their line of argument and accused him of preaching for money, not for love. He replied that travelling Quaker preachers received pay, both from Friends in London and from the meetings they visited. He himself had received pay from that very meeting. He was then accused of misappropriating money entrusted to him. This he denied.

On the third of December, Keith returned to Flushing, armed with a letter from Lord Cornbury, and protected by two justices of the peace. He read the letter, without effect, in the meeting house. The Quakers again brought up the Act of Toleration, and Keith again turned it against them. They then said it did not apply to the American colonies. The Quakers tried to talk him down. He remained to hear three of their speakers, though, he says: "It was very grievous to us to hear such nonsense."[9]

Whether the Church of England service was at this time established in Flushing, as a result of the visit of Keith and Talbot, it is impossible to state.

Between these two visits of Keith and Talbot viz., on the 29th of November, 1702 the meeting-house in Flushing was the scene of another disturbance. Samuel Bownas, a Quaker preacher from England, was accused by William Bradford[10] of having, at a meeting recently held in Hempstead, spoken with contempt of the Church and her Sacraments. Bradford's deposition was supported by a similar one, made by Richard Smith. A warrant was issued for Bownas's arrest. This was accomplished in Flushing. We shall allow Bownas to tell his own story. "On the twenty-ninth of the same month, [November, 1702] I was at Flushing on Long Island, it being the Half yearly Meeting, which

---

9 *Journal of Travels.*

10 William Bradford came to America with William Penn, in 1658, and set up a printing press in Philadelphia. He was a Quaker, but left the Society and joined the Church of England. This threw him out of sympathy with the authorities in Philadelphia. In 1693, he was invited to come to New York. Here he set up the first press in the Province, and was appointed public printer. In 1725 he established the New York Gazette, the first paper published in the Province. He died in 1752 and was buried in Trinity Churchyard.

was very large, Keith being expected there. When the meeting was fully set, the High Sheriff came with a very large company, who were all armed: some with guns, others pitchforks, others swords, clubs, halberts, etc. as if they should meet with great opposition in taking a poor harmless sheep out of the flock. The Sheriff, stepping up into the gallery, took me by the hand, and told me I was his prisoner. 'By what authority?' said I; he pulled out his warrant and showed it me. I told him that warrant was to take up Samuel Bowne, and my name was not Samuel Bowne, but that Friend's name is so, pointing at the Friend by me. 'We know him,' said he, 'this is not the man, but you are the man: pray then what is your name?' 'That is a question which requires consideration, whether proper to answer or not, for no man is bound to answer to his own prejudice; the law forces none to accuse himself.' Thus we pro'd and con'd a little time, and I got up from my seat, and John Rodman, Samuel Bowne, and sundry other Friends, walked out of the meeting, it not being proper to discourse there at that time: and they, on conversing with the Sheriff, who in his nature was a very moderate man, having known Friends in England, easily prevailed on him to stay the meeting, with all his retinue, and afterwards they would consider what was best to be done. They willingly laid down their arms on the outside of the door, and came in, which increased the throng very much."[11]

Bownas was allowed to remain undisturbed, until the days of the Half yearly Meeting had passed. He was then taken to Jamaica for examination. Refusing to give bond, or to allow any of his friends to do so, he was commmitted to jail. Among others, one of the justices of the peace offered to be surety for him, but Bownas would not allow it- preferring to go to jail. To follow the fortunes of Bownas, would take us too far afield. During his imprisonment, he supported himself by making shoes. After a year's imprisonment, he was set at liberty.[12]

The Friends took the initiative in Flushing, in two great works of beneficence, i. e. education, and the freeing of slaves. In 1703, 5th. of 6th. mo., the meeting decided: "A schoolmaster being judged necessary for the town of Flushing, it is thought fit by this meeting that Samuel Hoyt and Francis Doughty do seek out for a convenient piece of ground, to purchase it and build a school-house thereon, for the use of Friends, about Richard Griffin's lot

11 *Life of Samuel Bownas, in the Friends Library, III, 25.*

12 Bownas again visited Flushing, in 1726. "The meeting of ministers and elders was of good service, among them were some young ministers; and at this Quarterly Meeting we had a solid time, a large appearance of young Friends of both sexes being there." *Life, p. 56.*

upon the cross way, which is near the centre of the town."[13] This school-house was probably built, though we find no record of the fact. Six years later, however, we find this record: "Thomas Makins, schoolmaster hath signified to this meeting his willingness to sit with his scholars in the meeting and take care of them, which the meeting think well of, and desire him as much as may be to bring all Friends' children with him on Fifth day, and also unto the meeting-day appointed for the youth's meeting."[14] These youth's meetings were held on the last Tuesday in February, May, August, and November.[15] Though not held on Sunday, these youth's meetings seem to be the beginning of the modern Sunday School idea, i. e. a special season for the religious instruction of the young. The first school held on Sunday was also conducted by Friends. It began about 1819 and was devoted to the education of negro children, in the elementary branches of secular learning.[16]

The first agitation of the subject of slavery appears to have been at a meeting held in Flushing, in 1716, when the

---

13 *Minutes of Meetings, I, 2.*

14 *Minutes of Meetings, I, 54.*

15 *Manuscript History of the Society of Friends in Queens County, H. Onderdonk, Jr., p. 139.*

16 *Manderille, p. 713.*

subject was brought up by John Farmer. It occupied the attention of Friends for four subsequent yearly meetings. In 1718, William Burling, of this meeting, published an address on slavery, which is probably the first anti-slavery publication in this country.[17]

The traditional history of the Flushing Meeting-House does not agree with that to be gathered from the original records. On the third day of the ninth month, 1693, orders were given to cut the timber and have it ready for "raising" in the next first month, i. e. January 1694. The first meeting was held in the Meeting House on the fourth day of the eighth month, 1694.[18] This is one year earlier than the traditional date. But the Meeting House then built was not

---

17 *Manuscript History, p. 153-155.* The Friends in Flushing had not always opposed slavery. We have at least one instance of the meeting's raising money to enable an impecunious Friend to buy a slave. In 1684, John Adams bought a negro and was not able to pay for him. His "necessity" was laid before the meeting, on the 14th. of 8th. mo. "The meeting did appoint and desire John Bowne of fflushing and William Ricardson of West Chester to take ye charge in behalf of ye meeting, to procure the sum of money . . . the meeting dooth promise and Engage to ReImburs and pay the said sumb soe procured." *Minutes of Meetings.*

18 On the 28th of 9th. mo. 1702. Samuel Haight was paid £50 for the money he had "layd out" in building the Meeting-House.

the one which now stands. It is sad thus to disturb a fond tradition, and to deprive our Meeting-House of its claim to so great antiquity, but the records seem to show that the present building was not erected until 1718 or 1719. We give in full the entries concerning this subject: "At a Quarterly Meeting at ye meeting-house at Westbury ye 23d. 12mo., 1716-7. It is Concluded at this meeting, Unanimously, that ye meeting house proposed to be built at ffiushing upon friends land there, neare ye Ould Meeting, be left to Hugh Cowperthwait, Samuel Bowne, francis Dowtey, James Jackson: for Westbury: William Willis, Nathaniell Jonson, John Titus, Jeremiah Williams, Thomas Percon: for Newtown: Robert ffeald: for New Yorke: Joseph Lathem: for West Chester: Jeremiah Hunt: and that the men above said shall have power to form ye said house and agree with workmen and carrey it on, according to their discression and Receave ye seaverall subscription to pay said workmen." This building was completed sometime before the close of 1719. At the Quarterly Meeting held on the 28th of 9th month, 1719, the following minute was recorded: "Inasmuch as mention hath bene mad that severall men are out of what may be dew them about building of ye meeting house at ffiushing, there for ye meeting hath appointed James Jackson, Francis Dowtey, Robert ffeld, William Burling, Nathanael Simens and John Rodman to in spect ye accoumpts a bout ye dis bursement and what Remains yet Unpaid, and give accoumpt to ye next Quarterly Meeting."[19]

The present Meeting-house was not originally a two-storied building. A gallery occupied the position of the present upper floor, until 1763.

The meeting kept a very close supervision over the conduct of Friends, and never hesitated to enforce its rules of discipline. Penitents were compelled publicly to "condemn" their action. If offenders refused to do this, after being "tenderly dealt with," they were "disowned." Here in a sample (1705) of many similar entries. "William Thorne condemns his disorderly and evil action in accompanying William Ford and Mary Hait, his cousin, in their rebellious endeavor to accomplish marriage without and altogether against the consent of her parents. The meeting advise him to give Samuel Hait satisfaction by desiring his forgiveness, and to make his paper of condemnation public, as far as his action was known: That truth may be cleared, a committee visit Thomas Ford who was concerned in assisting his brother William with great endeavor to perform a disorderly

---

19 *Minutes, I, 14, 39* No further reference to the subject can be found.

marriage by a priest. Thomas condemns his outrunning in going to New Rochelle about his brother's disorder in attempting to get married."[20]

20 Many similar cases of discipline may be gathered from the records. 1739, 7th of 12mo., R—— L—— condemns himself for consenting to his daughter marrying outside of meeting, and for being with her where there was "fiddling and dancing." Another offence was, giving her a dinner at his own home. 1782, E—— L—— is disowned. He plays cards, is extravagant in dress and address—uses vain compliments. 1784, E—— daughter of S—— D—— is disowned "for superfluous, and extravagance in, dress and address." 1775, "O—— W—— was at a horse race, attended with a fraudulent circumstance. He now condemns it and returns what he had so obtained." In 1774, it was reported: "Friends are clear of chewing tobacco in meeting, not clear of sleeping, no buying or importing of negroes." *Manuscript History*, p. *139, 173, 175, 181.*

CHAPTER XI

THE CHURCH OF ENGLAND IN FLUSHING GOVERNOR CLINTON

1704 Two years after the visit of Keith and Talbot, the services of the Church of England were regularly held in Flushing, if not at an earlier date. The first Rector of Jamaica, the Rev. Patrick Gordon, who had come out from England with Keith and Talbot, died of yellow fever before he had begun his work. Until his successor should be appointed, the Rev. James Honeyman was licensed, by Lord Cornbury, to conduct services at Jamaica, Flushing and Newtown. He spoke of Flushing as "famous for being stocked with Quakers." The regularly appointed Rector of these three towns, the Rev. William Urquhart, was inducted in July, 1704. Of the inhabitants of Flushing, he wrote: "Most of the inhabitants thereof are Quakers, who rove through the county from one village to another, talk blasphemy, corrupt the youth, and do much mischief." He visited Flushing once a month, and held services in the

Guard House, which stood near the corner of Broadway and Union street.[1]

Mr. Urquhart lived in Jamaica. He held services in Flushing twice a month once on Sunday, and once on a week day. He died in 1709. His controversies with the 1709 Nonconformists, concerning the possession of the church and glebe, belong to the history of Jamaica.

Lord John Lovelace, who succeeded Cornbury as 1708 Governor of New York, arrived on Dec. 18, 1708. He came down the Sound, on the Kingsale, and landed at Flushing.[2] Thence he proceeded to New York, where he was cordially received by the people. He died in the following year, and 1710 was succeeded, 1710, by Robert Hunter.

The same year brought to the three united parishes of Jamaica, Newtown, and Flushing, a new Rector, in the person of the Rev. Thos. Poyer. Mr. Poyer was a native of Wales. He sailed for America, in December, 1709. After a voyage of over three months, he was shipwrecked on the coast of Long Island, about a hundred miles from his parish. Mr. Poyer proved to be a faithful and hard-working 1711 pastor. In his report to the Society, May 3, 1711, he

1 *History of St. George's Parish, 21, 22. Antiquities of the Parish Church of Jamaica, p. 16-20.*

2 *Documents, V, 67.*

wrote: "I thank God the Church of England increaseth, for among the Quakers at Flushing . . . I have seldom so
1713 few as fifty hearers." Again, two years later: "The Churches increase beyond expectation, and among the Quakers in Flushing . . . I seldom have so few as fifty, and often more than a hundred hearers." Mr. Poyer received £50, a year from the Society, and very little from any other source. The friction between the Church of England and
1717 the Nonconformists continued. Mr. Poyer wrote, in 1717: "They make it their constant endeavour to tire me with their ill usage and to starve me."[3] The shop-keepers would not sell him provisions; the miller would not grind his corn. The miller told him to eat his corn whole, as the hogs do.
1731 In 1731, Mr. Poyer asked to be relieved of his duties, that he might return home; but he died of small-pox, in the same year, and was buried in Jamaica. Two manuscript sermons, preached by Mr. Poyer in Flushing, are still preserved in St. George's Church.

1733 The Rev. Thomas Colgan succeeded Mr. Poyer, in 1733. He had been an assistant minister in Trinity Church, New York. His wife was the daughter of John Reade. Mr. Colgan's conciliatory methods did much to overcome the opposition to the Church of England. The first Episcopal

3 *Documentary History of New York, III, 171.*

Church, in Flushing, was built during his rectorship. He wrote, in 1746, that they were "in a very likely way of 1746
having a church erected in the town of Flushing, a place generally inhabited by Quakers, and by some of no religion at all."[4] He expressed the hope, that the church would be ready for service in three months. The Society for the Propagation of the Gospel sent, for use in the new church, a copy of the Bible and the Book of Common Prayer, bound together, which may still be seen in St. George's Church. "A Quaker gave some money, at the opening of the new church" Mr. Colgan writes "and afterwards thought he had not put enough in the plate, and gave more to the collector." The churchyard was the gift of Capt. Hugh 1749
Wentworth[5] and Mary his wife. Capt. Wentworth was a merchant in the West Indian trade. The deed is dated, April 7, 1749 three years after the completion of the Church.

1753
It was during the rectorship of Mr. Colgan, that Flushing became the temporary residence of Sir George Clinton,

---

4 *Documentary History of New York, III, 194.*

5 *The New York Post Boy*, of October 25, 1756, contains the following: "Capt. Wentworth, being at St. Thomas, mustered as many New Yorkers as he could find (twenty-four hands in all), and in his own vessel, indifferently mounted with great guns, put to sea in pursuit of a French Privateer cruising off the harbor and chasing New York vessels. The Privateer thought best to disappear."

the Governor of the Province.[6] How long the Governor lived in Flushing, we are unable to say. It is certain that he was here in 1753.[7] On May 3, 1753, the Provincial Council met in Flushing present: the Hon. Jas. Alexander, Speaker, Archibald Kennedy, and Edward Holland. An address was presented to his Excellency, the Governor, who responded, in these words: "Gentlemen: I thank you for this kind address, as it is a great satisfaction to me to have my conduct and administration meet with your approbation."

One of Governor Clinton's letters to the Lords of Trade, is dated: "Flushing upon Long Island, ye 30 June, 1753." In this letter, he speaks of his lack of health, and expresses the

---

6 Sir George Clinton was the youngest son of the sixth Earl of Lincoln. He became Commodore in the navy, and later, in 1732, Governor of Newfoundland. He was appointed Governor of New York, in 1743, and retired in 1753. Returning to England he was appointed Governor of Greenwich Hospital: later, in 1757, Admiral of the Fleet: finally, a second time, Governor of Newfoundland, where he died, in 1761.

7 "He committed the error of secluding himself in the fort, or at his country seat, where he spent his time over his bottle, with a few dependents, who played billiards with his lady and lived on his bounty. He seldom went abroad: many of the citizens never saw him; and he did not attend Divine worship more than three or four times during his whole administration." *New York Gazetteer, p. 52.*

desire to return to England.[8] He also speaks of the threatening movements of "the French and their Indians," and states that he had sent notice of this danger to Governor Hamilton of Pennsylvania. It was probably in consequence of this notice, that Governor Hamilton sent Conrad Weiser, an interpreter, on a mission to the Mohawks. Weiser arrived in New York, on the first of August, on his way north. Being unwell, he sent his "son Sammy, with one Henry Van den Ham, to Flushing, on Long Island, to wait on Governor Clinton, and deliver Governor Hamilton's letter to him. Governor Clinton being gone to the plains, they left the letter with his lady and returned the next day." Weiser proceeded on his journey, and returned to New York, August 24th. Mr. Kennedy, a member of the Council, who was going to Flushing on the following day, offered to notify his Excellency of Weiser's return. Mr. Kennedy, however, found "that all the horses and chairs over the river were employed, and that he could get none, which prevented his going to Flushing."[9] Two days later, Weiser was able to reach Flushing. "I went" he says – "to Flushing, on Long Island, seventeen miles from New York, to wait on Governor Clinton -he happened to be from

8 *Documents, VI, 778.*
9 *Documents VI, 795-798.*

home, but came in by one o'clock. I paid him my compliments at his door he called me in and asked me how far I had been, and signified to me that it was a wrong step in me to proceed to Albany before I had his directions. I asked pardon, and told him my reason why I proceeded. His Excellency said it was well: he did not disapprove so much of my proceeding, as of my son's not staying for an answer. His Excellency seemed well enough pleased with my return, and of my not proceeding to Onondago, and was pleased to tell me that he intended to be in New York next Wednesday, and would then have me to wait on him and take a letter to Governor Hamilton, and so dismissed me, but would have me stay and eat a bit of victuals first, and ordered his attendance accordingly to get it for me and my companion. After dinner, I left Flushing and arrived in New York the same evening."[10]

Weiser did not see the Governor again. Clinton sent him his compliments, wished him a safe journey, and requested Weiser to present his compliments to Governor Hamilton.

These, not important, incidents are cited to enable the reader to gain something like a correct picture of the times.

---

10 *Documents, VI*, 798.

and to realize how Flushing entered into the life of the whole Province.

The French and Indian war broke out, two years later. 1755
William Johnson, in command of the expedition against Crown Point, wrote, in October, to thank the inhabitants of Queens County for "sixty nine cheeses and two hundred sheep, being part of one thousand raised in Queens County, on Long Island, as a present to the army."[11]

The Rev. Mr. Colgan died during this troublous year, "lamented and respected by all who knew him." He had done much toward accomplishing the work he laid out for himself, when he wrote, in the second year of his incumbency: "We are at peace with those several sectaries that are round about us, and I hope that, by God's help, peace will subsist among us. To sow the seeds thereof shall be my endeavor: to be of a loving, charitable demeanor to all men, of whatever persuasion, in matters of religion, shall be, by God's help, my practice, that so discharging my duty therein, I may contribute my mite to the good of the Church of Christ."[12]

Peace among the Churches was not, however, permanently secured. At the death of Mr. Colgan, the old feud

11 *Mandeville, p. 55, 56.*

12 *Documentary History of New York, III, 191.*

again broke out. The dissenters secured a majority in the vestry at Jamaica, and elected a Presbyterian Minister to the rectorship of the three parishes. Governor Hardy would not allow his induction. The vestry declined to elect any one else. After waiting some time, the Governor "was pleased to collate to the care of the parish, the Rev. Samuel Seabury Jr."

1756 The unwillingness on the part of the Quakers to serve in the militia, or in any way to assist in warfare, probably accounts for the fact that fines are recorded against many of them at this time.[13]

"Nine neutral French"[14] were sent to Flushing, in May, to be cared for by the magistrates. On Nov. 29, the General Assembly paid Christopher Roberts £4.2.1 for their support.

---

13 John Thorn, James Burling, James Bowne, Benj. Doughty, Stephen Hedger, Dan'l. Bowne, James Parsons, Dan'l Lathum, Sam'l. Thorn, Caleb Field, John Thorne, were fined £2 each, except the last-named, whose fine was 1£. *Documentary History of New York, III, 623.*

14 These so-called "neutral French" were the residents of Nova Scotia who were drawn from their homes by the British, because, it was alleged, they, under the guise of neutrality as non-combatants, had given aid to the enemy. A great number of them were distributed throughout the Island.

Quebec fell on Sept. 13, 1759.[15] The current number of the New York Mercury tells us how the event was celebrated, on the ninth of November. "The inhabitants of Flushing celebrated the reduction of Quebec, that long dreaded sink of French perfidy and cruelty. An elegant entertainment was provided, at which the principal persons of the place were present.. After dinner, the paternal tenderness of our gracious Sovereign for these infant colonies, the patriotism and integrity of Mr. Pitt, the fortitude and activity of our generals and admirals, etc., with every other toast that loyalty and gratitude could dictate, were drank. Each toast was accompanied by a discharge of cannon in all, about one hundred. The evening was ushered in with a large bonfire and an illumination."[16] 1759

One year later, Sept. 8, 1760, Canada passed into the hands of the English. Peace was once more established. The inhabitants of Flushing again turned their attention to 1760

---

15 One of the heroes at Quebec was Lieutenant Colonel Isaac Corsa. He, with the Long Island men, volunteered to erect a battery under the fire of the enemy, during the night of August 26th. This battery was chiefly instrumental in the capture of Fort Frontenac. After the war, he returned to his farm in Flushing and resigned his commission. During the Revolution, he was arrested as a British sympathizer and released on parole. He died in 1807, aged 80 years.

16 *Queens County in Olden Times*, p. 31.

religious affairs. The Rev. Samuel Seabury, the Rector of the Church of England, does not give a flattering picture of the spiritual condition of the town. He writes: "Flushing, in the last generation the ground seat of Quakerism, is in this, the seat of infidelity." Again: "Quakerism has paved the way" for "deism and infidelity."[17]

The Charter of St. George's Church is dated June 17,
1761 1761 the first year of the reign of George III.[18]

Mr. Seabury was assisted in his work, in Flushing, by John Aspinwall, Thomas Grennell, and a Mr. Treadwell.
1762 George Harison writes, in 1762: "Mr. Aspinwall,[19] a friend of the Church, a man of fortune and public spirit, has retired from business in New York, and settled in Flushing, where he found the inhabitants, chiefly Quakers, almost void of all sense of religion, a total dissolution of all manners, and a horrid contempt of the Sabbath. He immedi-

17 *Documentary History of New York, III*, 195, 196.

18 The petition for the charter was signed by the following residents of Flushing: John Aspinwall, Thomas Grennell, Daniel Thorne, Joseph Bowne, Joseph Haviland, Jacob Thorne, Francis Brown, Foster Lewis, William Thorne, Charles Cornell, John Morrell, Benjamin Thorne, John Dyer, Jeremiah Mitchell, Nathaniel Tom, Benjamin Fowler, John Marston, Charles Wright, Isaac Doughty, Christopher Robert, John Wilson.

19 Mr. Aspinwall lived in a house which still stands on the south side of Broadway, between Union street and Bowne avenue.

ately set about a reformation. The first step was to engage Mr. Treadwell to come and settle there as a teacher of the Latin tongue, and on Sundays to perform the service of the Church. His next step was to finish what was only the shell of a church.[20] He built a handsome steeple and gave a very fine bell. It is now one of the neatest churches in America, for its bigness: all of which was done at an expense of £600 currency to himself. He and Mr. Treadwell, by their good example, have brought over many Quakers

20 On Oct. 6, 1760, Mr. Seabury wrote: "They are now finishing the Church, which before was only enclosed so as to keep out the weather, and I hope in my next letter to acquaint the Society of its being completed."

March 26, 1761: "The severe cold weather, the past winter, obliged them to suspend the work some months, but they have now resumed it and are likely to complete it in a short time, together with a handsome steeple, which was begun last autumn. The principal expense of this work is defrayed by Mr. John Aspinwall and Mr. Thomas Grenall, two Gentlemen who have recently retired thither from New York. Mr. Aspinwall has besides made them a present of a very fine bell of about 500 pounds weight, and I hope the Influence and example of these gentlemen in their regular and constant attendance on Divine service will have some good effect on the people of that town. Thro' Mr. Aspinwall's means also, the church has been constantly supplied the last half year with a lay-reader, one Mr. Tredwell, a young gentleman educated at Yale College, in Conn., of an amiable character and disposition, and who intends to offer himself for the service of the Society and with their permission to go to England next Autumn." *Documentary History of New York*, 196, 197.

and Calvinists, so that I myself have been a joyful witness of a numerous congregation in a church, wherein, within three or four years, seldom assembled above ten or twelve persons."[21]

From the above, we learn that the church, built during Mr. Colgan's rectorship, was not, at that time, finished; and that the congregation collected by him had lost interest and become scattered. While both Mr. Seabury and the writer of this letter seem, justly or unjustly, to hold the Quakers responsible for the irreligious condition of the inhabitants of Flushing, we are not to understand that they accused the Quakers themselves of having lost "all sense of religion," or having fallen into dissolute manners or having a "contempt for the Sabbath."

1763 Mr. Treadwell, the school master and lay-reader, went to England for ordination, and returned to this country in 1763. He was stationed, by the Society, at Trenton, New Jersey. An unsuccessful effort was made, at this time, to separate St. George's Church from the other two neighboring parishes, and to secure Mr. Tredwell as the Rector of Flushing.[22] Mr. Seabury resigned the rectorship of the

---

21 *Onderdonk's Antiquities of the Parish Church of Jamaica*, p. 62.

22 This caused an estrangement between the Rev. Mr. Seabury and John Aspinwall. Mr. Seabury wrote to the

three parishes, in 1765, and removed to West Chester.[23] After the resignation of Mr. Seabury, the three parishes were without a Rector for more than three years, when the Rev. Joshua Bloomer was inducted to the rectorship. He was to receive from the Society in England, £20 per annum, and £30 per annum from each of the three parishes. The new Rector wrote, in 1770: "I preach at the three churches of Jamaica, Newtown and Flushing, alternately, and generally to crowded assemblies, who behave during Divine service with the utmost decency and decorum. The churches are neat, well-finished buildings, but those of Newtown and Flushing, rather small for the congregations."[24] 1765

Secretary of the Society, March 26, 1763, complaining of Mr. Treadwell's intrusion into the parish, and of his forcing an entrance into the Flushing Church. "I am utterly unable to guess at the motive of Mr. Tredwell's conduct, unless he acted under the Influence and direction of Mr. John Aspinwall of Flushing, a man of low Birth and strong passions and violent in his resentments, who, having acquired a great fortune by privateering, removed thither from New York, and who has really done very considerably towards finishing the church and gave a good Bell." *Documentary History of New York, III, 198.*

23 During the Revolution, he was imprisoned as a British sympathizer. At the close of the war, March 25, 1783, he was elected Bishop of Connecticut. On November 14, of the following year, he was consecrated, in Aberdeen, Scotland, the first Bishop of the Protestant Episcopal Church.

24 *History of St. George's Parish, p. 55.*

PART IV The Revolutionary Period

CHAPTER XII

MEN OF THE TIME

There were several Flushing men, identified with events of this period, who deserve more than a passing notice.

The first to claim our attention is Col. Archibald Hamilton. Hamilton entered the British army in 1755. In 1757, he received his commission as a Lieutenant. He served against Louisburg, in 1758; was made Captain, in 1761; served in America until 1774, when his regiment returned to England. He then left the army and settled in Flushing. He married Alice Colden, daughter of Alexander Colden and grand-daughter of Lieut. Gov. Cadwallader Colden. On June 5, 1776, he was arrested, as a British sympathizer, by order of the Provincial Congress of New York, but was soon released on parole.[1] In August, of the

---

1 June 24, 1776. Archibald Hamilton gave parole that he would not, directly or indirectly, oppose or contravene measures of the Continental Congress or of the Congress of New York.

same year, he was again arrested, brought before the Continental Congress, and sent to New Brunswick. On September 23rd., he was allowed to return home to his family. He soon joined the Loyalists, and was made Colonel of the Queens County Militia and Aide-de-camp to Governor Tryon.[2] His headquarters were at "Innerwick," Flushing. Judge Jones, a contemporary, speaks of him as "a man of an opulent fortune, a supernumerary aide-de-camp to his Excellency—for which he received ten shillings a day, for doing nothing, with rations of all kinds for his family."[3]

Hamilton was a man of an almost ungovernable temper, if we may judge from contemporary testimony. In October, 1778, he beat Thomas Kelly with the but-end of his riding-whip, because Kelly did not take off his hat to him. John Willet, seeing a negro taking from his farm a load of rails by order of Col. Hamilton, asked Hamilton why he had given the order. Hamilton leaped from his horse and ran at Willet, with a cutlass in his hand. Willet defended himself with a stick. Col. Hamilton fell upon his knees,

---

2 Gov. Tryon writes to Lord Germaine, Dec. 16, 1778: "I have been obliged, from the frequent duties the militia of Kings and Queens counties have been called on to perform, to appoint Archibald Hamilton Aid-de-camp and Commandant of the Militia of Queens County." *Documents and Letters*, p. 237.

3 *History of New York During the Revolutionary War*, II, 46.

and called God to witness that he would cut any one to pieces who opposed his orders. The same day, he fell upon James Morrell with a sword, and almost killed him. Walter Dalton also deposed, that Hamilton had twice knocked him down with a heavy weapon.[4] At least a dozen similar affidavits were sent to Governor Tryon, who appointed David Colden to investigate the charges. The result of the investigation is not known. At the close of the war, on the last day of December, 1783, Hamilton sailed for England. Twelve years later, he died in Edinburgh. His farm in Flushing became the property of John Hoogland.

One of the most distinguished families in Flushing, at this period, was the Colden family. Cadwallader Colden was born in Scotland, Feb. 17, 1688. He graduated from the University of Edinburgh in 1705, and came to Philadelphia three years later, where he practised medicine until 1715. He then spent a year in London, where he met many noted literary and scientific men, and returned to Philadelphia, in 1716. Two years later he came to New York, and was made Surveyor-General. In 1755, he received a patent for land near Newburg. In 1760, he became President of the Provincial Council. In 1761, he was appointed Lieutenant-Governor of New York, and held the office

---

4 *Onderdonk's Queens County in Olden Times, p. 54.*

until his death, in 1776. During this time, he was repeatedly placed at the head of the Government, by the death or absence of the various governors. In 1762, he purchased in Flushing, from John and Thomas Willet, for £200, an estate of 120 acres, known as Spring Hill. Reservation was made in the deed for this property, of "a certain antient burying Place, fenced in with a stone fence, or stone Ditch, (where the family of the Willets have hitherto been interred) to and for the use of the family of said Willets, to bury and deposit their dead henceforth forever."[5] This estate has recently become the Cedar Grove Cemetery. The "antient burying Place" may still be seen, though sadly neglected.[6] Mr. Colden used Spring Hill as a summer home until 1775, when he retired hither to end his days. Here he died on Sept. 20, 1776, at the age of eighty-eight. He was one of the most learned men of his time, in America, and carried on a correspondence with most of the scientific men of Europe. He was especially interested in botany, and was the first to introduce the Linnaean system into this country. He furnished Linnaeus with descriptions of between 300 and 400 American plants. Besides the History of the Five

5 The Colden Family, *E. P. Purple, p. 7.*

6 Mandeville says he carefully examined this burial-plot, in 1859, but could find nothing to mark the grave of Cadwallader Colden who was buried there, in 1776.

Indian Nations, Colden was the author of a number of medical and scientific treatises.

David Colden, son of Cadwallader Colden, inherited Spring Hill from his father. He married, in 1767, Ann Willet, daughter of John Willet. Judge Jones says that David Colden was "a gentleman of the first character and reputation, as to honesty and veracity."[7] David Colden studied medicine, though he never practised it, except among his friends. He devoted most of his time to scientific pursuits. Like his father, he was an ardent Loyalist.[8] At the close of the war his property was confiscated, he was proscribed and sentenced, if found in any part of this state, to suffer death as a felon, "without benefit of clergy."[9] In vain Colden begged Gov. Clinton for protection. He was compelled to flee to England, where he died, July 10, 1784, and was buried at St. Ann's Church, Soho. His farm was sold ten days later, by the Commissioners of Forfeiture, to William Cornwell, for £1800. Colden was, for a number of years, a vestryman of St. George's Church.

---

7 *History of New York During the Revolutionary War*, *I*, *363*.

8 David Colden was appointed, July 15, 1780, Assistant Master of the Rolls and Superintendent of the Police on Long Island. George Duncan Ludlow was the Chief. They acted as judges in all controversies, during the suspension of the civil government. *Onderdonk's Documents and Letters*, *p. 239*.

9 *New York During the Revolutionary War*, *II*, *269*.

Cadwallader David Colden was a son of David Colden. He was born at Spring Hill, April 4, 1769. He began his studies at Jamaica, Long Island, and afterwards continued them in London. He returned to the United States in 1785, after the death of his father, and began the practice of law in 1791. In the war of 1812, he was Colonel of a regiment of volunteers. In 1818, he was elected Mayor of New York, was sent to Congress in 1821, and served in the State Senate from 1824 to 1827. He married a daughter of Bishop Provoost, and died in Jersey City, Feb. 7, 1834. He was the author of the Life of Fulton, and of several other works.

Another distinguished Flushing family, at this period, was the Lewis family.[10] They espoused the cause of the Colonies. The head of the family, Francis Lewis, was born in Wales, in 1713. His father was the Rector of Landaff parish. His mother was the daughter of Dr. Pettingal, a Church of England clergyman. Francis was their only child. He lost both parents while young, and was educated under the care of his maternal uncle, the Dean of St. Paul's. When he reached the age of twenty-one, his first act was to convert his patrimony into merchandise and embark for New

---

10 *Biographies of Francis Lewis and Morgan Lewis, by Julia Delafield.*

York. Here he formed a partnership with Richard Annely, whose sister he afterwards married. When the French war broke out, in 1752, Lewis obtained a contract to clothe the British army. While at Oswego, superintending this business, he was taken prisoner by the French and committed to the care of the Indians.[11] It is said that his

---

11 Lewis's contemporaries do not give so flattering an account of him as does his descendant, Miss Delafield, whose biography has been followed in the text of this history. Among the manuscripts in the Library of the N. Y. Historical Society, is one endorsed "Annely v. Lewis, Instructions to draw a Bill." From this we learn that Richard Annely, of Bristol, England, came to New York, in 1734, with goods advanced by certain Bristol merchants. In 1739, Annely's consignors urged him to take Lewis as a partner. Lewis was at that time a shopman in the employ of Sydenham Shipway, at a salary of £15 a year. In 1743 Richard Annely died, at Whitestone. After four years, Edward Annely came out to settle his brother's estate. In the document cited above, he accuses Lewis of defrauding the estate. The New York Gazette and Post-Boy, for 1849, also contains charges by Edward Annely against Francis Lewis. Lewis replies, by charging his late partner with taking large sums of money without accounting for the same. He adds: "I am ready upon Oath to lay all Books and Papers before any judicious Persons; and nothing would be more agreeable to me than having the Accounts fairly adjusted, which have been so unaccountably perplexed by the Deceased. I only desire to be secured myself, which every judicious Man would think but reasonable." *New York Gazette and Post Boy, Sep. 6, 1749.*

Judge Jones, another contemporary, says that Lewis failed in business three times before 1752. He then made two voyages to the Baltic as supercargo. Returning to New York, he opened a lodging house. In 1755, he left the lodging house to be conducted by his wife, and went as sutler

knowledge of Gaelic and Cymraeg enabled him to converse with the Indians and thus he saved his life. He was sent to France and afterwards exchanged. The Colonial government presented to him a tract of land, of 5000 acres, in acknowledgment of his military services. About the year 1765 Lewis bought a farm of 200 acres, in Flushing. It was located where Whitestone now stands. In 1775, Lewis was chosen, with others, to represent New York in the Continental Congress. In July, of the following year, he was one of the signers of the Declaration of Independence. He served in the vestry of St. George's Church, Flushing, when at home, between 1770 and 1790. In 1790, he removed to New York, where he died, in 1802. He was buried in Trinity churchyard.[12] During the Revolutionary War, his business capacity made him a valuable member of Congress. Lewis was

---

with the army, on the expedition against Niagara. During the winter he remained at Oswego, where a large garrison was left. "By selling his tobacco, his pipes, his sugar, and his salt, at a most exorbitant price, he extorted a great deal of money from the poor soldiery." Returning to New York he entered into partnership for fraud with a corrupt Judge of the Admiralty, and made much money from privateering. During the Revolution, continues Jones, Lewis and his sons speculated in soldiers' certificates which they bought at the rate of 6 pence for 40s. With these certificates they bought confiscated lands. *Jones's New York During the Revolution II, 357 et sq.*

12 When Lewis died, not a single obituary notice appeared in any New York City paper, so far as can be ascertained.

a zealous supporter of Washington, when the attempt was made to supplant Washington and give the command of the Continental forces to General Gates.

Francis Lewis, Jr., succeeded his father as owner of the Whitestone estate, when the latter removed to New York. He appears to have been a prominent man in local affairs, and was a warden of St. George's Church, from 1791 to 1794.

A more distinguished son of Francis Lewis was Morgan Lewis. He was born in 1754. It does not appear that he was in any way identified with Flushing, though it is probable that this was his home, until 1779, when he married Gertrude Livingston, a daughter of Judge Robert Livingston. Morgan Lewis served in the Revolutionary War, as Captain, Major, and finally as Chief of General Gates's staff. He commanded the troops that met and escorted Washington, when Washington came to New York, in 1790, to be inaugurated as the first President of the United States. Morgan Lewis was elected Governor of New York, in 1804. He again served his country in the War of 1812. He died in 1844.

CHAPTER XIII

BEGINNING OF THE REVOLUTION

The Stamp Act was passed in 1765. The Lieutenant Governor, Cadwallader Colden, whose country home was in Flushing, was at the time acting Governor of the Province. He declared his intention of enforcing the act. On the evening of November 1st., a torchlight procession came down Broadway, New York, from the fields, carrying images of Colden and the devil. The Lieutenant Governor's coach-house was broken open, and his best chariot was seized. The two images were placed in the chariot, and the procession proceeded to Bowling Green. There chariot and images were burned. Not long after this, Zacharias Hood, a stamp officer, was pursued to Flushing, where the alarmed officer had taken refuge in Colden's residence. Hood was seized, taken to Jamaica, and compelled to swear loyalty to the colonies.[1] This is the extent of Flushing's connection with the detested Stamp Act. 1765

---

1 "Volunteer parties of the Sons of Liberty soon after went to Flushing by land and water, when fifty of them

The idea of appointing committees of correspondence in the various colonies originated at a Boston town meeting.
1772 in 1772. It was soon adopted by other colonies. This was the beginning of the Union. It was a thing unknown to law, but it was not a violation of any law.[2] The object of these committees was to arrange for some concerted action to protect the colonists in their rights. The result of their conference was the call of the first Continental Congress,
1774 which assembled in Philadelphia, Sept. 5, 1774. Local committees were appointed everywhere, to carry out the recommendations of Congress. With the exception of Suffolk County, Long Island opposed the assembling of a Congress, and declined to send delegates to co-operate with the New York Committee. Colden wrote, in October, to the Earl

---

surrounded Hood's lodgings and forced him to resign. Then one hundred persons on horseback and in carriages, in regular order, escorted him to Jamaica (Mr. Hood and another gentleman riding in a chair, in the centre) where he took the oath before Justice Samuel Smith. Mr. H. then thanked the company for their politeness, when he was complimented and huzzaed and invited to an entertainment, but he excused himself inasmuch as he was in such a frame of body and mind that he should be unhappy in company. Many constitutional toasts were drank, and next morning the company (except those who lived on Long Island) set out for New York, in several divisions, carrying the flag of liberty with the words *Liberty, Property and No Stamps*, inscribed thereon." *N. Y. Journal, Dec. 5, 1765. Queens County in Olden Times, p. 37.*

2 *Fiske's American Revolution, I, 89.*

of Dartmouth: "In Queens County, where I have a house and reside the summer season,[3] six persons have not been got together for the purpose, and the inhabitants remain firm in their resolution not to join the Congress."[4] But the Sons of Liberty, though few, were not idle. Early in January, 1775, a funeral in Flushing brought together a large 1775
number of people, and gave the Patriots an opportunity of creating a local committee of twelve.[5]

The New York Provincial Assembly met, January 10th, 1775. It refused to endorse the action of the Continental Congress, or to send delegates from New York to the next Congress, which was to meet on the tenth of May. The New York Committee, despairing of assistance from the Provincial Government, sent out, on March 16th, circulars to the different counties, requesting them to send delegates to a convention to be held in New York, on April 20th, for the purpose of electing delegates to the next Continental Congress. On April 3rd, the Provincial Assembly of New York, adjourned, never to meet again. Queens County

---

3 "Saturday last, the Hon. Cadwallader Colden, Esq., Lieutenant-Governor of this Province, arrived here from his seat at Flushing, in good health." *New York Journal, March 24, 1774. Queens County in Olden Times, p. 47.*

4 *Flint, p. 350.*

5 *Onderdonk's Documents and Letters, p. 21.*

voted against sending delegates to the New York Convention, but four delegates, chosen by minorities or otherwise irregularly, were sent from the county. Among these was John Talman, chosen, April 4th, by the town meeting of Flushing. The delegates met at the Exchange, in New York, April 20th, and formed themselves into a Provincial Congress, thus usurping the powers of the Royal Government. The delegates from Queens County were allowed to attend the sessions of the convention and to offer advice; but, because of the irregularity of their election, were not permitted to vote. Among the delegates chosen by this Provincial Congress, to represent New York in the next Continental Congress, was Flushing's patriotic citizen—Francis Lewis. The Provincial Congress adjourned, April 23rd.

On the following day came the news of the battle of Lexington and Concord. Another Provincial Congress was at once called, to "deliberate on and to direct such measures as may be expedient for our common safety." Queens County still refused to choose delegates. However, on May 22nd, delegates were chosen by Flushing; viz., Nathaniel Tom and Thomas Hicks. This second Provincial Congress, of New York, which met on May 24th, entirely ignored the Royal Governor and his Council, and assumed the functions of the Provincial Government. It recommended the various counties to appoint committees, with sub-committees for the towns, to carry out the resolutions of the Continental and Provincial Congresses. The sub-committee for Flushing, chosen in accordance with this recommendation, was: John Talman (Chairman), John Eagles, Thomas Rodman, Thomas Thorne, Edmund Pinfold, Joseph Bowne (Clerk).

In November, Queens County was again called upon to send delegates to the Provincial Congress. Every freeman in the County voted. An overwhelming majority (788 to 221) voted against sending delegates. Soon after this, Congress published "A List of Queen's Co. Tories," known as "The Black List," who were suspected of having received arms and amunition from the British war-ship Asia, and of having formed a militia to oppose the Colonies. Among these Tories was John Willet, a prominent and respected citizen of Flushing. The persons whose names were on "The Black List" were cited to appear before Congress, on Dec. 19th, "to give satisfaction in the premises."[6]

Queens County Tories became notorious. Their case 1776
was taken up by the Continental Congress. The pole list was forwarded to Philadelphia. Congress ordered that all who had voted against sending delegates to the New York

6 *Flint, p. 356 et sq*

Congress should "be put out of the protection of the United Colonies and that all trade and intercourse with them cease."[7] Col. Nathanael Heard, of Woodbridge, N. J., was ordered to take with him "five or six hundred minutemen, under discreet officers," march into Queens County, disarm every man who had voted against sending deputies, and arrest all who resisted. Nineteen "disaffected" persons were carried away to Philadelphia. Among them was John Willet of Flushing. They were afterwards handed over to the mercies of the New York Congress and later released, under bond to appear "within six days after summoning before any Provincial Congress or committee of Safety."[8]

Boston was evacuated by the British troops, March 17, 1776. General Howe sailed with his forces to Halifax. Later he sailed west again, and, toward the end of June, appeared before New York. He had with him about 30,000 soldiers, including 12,000 Germans, under General De Heister.[9] Washington hurried toward New York. Flushing now became the refuge of two classes of persons; viz., the

---

7 *American Archives, 4th Series, IV, 1030.*

8 *Flint, p. 368.*

9 *Losing's Empire State, p. 244.*

Loyalists,[10] who sought protection among their many sympathizers, and certain poor families who were sent hither by the Provincial Congress.[11] Among those of the former class, was the Rev. Chas. Inglis, Rector of Trinity Church, N. Y.[12] The local committee considered the advisability of seizing him, but his friends removed him to more retired quarters, and he escaped further notice. How many of the second class came to Flushing, it is impossible to say. The Provincial Congress paid John Talman £200, to defray the expense of their support.[13]

Governor Tryon, the Royal Governor of the Province had established his headquarters on one of the British ships. Thence he sent out a declaration from Lord Howe and General Howe, offering pardon to all who would submit to the authority of England. This declaration was published by Thomas Willet, in his capacity as Sheriff. Willet was

---

10 "Long Island became an asylum for the Loyalists, to which they fled from all parts of the continent for safety and protection, to avoid oppression at least, if not murder." *Hist. N. Y During the Revolution, II, 116.*

11 Washington recommended that women, children and infirm people be removed from the city, because their shrieks and cries tended to dishearten the young and inexperienced soldiers. *Documents and Letters, p. 85.*

12 At the close of the war, 1783, Inglis went to Halifax. In 1787 he was consecrated Bishop of Nova Scotia.

13 *Documents and Letters, p. 85.*

arrested and, on admitting that he had caused the declaration to be published, was committed to jail in New York, by authority of the Provincial Congress.[14] The nearness of the English caused the committee-men of Flushing to organize a militia. Nathanael Tom was elected Captain and Jeffery Hicks, Lieutenant.[15] Nathanael Tom afterwards

---

14 *Journals of the Provincial Congress, I. 558.*

Willet's brother, Edward Willet, and Edward Willet, Jr., together with Lawson the schoolmaster of Flushing, who acted as the scribe, and Thomas Hicks, attorney at law, were also arrested. *Queens Co. in Olden Times, p. 51.*

15 *Calendar of Historical Manuscripts, I, 335.*

Another company was organized at Flushing, July 27, 1776, to become part of Col. Josiah Smith's regiment, which was used to protect the live stock on Long Island. Below is the muster roll. The lieutenants and sergeants received $\$8$, pr. month: the corporal and drummer, $\$7\frac{1}{3}$ pr. month; the fifer, $\$7\frac{1}{2}$ pr. month: and the privates, $\$6\frac{2}{3}$ pr. month.

John Robert, *1st Lt.*	William Lowree, *Corp.*
Isaac Hicks, *2d Lt.*	John Smith, *Corp.*
Joseph Beesley, *Sergt.*	James Doughty, *Drummer.*
Lewis Cornwell, *Sergt.*	Moses Fowler, *Fifer.*

Privates.

Benjamin Farrington	John Moore
John Mills	Jarvis Dobbs
John Smith	Jacob Manney
Matthew Farrington	Thomas Talman
Stephen Wright	Jacob Huber
Thomas Fowler	John Parker
Oliver Thorne	Jacob Grifling
William McDeane	Robert Wilson
John Hulsifer	Daniel Hitchcock
James White	Robert Betts
Malcomb McAuley	George Miller

Documents and Letters, p. 98, et sq.

became Captain of a company of Continentals, raised at Kingston. He served through the war, and died at Kingston, aged 73 years. The Rector of St. George's Church was ordered to omit the prayers for the King and Royal family; but, rather than do this, he closed his church for five Sundays—until the British troops entered the town.[16]

16 "The courts were closed in Queens County, from September, 1773, until May, 1784. The Whig Committee of Safety served, in lieu thereof, until Aug. 27, 1776. Martial law then prevailed until the establishment of peace." *Flint's Early Long Island, p. 449.*

CHAPTER XIV

THE BRITISH OCCUPATION OF FLUSHING

1776 to 1783

On the 27th of August, occurred the battle of Long Island. On the 28th, the American army, under the direction of Washington, retreated to New York and later to Harlem Heights. New York fell into the hands of the English. So did Flushing.[1] A company of light-horse galloped into "the town spot" of Flushing and inquired at the Widow Bloodgood's for her sons. On being told that they had fled, the soldiers threatened to burn her house, but were persuaded to desist. Thomas Thorne, the blacksmith and inn-keeper, was seized, and ended his days on one of

1 The Rev. Joshua Bloomer, Rector of St. George's, wrote to the secretary of the S. P. G., in London: "I feel myself happy to have it in my power to write to you from a land restored from anarchy and confusion to the blessings of order and good government . . . The principal members of my congregation who conscientiously refused to join in their [i. e. the Patriots'] measures excited their highest resentment. Their homes were plundered, their persons seized, some were committed to prison, others sent under a strong guard to the distant parts of Connecticut, where they were detained as prisoners for several months." *Documentary History of New York, III, 205.*

the prison-ships. James Burling and John Vanderbilt were also carried away, but later came out of prison alive. Cornelius Van Wyck, the member of Congress from Flushing, was imprisoned until October.[2]

A report of this raid being brought to the headquarters of the Continental army, at Kings Bridge, Gen. Heath commanded Col. Graham to confer with Messrs. Eagle and Pinfold, committee-men for Flushing, and, if the enemy were not more than a hundred, to go and scatter them.[3] This expedition of relief was probably never undertaken, for, soon after the battle of Long Island, the 71st Highlanders marched into Flushing.[4] On October 12th, the 1st, 2nd, and 6th brigades of Howe's army passed through Flushing to Whitestone, where they crossed to the mainland, preparatory to the battle of White Plains. It required half a day for the troops to pass a given point.[5]

Flushing was occupied by the English until the close of the war.[6] During the summer, there were not so many

---

2 *Documents and Letters*, p. 109.

3 *American Archives, Fifth Series, I, 1216.*

4 They brought with them fifty or sixty head of cattle from Kings county. These were butchered about a mile east of the village, and cooked. *Documents and Letters*, p. 103.

5 Id.

6 The inhabitants of Flushing, as a class, were Loyalists. The only persons of property reported, in 1778, as being "now in actual rebellion," were: Francis Lewis, White-

soldiers on Long Island; but as winter approached, each year, the officers began to seek for protection for themselves and their men, among the farms and in the villages of Long Island. An officer, accompanied by a Justice of the Peace or some other prominent Loyalist, would go about to inspect the houses, and decide how many soldiers each house was capable of accommodating. The only notification was: "Madam, we have come to take a billet on your house." The rooms occupied by the soldiers was separated from the rest of the house by nailing up the connecting doors; though the soldiers often mingled with the members of the family, and sometimes intermarried with them.[7]

The Quaker Meeting-house, in Flushing, was used as a prison, a hospital, and a hay magazine. Meeting was in session when the British officers came to take possession. They respectfully waited until the Friends rose to leave, before they carried their orders into effect. The Friends suffered in the confiscation of their property, from both sides, because of their refusal to contribute to the support of the armies.[8] Some of them were suspected of giving aid to

---

stone, whose estate was valued at £4000: Joseph Robinson, Whitestone, £2000: —Cornell, Success Pond, £200. *Steven's Manuscripts in European Archives. Document 1234.*

7 *History of Queens County, p. 38.*

8 Appendix.

the Patriots, while professing strict neutrality. Colonel Hamilton issued the following order: "Any of those people, commonly called Quakers, who were aiders or abettors of this unnatural rebellion, are to be constantly warned to appear, and to be fined for a non-compliance. At the same time every lenity will be shown to those few who held fast their integrity."[9]

West of the Meeting-house was a hospital, where small-pox raged. South of the Meeting-house was a parade ground. A guard-house, which stood west of the Aspinwall house, was pulled down by the soldiers for fire wood. The Aspinwall house was the headquarters for the officers. Col. Hamilton's headquarters were in the Mitchell house, corner of Whitestone and Bayside avenues. The old Duryea house, south of the Cemetery was also used as headquarters. Many soldiers were at times encamped beyond this house, near

---

9 *Documents and Letters, Second Series, p. 31.*

One of the German officers, Lieut. Hinrich, writes thus about Long Island, Sept. 18, 1776: "Long Island is a beautiful island. It has a great number of meadows, orchards, fruit trees of all descriptions, and fine houses . . . The Quakers are not rebels: on the contrary they have publicly proclaimed in all their gatherings and churches that whosoever went armed would lose their membership . . . The whole island forms an exquisite picture . . . The ladies on this island are not ugly, and upon the mainland are even said to be pretty." *Letters of Brunswick and Hessian Officers, p. 188 et sq.*

Fresh Meadows. Cannon were mounted on the ridge east of Whitestone avenue, between Broadway and State street. A beacon was erected on Washington street, east of Main street. It consisted of a pole wrapped with straw, and bearing aloft a tar barrel. This was one of a system of signals, extending from Norwich Hill to New York, via Flushing.[10]

Flushing furnished comfortable quarters for both officers and men. The favorite toast was: "A long and moderate war." For amusement, the officers played at fives against the Meeting-house, or rode to Hempstead plains to take part in the fox-hunting, horse-racing, bull-baiting and other

---

10 "Signals by day and night for Long Island and Kings bridge, to be made from Norwich Hill, Sutton's Hill and Flushing Heights.

MEM.—Norwich Hill is two miles south of Oysterbay, Sutton's Hill is three miles from Cow Neck Point, Flushing Heights are near Ustick's house." General Order of William Tryon, Major General. *Documents and Letters. Second Series, p. 36.*

There was a small fort at Whitestone, at Bogart's Point. The militia from Jamaica were sent over in squads of six or eight to man the fort. They stood guard for about a fortnight, and were then relieved by others. The fort was cold, and sentinels found the neighboring tavern more attractive. Col. Hamilton one day surprised Stephen Higbie, sergeant, smoking in the tavern. He knocked the pipe out of Higbie's mouth and, pointing a pistol at his breast, cried: "Are you a d—d old Presbyterian or not?" "No!" "'Tis well you said no, or I'd blown your brains out. Now I've some hopes of you." *Documents and Letters, p. 46.*

"good, old English sports." The soldiers also had their fun. They rolled large cannon-balls about a course of nine holes: they ran races, tied in sacks; they made wry faces for wagers: they tried to catch pigs whose tails had been soaped.

"The Royal and Honorable Brigade of the Prince of Wales Loyal American Volunteers," was quartered at "the famous and plentiful town of Flushing," early in 1777.[11]

Colonel Hamilton was appointed in command of the Queens County militia, and from his headquarters, "Innerwick," issued many orders that are still preserved.

At Whitestone stood the home of Francis Lewis, an uncompromising Patriot. A party of light-horse, under Col. Birtch, surrounded the house, seized Mrs. Lewis, and destroyed books, papers and furniture. Mrs. Lewis was sent to New York. Here she was imprisoned for several months. She would have been without the common necessaries of life, but for the faithful attendance of negro servants who followed their mistress, and ministered to her wants. She was finally released by the intervention of Washington, who ordered the wives of two British officials to be imprisoned in Philadelphia, until Mrs. Lewis was restored to freedom.

---

11 *Documents and Letters, p. 142.*

The war did not stop the usual course of events in human life.[12] People married, carried on their business, and died. Lieut. Col. Beverly Robinson, Jr. was married, in Flushing, Jan. 26, 1778, to "the amiable and accomplished Miss Nancy Barclay."[13] Henry Nicoll was married to Elsie Willet, of Spring Hill, June 21, 1779. The events of Nov. 27, 1780, must have caused no small stir in Flushing society. On that day, the Rector of St. George's solemnized three weddings: Capt. Jarvis Dobbs, of the sloop Abigail, was married to Miss Hettie Worthman: Capt. Heymen Clarke, of the Industry, to Miss Annatie Worthman; and Capt. Matthew Farrington, of the Nancy, to Miss Phebe McCullum.[14] Thus Flushing surrendered to the British Navy. The newspaper comment on this tripple wedding was as follows: "The amiable accomplishments of

---

12 "Long Island (from the Tour of which I am just returned) is the only peaceful and happy spot at present in this Part of America. The Inhabitants are exceedingly benefited by supplying the Army, and are, excepting a few Presbyterians to the Eastward, eminent for their Loyalty, on which Account they suffered much while under the Terror of the Rebels." Ambrose Serle to the Earl of Dartmouth, April 25, 1777. *Steven's Manuscripts in European Archives, Documents 2057.*

13 Nancy Barclay was the daughter of the Rev. Henry Barclay, D. D., of New York. Doctor Barclay and his family were probably among the refugees in Flushing.

14 *Queens County in Olden Times, p. 56.*

the young ladies presage the most perfect happiness that the marriage state can afford."

William Prince advertised his "large collection of fruit trees, "and directed orders to be left at "Gaine's, or on board the Flushing boat, near Fly Market, Ferry Stairs, Oliver Thorne now Master."[15] Houses and lands were bought and sold. So were negroes. David Colden advertised for sale a healthy man and woman, "neither in the least infatuated with a desire of obtaining freedom by flight."[16] "A likely negro wench, aged twenty-two, and her male child, aged twenty-two months," were offered for sale in New York, with the recommendation that the woman understood all kinds of house-work, and "was brought up in Flushing." The farmers found ready market for their crops and wood. It is true the sales were often

---

15 William Prince established his nursery in 1737. It is supposed to have been the first nursery in America. When the British took possession of Long Island, Gen. Howe placed a guard to protect the Linnean Botanic Gardens, as the nursery was called. The war seriously affected Mr. Prince's business. He was compelled to sell a large number of grafted cherry trees for hoop poles.

16 *Documents and Letters, p. 146.*

"May 22, 1780. £5 Reward—Ran away from his master, David Colden, a negro named Kelso. He had eight days' leave of absence to find a purchaser. He speaks English only, and wore apple-tree buttons on his coat."

Queens Co. in Olden Times, p. 56.

compulsory, but in most cases a fair price was paid.[17] For instance, an order was issued, April 23, 1778, notifying farmers from whom the soldiers had taken hay, that if they would present their claims "to Mr. Ochiltree, Deputy Commissary of forage at Flushing, with proper certificates," they would be paid.[18]

Education appears not to have been neglected. Among the advertisements in a New York paper, we find one for "a private tutor, to teach Latin, etc., to go in a gentleman's family at Flushing."[19]

Mixed in with these occasions of joy, and events in every day business life, were also occasions of sorrow. Mrs. Susanna Cornell, the wife of the Hon. Samuel Cornell, a member of His Majesty's Council, in North Carolina, came to Flushing as a place of safety, during the war. Here she

---

17 The price of wood, per cord, was as follows:

	Oak	Hickory
From Flushing to Cow Neck	£3	£4.10
From Cow Neck to Huntington	45s.	70s.
From Huntington to Setauket	35s.	45s.

Hay and grain brought the following prices, in 1778:

Upland hay	8 *s. per cwt.*	Rye	10 *s. per bu.*
Salt hay	4 *s. per cwt.*	Buckwheat	7 *s. per bu.*
Straw	3 *s. per cwt.*	Wheat flour	80 *s. per cwt.*
Wheat	26 *s. per bu.*	Rye flour	30 *s. per cwt.*
Corn	10 *s. per bu.*	Buckwheat flour	26 *s. per cwt.*
Oats	7 *s. per bu.*	Indian meal	28 *s. per cwt.*

Flint, p. 447.

18 *History of Queens County, p. 38.*

19 *Documents and Letters, Second Series, p. 28.*

died of small pox, Feb. 16, 1778, contracted by inoculation. She left five daughters. "The Hon. Mrs. Napier, lady of the Hon. Capt. Napier, of the 80th Grenadiers," died of consumption, at Mr. Vanderbilt's house, Jan. 10, 1780. She was but twenty-three years old. "Her remains were deposited in the Colden vault, at Spring Hill, attended by the officers of the 22nd, 38th, and 80th Regiments."[20]

Religious services were uninterrupted. The Friends, though deprived of the use of their Meeting-house, held regular meetings in private houses and barns. Abel Thomas, a traveling Quaker preacher, testifies to the courteous treatment received at the hands of Col. Hamilton. Arriving at Flushing, Thomas was taken before Hamilton, as were all strangers. "We informed him," writes Thomas, "that we intended to hold meetings on the Island. His answer was that 'if that was our business, it was a pity to hinder us.' He readily gave us a permit to travel through the Island."[21] Regular services were held at St. George's

---

20 *Documents and Letters, p. 145.*

"She left the world with the most perfect serenity and resignation; her two daughters, one, three and the other, two years of age, are under the protection of Col. Archibald Hamilton, nearly related to the Hon. Capt. Napier, by the Marquis of Lothian's family." *Royal Gazette, New York, Jan. 15, 1780.*

21 *Documents and Letters, Second Series, p. 59.*

Church. The Rector was, for a time, assisted by the Rev. John Sayre, a refugee from Fairfield. Conn.

It is impossible to say just how many soldiers were quartered in Flushing, during the war. We have already mentioned the 71st Highlanders. and the Brigade of Loyal American Volunteers.[22] An advertisement in Rivington's Gazette tells us that the 1st Bat. of Delancey's Brigade was in camp, at the head of the Fly, in January, 1778.[23] From similar sources and from the reports of American spies, we

---

22 Page 135 Col. Beverly Robinson was in command of the Loyal American Volunteers; Lt. Col., Beverly Robinson, Jr.; Maj., Thomas Barclay. *Documents and Letters, p. 247.*

Col. Beverly Robinson was born in Virginia, 1723. He served, under Wolfe, against Quebec, in 1759. Though opposed to the action of England which brought on the war of the Revolution, he remained loyal to the English government. He was implicated in Arnold's plans of treason. He went with the commission, sent by Clinton, to plead for the life of Andre, and reminded Washington of their former friendship. At the close of the war, he went to New Brunswick. and subsequently to England, where he died in 1792. Beverly Robinson Jr. was born in New York state in 1755. He served in his father's regiment as Lt. Colonel through the war. In 1783 he went with the emigrants to Nova Scotia, and later to New Brunswick. He resided at St. John's and served as a member of the Provincial Council. He died in 1816 while on a visit in New York.

23 "Sutler wanted for the 1st Bat. of General Delancey's Brigade, who is capable of furnishing a large mess. Apply to the gentlemen of the Reg., at the camp, head of Flushing Fly. *Rivington's Gazette, Jan. 17, 1778, Doc. and Let., p. 143.*

gather the following information. It will be seen that it is impossible to state how many soldiers were here at any given time, for frequently only the arrival or departure is noted, or from an advertisement we learn that a certain regiment was here on a given day. How long was its stay cannot be ascertained.

"One regiment of Scotch" was in Flushing, in February, 1778. The 17th. Reg. of Foot,[24] and the Maryland Loyalists' Regiment, were in camp at the head of the Fly, in September of the same year. The 64th[25] was also some where in the town during the year. It embarked at Whitestone, in September, and went into camp at Bedford. The 1st Bat. of Hessians was reported at Flushing, in February, 1779.[26] The 82nd was at Whitestone,[27] in July of the same year. The 3rd Bat. of Hessians was here early in 1780.

---

24 Col. Moncton; Lt. Col. Johnson; Maj. Armstrong. Capt. Darby advertises for a strayed horse. *Rivington's Gazette, Sept. 5, 1778. Doc. and Let., pp. 143, 250.*

25 Col. Pomeroy; Lt. Col. Ed. Eyre; Maj. Brereton. Uniform—Red, faced with black. *Rivington's Gazette, Sept. 23, 1778. Doc. and Let., pp. 144, 251.*

26 Report of Spies. *Doc. and Let. p. 260.*

There were 350 Hessian Chasseurs at Flushing on Feb. 16, 1779. *Queens Co. in Olden Times, p. 54.*

27 Col's. Gunning and F. McLean; Lt. Col. Craig; Maj. Robertson. *Doc. and Let., pp. 144, 252.*

There is reason to believe that the 22nd, 38th,[28] and 80th, Grenadiers, also, were here, in January, 1780.[29] Simcoe's corps crossed the sound to Flushing, July 19th, and proceeded to Huntington. On the 19th of August, 9000 troops were reported at Whitestone and West Chester. Toward the close of the same year, General Sir Henry Clinton[30] returned from his campaign against Charleston, and went into winter-quarters on Long Island—"the main army of the British lay at Flushing, from Whitestone to Jamaica." During 1781, we find the 17th Dragoons—300 men—near Fresh Meadows, and Benedict Arnold's Legion of Provincials—200 men—near Black Stump.[31] The 38th and 54th were here in February, 1782.[32] During the summer we find the King's American Dragoons, consisting of four troops mounted and two unmounted, under the command of Col.

---

28 Col. Sir Robert Pigot; Lt. Col. Henry Edw. Fox; Maj. French. Uniform—Red, faced with yellow. The 38th was near Fresh Meadows, with headquarters at Duryea's, during the summer of 1783, also. *Doc. and Let., p. 250.*

29 Page 139.

30 Clinton's own regiment was the 84th. Royal Highland Emigrants. Col. Sir Henry Clinton, K. B.; Lt. Col. John Small, Maj's. Alex. Macdonald, Thos. Murray. *Doc. and Let., p. 252.*

31 Report of Spies. *Doc. and Let., pp. 244, 260.*

32 The officers of the 38th. have already been given. Those of the 54th were: Col. M. Frederick: Lt. Col. A. Bruce; Maj's. A. Foster and John Breese. *Doc. and Let., p. 251.*

Benjamin Thompson, encamped near Fresh Meadows. During the same year, 1782, the 1st Bat. Grenadiers was at "Ireland Heights, near Flushing."[33] Toward the close of the year, we find also Ludlow's corps, Fanning's corps, and Robinson's Loyal American Volunteers, at, or near, the head of the Fly.[34] During the next year, 1783, the 34th, 38th, 54th, 64th[35] regulars, as well as Delancey's 3rd Bat. and Robinson's Loyal Americans, are reported at Flushing.

With so many idle soldiers about, it is not surprising that we read of many cases of depredation.[36] Every effort was made by Gen. Delancey to restrain the soldiers and to protect the inhabitants from outrages.[37] Soldiers were not

---

33 *Rivington's Gazette, July 3, 1782. Doc. and Let., p. 150.*

34 *Doc. and Let., p. 260.*

35 "Any persons having demands against the late Lt. Steadman, 64th. Reg., are desired to send accounts to Lt. Hutchinson of the 64th. Gren., near Flushing." *Rivington's Gazette, July 19, 1783. Doc. and Let., p. 151.*

36 Ambrose Serle writes to the Earl of Dartmouth, Sep. 5, 1776, concerning the Hessians: "The injudicious Abuse and Menaces of the Rebels. and the Hope of Plunder (for I hear all the Hessian common Soldiers have a Notion of making their Fortunes), have stimulated them to Such a Degree, as by no Means inclines them to show Tenderness and Mercy. They are very expert in foraging, and have made great Use of their Time." *Steven's Manuscripts in European Archives. Document 2042.*

37 *The Orderly Book of the Maryland Loyalists Regiment* contains the following: "Flushing Fly, Sep. 4, 1778. The Genl Expects The Commanding Officers of Corps will use their utmost Exertion to Pertect the Property of the Inhab-

allowed to go more than half a mile from camp. After sundown, they were not allowed to leave the camp at all, without a pass. The roll was called several times a day, to assist in the enforcement of this order. When John Willet was attacked and robbed, on June, 1778, General Delancey offered a reward of $10 to the person who would discover and report the offender to Major Waller.[38] When James Hedger was murdered, Col. Hamilton offered a reward of 150 guineas for the arrest of the criminal.

Still, in spite of every precaution, many depredations were committed. They cannot, however, be all charged against the British soldiers. Flushing, like all other places on the North Shore, suffered from the bands of piratical plunderers known as "whaleboat men." These infested

---

itants and not Suffer the Corn-fields Orchards, gardens or fences to be Destroyed or Damaged without Severely punishing the offender."

"The soldiers not to be Allowed to Stray from the Incampment, and if any are found 1 Mile from Camp They will Be taken up and Deamed as Dissorters."

"Flushing Fly, Sep. 23, 1778. It is again Possitefly Ordered That No Wood is Cutt or fences Destroyed on any Portenc whatever or any other Injury Done to the Property of Late widdow Waters in the Rare and Left of the Incampment." *Pages 84 and 100.*

38 Major Waller died in 1780 and was buried at Jamaica, on the 24th of October.

the waters of the sound and robbed Whigs and Tories alike. Nor did they hesitate to commit murder.[39]

Judge Jones, a resident of Long Island during the Revolutionary war, complains bitterly of the conduct of officers and soldiers. He says that Clinton's men "robbed, plundered and pillaged the inhabitants of their cattle, hogs, sheep, poultry, etc."[40] Farmers were com-

---

39 *Gaine's Mercury and Rivington's Gazette* give accounts of the raids of these whaleboats at Bayside and Little Neck. Several houses were robbed at Bayside, among others that of John Thurman, a New York merchant. At Little Neck, Thos. Hicks was robbed of his law books and other property. *Documents and Letters, p. 146.*

David Haviland and Robert Lawrence offered a reward of ten guineas, Aug. 4, 1783, for the recovery of thirty-four sheep, which had been taken away in a boat at Abraham Lawrence's Point.

Documents and Letters, p. 151.

40 "David Colden, Esq., an inhabitant of Flushing, a gentleman of the first character and reputation as to honesty and veracity, told me that when the troops left that place, in the spring of 1781, there was not a four-footed animal left in the town (a few dogs excepted) nor a wooden fence standing within the township." *Jones I, 368.*

Holt's Journal, Aug. 10, 1778, contains information furnished by a "gentleman who left Flushing, last Lord's Day." He stated: "Bread was very scarce, pease and oatmeal being served out instead. Commissary rations were entirely stopped. Soldiers' wives were allowed quarter, instead of half rations. The Long Island people were selling off their small cattle and poultry, as they were daily robbed of them by the soldiery. Our friends on the island, since the battle of Monmouth, are in high spirits, and the formerly active Tories now begin to hang their heads and cry, *peccavi.*

Documents and Letters, p. 143.

pelled to put their turkeys, geese and chickens in the cellars at night, and keep strict watch over them in the fields during the day. "It was no uncommon thing for a farmer, his wife and children, to sleep in one room, while his sheep were bleating in the room adjoining, his hogs grunting in the kitchen, the cock crowing, hens cackling, ducks quacking and geese hissing, in the cellar." Horned cattle were locked up in barns. But, in spite of lock and bar, they were not always safe. David Colden had a fine stall-fed ox, which he was reserving for New Year's, but the barn was broken open and the ox was driven away. "This robbing was done," adds Jones, "by people sent to America to protect Loyalists against the persecution and depredations of rebels. To complain was needless; the officers shared in the plunder."[41]

The murder of James Hedger, already referred to, occurred in April, 1782.[42] He was living in the house of

---

41 *Jones's History of New York During the Revolutionary War, I, 262.*

This history was written between 1783 and 1788.

42 This was Hedger's second encounter with robbers. Some time before this he found two men choking his sister. He ran for his gun. They, thinking he was trying to escape, ran around the house to intercept him. Hedger killed one of them and wounded the other. The body of the dead man, who was named Sibly, was hanged on a gibbet, on the Hempstead plains, and the regiment paraded before it. The wounded man received 1,000 lashes, save one. *Documents and Letters, p. 147.*

his sister, the "Widow Talman, at the mill, four miles east of Flushing." Hearing a noise, Hedger went to the door to call his dog, and was shot dead. The murderers secured property valued at £200, in specie, clothing and plate. They were afterwards discovered to be members of the 38th and 54th regiments of Grenadiers. One of them, named Perrot, confessed. Five others fled. Three of them were captured and taken to Bedford, whither the regiments had gone. There, two, named French and Porter, were hanged.[43] Ten days after the murder, an address, signed by forty-seven inhabitants of Flushing, was presented to Lieut. Col. A. Bruce, of the 54th, commanding the 38th and 54th, thanking him for the quiet and security enjoyed by the community, for the politeness of the officers and the orderly and decent behavior of the soldiers. The address stated that, during the winter, there had been no occasion for murmuring or complaining.[44] Though this was after the murder, it must have been before the culprits had been discovered.

Samuel Skidmore, near Black Stump, was shot, while in his house—the ball having passed through the window.[45]

---

43 *Documents and Letters*, p. 147.

44 *Documents and Letters*, p. 148.

45 *History of Queens County*, p. 83.

The house of B. Areson, at Fresh Meadows, was robbed. One of Simcoe's men came and asked for cider. While Mr. Areson went to draw it, the soldier stole $10. He returned at night and carried away property valued at $100. Mr. Areson had a new, unfinished house. It and his barn were torn down by the 'Jagers.[46] James Bowne was awakened one night by a disturbance in his barn-yard. Going to the window to discover the cause of the noise, he received a musket ball through his arm. His son Walter, a lad about ten years old, in company with his cousin William Bowne, the son of Willet Bowne, went through the woods for Dr. Belden, to dress the wound. Willet Bowne also had an experience with lawless marauders. His house was entered at night, and he was aroused by a company of partially disguised men who demanded his money. 'On his refusing to give it up, they tied his hands to the bed-post and applied a lighted candle to the ends of his fingers. But the old man loved his gold more than his fingers. The would-be robbers, being unable to discover his treasure, were compelled to go away empty-handed. Bowne recognized them, in spite of their disguise, or at least thought he did; but magnanimously declined to prosecute them.

---

46 *Documents and Letters*, p. 150.

On Christmas Eve, 1779, the house of Col. Hamilton took fire, and was burned to the ground. Everything in the house was destroyed—"elegant furniture, a stock of provisions and various sorts of wines, spirits, intended to regale his numerous friends, the military and other gentlemen of the neighborhood, at this convivial season."[47]

On the first day of August, 1782, Flushing was honored by a visit from His Royal Highness William Henry, the Prince of Clarence, who was afterwards King William IV. While in Flushing, the Prince was the guest of William Prince. His Royal Highness came to present a stand of colors to the King's American Dragoons, then in camp about three miles east of the village, on ground afterwards owned by James Lawrence. Col. Benjamin Thompson, afterwards Count Rumford, was in command. The regiment, consisting of four mounted and two unmounted troops, was formed in front of the encampment, with two pieces of light artillery on the right. About sixty yards in front of the regiment was a canopy, twenty feet high, supported by ten pillars. East of this was a semi-circular bower, for the accommodation of spectators. The standard was planted under the canopy. At one o'clock, the Prince arrived, accompanied

47 *Royal Gazette, N, Y., Jan. 5, 1780. Documents and Letters, p. 144.*

by Admiral Digby, General Birch, the Hon. Lieut. Col. Fox, of the 38th, Lieut. Col. Small, of the 84th, and other officers of distinction. He received the usual salute, the trumpets sounded, and the band played "God save the King." The Prince and his attendants took their places under the canopy. The regiment passed in review before the Prince, dismounted and formed in a semi-circle before the canopy. The Chaplain, the Rev. Mr. Odell, delivered an appropriate address. After this, the whole regiment kneeled, laid their helmets and arms on the ground, held up their right hands, and took the solemn oath of allegiance to their sovereign, and fidelity to the standard. After the Chaplain had pronounced the benediction, the soldiers arose, returned to their former position, and fired the royal salute. They then mounted and saluted the standard. The standard was consecrated and placed in the hands of the Prince. He, with his own hands, presented it to Col. Thompson, who in turn delivered it to the senior cornets. At a signal, all the soldiers and spectators gave three cheers, the band played "God save the King," and the artillery fired the royal salute. Thus closed the impressive ceremony. A feast was then prepared for the soldiers. An ox was roasted whole, "spitted on a hickory sapling supported on crotches and turned by handspikes."[48]

---

48 *Royal Gazette, N. Y., 1782. Documents and Letters, p. 149.*

One of the most serious, indirect results of the Revolution, which fell upon the farmers of Flushing, was the "almost total destruction of the wheat crop by the ravages of the Hessian fly." It was believed that this pest was brought from Germany, in grain imported for the British army. The price of wheat flour advanced from 35s., per cwt., in 1777, to 80s., per cwt., in 1779. It was an inhabitant of Flushing, named Underhill, a farmer and miller, who discovered the remedy that saved the wheat crop, not only of Flushing, but of a large part of the country. The New York Packet tells the story thus: "The insect that has destroyed the wheat many years past continues to spread, but it has no effect on the white-bearded wheat raised on Long Island. This wheat was brought here from the southwest during the war, and a few bushels sown by a Flushing farmer, grew well, and afforded a fine crop. He kept on, and has supplied his neighbors. It grew twenty bushels to the acre, and weighs over sixty pounds. It is of a bright yellow color, and makes fine flour. The straw is harder, and resists the poison of the fly, and supports the grain, while bearded and bald wheat were cut off."[49] Farmers from different parts of the state sent to Flushing for seed, and found the result to be all that had been promised.

---

49 *New York Packet, July 20, 1786.*

The war came to an end, and New York was evacuated in November, 1783. The exit from Flushing is thus described by a contemporary: "In the morning there were thousands of soldiers around. In the afternoon they were all gone, and it seemed lonesome."[50]

Although the Friends of Flushing refused to take part in the war of Independence, they were at the same time engaged in efforts to accomplish another sort of freedom—the freedom of slaves from bondage. Samuel Underhill of New York is "dealt with," by the meeting held at Flushing, 5th of 6th mo., 1765, for importing negroes from Africa. He acknowledges his fault and hopes to conduct himself more agreeably to the Friends' principles.[51] In 1775 a committee is appointed "to visit such Friends as hold negro slaves, to inquire into the circumstances and manner of education of the slaves, and give such advice as the nature of the case requires."[52] In the next year the committee reported that many Friends had slaves, but seemed disposed to free them. Some had already done so: others justified slavery. Later in the same year, a committee is appointed "to labor with Friends who keep these poor people in bondage, in the

---

50 *Flint's Early Long Island, p. 455.*

51 *Minutes, V, 59.*

52 *Minutes, VI, 84.*

ability that truth may afford, for their release." It was further decided that Friends could "have no unity" with those who held slaves, and that the meeting would receive no collections from slave-holders.[53] It was at another meeting ordered, that Friends should do nothing that involved an acknowledgment that slavery was right.

---

53 *Minutes*, *VII*, *4 et sq.*

PART V—The American Period

CHAPTER XV

MANNERS AND CUSTOMS

1783 Before entering upon this, the last, period of Flushing's history, it may be well to stop long enough to take a brief survey of the condition, habits and customs of the people at the beginning of our nation's life. It is hard to realize that scarcely one of the inventions and discoveries which we today regard as the marks of modern civilization, had then been made. There was then no railroad, no steamboat, no telegraph. In going from Flushing to New York one had either to take passage in one of the sloops, which sailed from Flushing several times a week, or had to drive over the country road which led him to Brooklyn, by the head of the Fly, through Jamaica and Bedford—a distance of about seventeen miles. The passage across the river, from Brooklyn to New York, was not without danger, and was attended by frequent and annoying delays. The ferry-boats were either clumsy row-boats; flat-bottomed, square-ended scows, with sprit-sails; or two-masted boats, called periaguas.[1] When the wind blew with the tide, the passengers considered themselves fortunate, if they were landed on the other side within an hour. In winter, the boats were frequently held fast for hours in an ice-jam. Boats thus situated often went to pieces under the pressure of the ice. In January, 1784, a boat was thus crushed and sunk, within a few feet of the New York shore. There were eight passengers on board. One was drowned: the others took refuge on a cake of ice, and were carried down to the Narrows before they were rescued.[2] During the same year, a ferry-boat went down with five horses on board. Persons driving in from the country would sometimes wait two or three days for favorable weather to cross to New York.

There was no postoffice on Long Island at this time. People at the west end of the Island were supposed to receive their mail in New York; but, as early as 1775, a Scotchman, named Dunbar, rode once in two weeks through the Island, with the mail. Dunbar was not a public official, but had undertaken the work of post-rider as a private enterprise. He would go east by the North Shore, and

1 *McMaster's People of the United States, I, 47.*
2 *New York Packet, Jan. 22, 1784.*

return by the South Side. The day on which he was due at any place was called "post-day." Half the village would assemble at the inn to meet him. In addition to the few letters and the newspapers, a week old, he brought all the news of the road over which he had travelled. Persons who were unwilling to have the contents of their letters known to the post-rider, corresponded in cypher, for he did not hesitate to amuse himself, on his long and lonesome ride, by reading the letters he carried.

A gentleman of the period,[3] if he was a person of means, wore a three-cornered hat, heavily laced. His hair was powdered and done up in a cue. His coat was light-colored, with a diminutive cape, a marvellously long back, and silver buttons. His small-clothes came scarcely to his knees: his stockings were striped; his shoes were pointed, and fastened with large buckles; his vest had flap-pockets; his cuffs were loaded with lead. When he bowed to a lady, he took up half the sidewalk, as he flourished his cane and scraped his foot. The lady, in returning his salutation, courtesied almost to the ground. She was gorgeously attired. Her gown of heavy brocade or taffeta, was spread out over huge hoops, which extended two feet on each side.

---

3 *McMaster's People of the United States*, *I*, 65.

Her hat loomed up like a tower, or she wore a muskmelon-bonnet.

The farmer[4] had his one suit of broadcloth, which he wore on Sundays and on state occasions. It lasted him a lifetime, and was bequeathed to his son. His every-day suit of clothes was made from homespun. He had none of the agricultural implements used today. He plowed his land with a wooden bull-plow, sowed his grain broad cast, cut it with a scythe, and threshed it out on his barn floor with a flail. His house was never painted, and had no carpets. He lighted his fire in the huge open fireplace with a flint, for there were no matches in those days. The spinning wheel and the loom were important and conspicuous articles in the house of the well-to-do farmer. His food was simple and coarse, and varied little, from day to day, throughout the year.

The day laborer[5] wore a pair of yellow buckskin, or leathern breeches, a checked shirt, a red flannel jacket, a rusty felt hat, cocked up at the corners, a pair of heavy shoes with huge brass buckles, and a leathern apron. If he fell into debt to the extent of a few dollars, he was liable to be cast into one of those filthy prisons, where men and

---

4 *McMaster's People of the United States, I,* 19.
5 *McMaster's People of the United States, I,* 97.

women herded together—the lowest criminals and the unfortunate debtors. There he might stay until his clothes rotted on his back, or until he died. In those prisons, no clothes were provided for the naked, and such a thing as a bed was rare indeed.

We who know but one unit of value, can scarcely conceive of the difficulties encountered by our ancestors in their money transactions.[6] In every state there were two units of value—the State pound, and the standard Spanish dollar. These state pounds, shillings and pence had no existence outside of the account books. They were not coins, but units of value. The pounds were divided into shillings and pence in the usual way. It required eight New York shillings, or ninety-six pence, to make a dollar; in South Carolina and Georgia, four shillings and eight pence had the same value; in New Jersey, Pennsylvania, Delaware and Maryland, people counted seven shillings and six pence of their money to a dollar. Thus in New York State a customer would pay a Spanish quarter for an article marked at two shillings; in Georgia, he would probably pay the same price, but the article would be marked one shilling and two pence.

---

6 *McMaster's People of the United States, I, 23.*

The school houses were small, unpretentious buildings. They were not painted, outside or inside; nor were the walls ceiled or plastered. A Dutch wood-stove was used to raise the temperature in the school-house somewhat above the freezing point. The parents of the pupils carted the wood, the older boys cut it, and the younger ones carried it in. The first pupil to arrive in the morning started the fire with live coals brought from the nearest house. The larger boys attended school only in the winter, the larger girls only in the summer. The girls swept the school-room once a week, and occasionally scrubbed it. On these latter occasions, the boys assisted by carrying the water.

Dilworth's speller was a standard text-book. After the Revolution, it was gradually supplanted by Webster's spelling-book. The master was generally the only person who had an arithmetic. He wrote the "sums" in the pupils' "ciphering books," into which books the pupils copied the correct solutions after their work on the slates had been approved.

The masters were generally single men, were engaged for a quarter, and would go from one school to another. They did not spare the rod. There were no steel pens, in those days, no ready-made writing books, there was no ruled paper. The school-master made and mended the quill-pens, and ruled the paper for writing-books, with a piece of lead. Ink was made by mixing Walkden's ink-powder with vinegar and water.[7]

The population of the town of Flushing was about 1600, at the close of the Revolutionary war.[8] There were not more than fifty houses in the village. Main street and Broadway were the principal thoroughfares. The village pond, about seventy-five feet wide and two hundred feet long, occupied the place where the park now is. East of the pond, and in front of the Friends' Meeting-house, arose a perpendicular bank of earth about eight feet high. It has been graded down to give the gradual incline of Broadway. The grade of Main street rose to the top of the wall in front of the Garretson property, at that point.

The Quaker Meeting-house, sadly desecrated by the war, was, in outward appearance, about as it is to-day. St. George's Church was a small wooden building, with a slender spire, and occupied the site of the present church. John Holroyd was proprietor of the Queen's Head tavern. The Guard House, which was built as a means of defence, and afterwards used as a town jail, and which stood east of the Meeting-house, near the corner of Union street and Broad-

---

7 *Alden J. Spooner, in History of Queens County*, p. 55.

8 *Mandeville*, pp. 27, 75, 76.

way, had been destroyed during the war. The whipping-post stood in front of what is now the Flushing Hotel. The Bowne House, the Garretson House, the Aspinwall House, the Duryea House, and a few other buildings, belong to this period. The localities known by the names of Head of the Fly (or Vleigh), Fresh Meadows, Black Stump, Bayside, Whitestone,[9] had the same names at the close of the Revolutionary War. The neck of land occupied by College Point was then known as Lawrence's or Tew's Neck.[10]

All elections were held at Jamaica, until 1799. All voting was *viva voce*, until after the Revolution, when secret ballots were cast for Governor and Lieutenant-Governor. The vote for assemblymen was *viva voce*, until 1787.

---

9 A part of Whitestone for some time bore the name of Cookie Hill. The village was first called Clintonville; but in 1854, when the postoffice was established, the old name Whitestone was restored.

10 Tew's Neck was later known as Stratton Port. Its present name of College Point owes its origin to the fact that St. Paul's College was established there by Dr. Muhlenberg in 1846.

Other local names, such as "Quarrelsome Lane" and "Lonely Barn," have long disappeared.

CHAPTER XVI

RECONSTRUCTION

1779 New York was not evacuated until Nov. 25, 1783; but the work of reconstruction and of the punishment of Loyalists began four years earlier. The Act of Attainder and Confiscation was passed in 1779. By this act, fifty-eight of New York's best inhabitants were adjudged and declared guilty of felony, and were sentenced "to suffer death as in cases of felony, without benefit of clergy, for adhesion to the enemies of the State." Among this number was David Colden, of Flushing. The act was supposed to have originated with Sir James Jay. His brother, John Jay, wrote from Madrid, concerning this act: "An English paper contains what they call, but I can hardly believe to be, your Confiscation Act. If truly printed, New York is disgraced by injustice too palpable to admit even of palliation."[1] This act could, of course, have no effect until after the declaration of peace. It was then relentlessly enforced, though clearly opposed to Article Fifth of the treaty. The

1 *Flint*, p. 453.

emigration of Loyalists to Canada began as early as 1782. 1782

Negotiations for peace were then being carried on, and the end was plainly seen. The emigration that affected Queens County was the one which took place in the following 1783

spring, when "The Spring Fleet," consisting of twenty square-rigged ships, carried more than 3000 persons to New Brunswick, Canada.[2] These emigrants from Queens County founded the city of St. John's and gave the city its first mayor—Gabriel G. Ludlow, whose farm lay partly in North Hempstead and partly in Flushing.[3]

Early in the next year, Congress sent copies of the 1784

Fifth Article of the treaty to the several state legislatures, with the note: "It was the desire of the Congress to have it communicated to them for their consideration." New York was especially bitter against the Loyalists. The city and the surrounding country had been occupied by the British throughout the whole time of the war, and the Patriots had been driven from their homes. On their return, they determined that the Loyalists must go. They declared that if the Loyalists were allowed to remain they would

---

2 *Flint, p. 492.*

At the election for assemblymen, in 1786, there were only 25 votes cast in Flushing and 359 in the whole county. The majority of the voters had been disfranchised.

3 Ludlow's farm was confiscated and sold to Captain Berrien and Isaac Ledyard, of Newtown, for £800.

depart themselves. The New York legislature replied to the note of Congress: "That while this legislature entertain the highest sense of national honor . . . they find it inconsistent with their duty to comply with the recommendation of the said Congress."[4]

1785 The courts, which had been closed during the war, were again opened. The county seat was established at Jamaica, and Willet Skidmore and others, of Flushing, signed a petition for the erection of a new Court-house. Cadwallader D. Colden, the Assistant Attorney General, writes thus of the court, a few years later: "The Court of Queens County is at all times the least orderly of any court I ever was in. The entry to the Court-house is lined, on court days, with stalls of dram-sellers and filled with drunken people, so as to be almost impassable."

The Constitution of the United States was signed, Sept.
1788 17, 1787. It was ratified by New York, July 26, 1788. On August 8th the adoption of the Constitution was celebrated in Flushing by a large gathering of people from different parts of the country. A colonade, constructed of evergreens, was erected on the green. Above the colonade were the standards of the states that had ratified the Constitution. At the east end of this enclosure stood a canopy of white

4 *Flint, p. 467.*

linen, about which were curtains caught up with blue ribbons. Across the front of the canopy were the words: "Federal Constitution, September, 1787." Under the canopy, on a platform covered with a rich carpet, stood the president's chair. The day was ushered in with a salute by the artillery. At three o'clock, in the afternoon, the discharge of guns announced that the banquet was served. The president, Col. William S. Smith, was conducted to the chair, "and the gentlemen sat down with that hilarity usual on such an occasion." Many patriotic toasts were drunk, and Mr. John Mulligan, a student of Columbia College, delivered an oration.[5]

Washington was inaugurated, in New York, as the first
President of the United States, April 23, 1789. On the 1789
tenth of the following October, he came to Flushing to see the Linnean Gardens of William Prince. "Pursuant to an engagement formed on Thursday last," says Washington, in his diary, "I sett off from New York, about nine o'clock, in my barge to visit Mr. Prince's fruit gardens and shrubberies, at Flushing, on Long Island. The Vice President, Governor of the State, Mr. Izard, Colonel Smith and Major

5 "This unexpected exhibition to the auditory, the graceful manner and interesting subject, excited the admiration of the hearers and commanded loud plaudits to the youthful orator." *New York Daily Advertiser, Aug., 13, 1788.*

Jackson accompanied me. These gardens, except in the number of young trees, did not answer my expectations. The shrubs were trifling and the flowers not numerous. The inhabitants of the place showed us what respect they could, by making the best use of one cannon to salute."[6]

Mandeville states that, in 1858, there still lived in Flushing an old negro, James Bantas, who remembered the visit. He said: "A large tent, made of cedar bushes and other evergreens, was erected and extended diagonally from Alfred C. Smith's corner toward the Flushing Hotel. In this were tables abundantly spread, and dinner was served. When the people were shouting and swinging their hats, Washington, who wore a three-cornered hat, raised his and bowed in recognition of their approbation."[7]

The party crossed to the mainland and stopped, on their way to the city, at the country seats of General and Gouverneur Morris, in Morrisania. At Harlem they were met by Mrs. Washington, Mrs. Adams, and Mrs. Smith. They dined with the ladies at a small tavern kept by Captain Mariner.[8]

Shortly after Washington's visit, October 22nd, the house of Jeremiah Vanderbilt, the town Clerk, was burnt

6 *Washington's Diary, Saturday, Oct. 10, 1789, p. 17 et sq.*
7 *Mandeville, p. 64.*
8 *Washington's Diary, p. 18.*

and the town records were destroyed. That event has made the writing of the history of Flushing no easy task. Nellie, a slave of Capt. Daniel Braine, and Sarah, a slave of Vanderbilt, were the incendiaries.[9] They were brought to trial, 1790
September 8th, of the following year, convicted and sentenced to be hanged, on October 14th. Sarah, because of her youth, was afterwards reprieved. Judge Robert Yates presided at the trial and Aaron Burr, as Attorney-General, was the prosecutor.

During this year, Washington made a second visit to Flushing. There was much discussion about the selection of a permanent seat of government. The President took great interest in the question and inspected many places proposed.[10] Harlem Heights, Westchester, and various places on Long Island were proposed. "Washington, having previously sent over his servants, his horses and carriage, crossed to Brooklyn and drove through Flatbush, New Utrecht, Gravesend, Jamaica, and beyond." He spent nearly a week on the island. On his way back, he breakfasted at Henry Onderdonk's in Roslyn and dined at Flushing. From Flushing, the party drove to Newtown, thence to Brooklyn. Concerning this part of his trip, the President

---

9 *New York Journal, October, 1789.*
10 *Lamb's History of New York, II, 372.*

said: "The road is very fine and the Country in a higher state of cultivation and vegetation of Grass and grain, forwarder (?) than any place also, I had seen, and occasioned in a great degree by the Manure drawn from the City of New York—before sundown we had crossed the Ferry, and was at home."[11]

1791 The inhabitants of Flushing and of the neighboring villages now turned their attention to the subject of providing themselves with better educational facilities than they had hitherto enjoyed. A number of residents of Flushing and of Jamaica met at the residence of Mrs. Joanna Hinchman, in Jamaica, March 1, 1791, to make arrangements for building an academy in Jamaica. A committee of twelve was appointed to solicit subscripitons. The academy was
1792 completed, and was opened for students, May 1st, of the following year. It was called Union Hall, because built by the united efforts of Flushing, Jamaica and Newtown. The opening of the academy was the occasion of much rejoicing, and was celebrated by a dinner at Hinchman's inn, Jamaica.[12] Maltby Gelston was the first Principal. The academy did good work for many years. It was closed in 1873.

---

11 *Washington's Diary*, p. 126.

12 *Queens County in Olden Times*, p. 79 *et sq.*

The freeholders of Flushing, who had already secured patents from the Dutch and the English, were now compelled to have their rights confirmed by the authorities of the State of New York. This was done, Feb. 24, 1792, by a lengthy document, called: "Exemplification of Flushing Patent." It rehearses the Patent granted by Governor Dongan, and adds: "All which we have caused to be exemplified by these presents. In testimony whereof we have caused these our Letters to be made patent, and the Great Seal of our State to be hereunto affixed. Witness our truly and well-beloved George Clinton, Esquire, Governor of our Said State, General and Commander in Chief of all the Militia and Admiral of the same, at our City of New York, the twenty-fourth day of February, in the year of our Lord one thousand seven hundred and ninety-two, and in the sixteenth year of our Independence."[13]

In the summer of 1798 Congress passed two laws, com- 1798
monly called the Alien and Sedition Laws, which caused great discontent and excitement throughout the country. They were occasioned by the trouble with France. They gave the President power to send out of the country all aliens who were thought to be dangerous or who were suspected of plotting against the Government. If such sus-

13 *Mandeville*, p. 23.

pected persons did not leave the country, they were liable to imprisonment and would never be allowed to become citizens. Writing or speaking false, scandalous or malicious things against the Government, the President, or Congress, were made punishable offences. These acts threw the country into great excitement. The people were divided into two factions. The Federalists, who were accused of being under British influence, wore black cockades on their hats, demanded the orchestras in the theatres to play the "President's March," "Yankee Doodle," and "Stony Point." They tore down the French liberty-cap from poles and put the American Eagle in its place. The Republicans were termed Jacobins. They were French sympathizers. They wore the tricolor cockades, tried to drown the sounds of "Yankee Doodle" in the theatres with demands for "Ca-ira" or the "Marseillaise" hymn. They waylaid young men at night and tore off their black cockades. Musicians in the theatres were pelted, and fiddles were smashed, because the music did not suit one or the other faction. Meetings were held all over the country, protesting against the Alien and Sedition Laws, or endorsing them.[14]

---

14 *McMaster's People of the United States, II, 308-416.*

Newtown declared against the laws, and called upon Flushing to cooperate with them in petitioning for the repeal of the laws. A meeting was called in Flushing. It was held some time in December, at the inn kept by John Bradwell. Lewis Cornwall was chosen chairman and David Gardner, clerk. Flushing declared for the Federalists and the black cockade. The meeting resolved that: "We place the utmost confidence in the wisdom, patriotism and integrity of the President of the United States and both houses of Congress, and cannot believe they would pass an act contrary to the Constitution or the interest of these States . . . We shall use our endeavors to assist the Government in the execution of these laws and all others."[15]

15 *Queens County in Olden Times*, p. 89.

CHAPTER XVII

FLUSHING'S NEW LIFE

1800 Up to the beginning of the present century the road to New York ran through Jamaica to Brooklyn, where the river was crossed by means of a ferry. In 1800, a company was formed in Flushing, to build a bridge over the creek. William Prince was President of the company. The bridge, then erected, was washed away two years later; but it was soon rebuilt. Since then, several bridges have been erected at the same spot. Before the construction of this bridge, foot-passengers were taken across the creek in small row-boats. James Rantas and Thomas Smith, two colored men, acted as ferrymen for many years. The construction of the bridge was soon followed by the opening of a road from the bridge to Newtown. This was accomplished only after much opposition on the part of the farmers. William Prince and John Aspinwall were especially active in securing this improvement. A stage was now established by William

Mott, to run between Flushing and Brooklyn, by way of Newtown and Bedford.[1]

Union Hall, in Jamaica, does not appear to have satisfied the educational needs of Flushing. St. George's parish, therefore, built, and for a short time maintained, an academy in Flushing. It stood on the church property, at the corner of Main and Locust streets. After two years' experiment, the parish conveyed the academy to a board of trustees, for the term of nine hundred ninety-nine years, "at the annual rent of six cents when legally demanded." The trustees were: William Prince, Thomas Philips, David Gardner, Samuel H. Van Wyck, Daniel Bloodgood.[2] They called the academy Hamilton Hall. The prospectus of the school stated that it was "situated at the pleasant and healthy village of Flushing," with a Principal who had been "regularly educated in the University of Gottingen;" and describes the curriculum as embracing "Greek, Latin, French and English languages—German and Hebrew if required—also the various branches of Mathematics, Read-

1803

1 Mott was on the road for seven years. He was succeeded by Carman Smith, Greenwall, Kissam, John Boyd and others. Boyd drove for seventeen years. His was the first stage from Flushing that crossed the ferry to New York. His route was across the Grand street ferry, up Grand to the Bowery, and down the Bowery to Chatham square. *Mandeville, p. 71.*

2 *History of St. George's Parish, p. 75.*

ing, Writing, Arithmetic, English Grammar, Bookkeeping." The patrons were assured that attention would be given to "the health and morals of young persons sent for education."[3]

1810 Hamilton Hall was not successful. It was returned to the vestry of St. George's Church, in 1810, for $1,125. The vestry again attempted to maintain the school: but, after a few years' struggle, abandoned the undertaking and converted the building into a Sunday School. The building was subsequently removed to the southwest corner of Washington and Garden streets, where it still stands.

1811 Up to this time, the Quaker meeting and St. George's Episcopal Church were the only religious organizations in the town. The next to appear was the African Macedonian Church. The Rev. Benjamin Griffin, a white preacher, officiated for this negro congregation in his circuit. There were at this time no Methodists among the white people of Flushing.[4]

---

3 *Queens County in Olden Times, p. 94.*

4 The African Methodist Church was not built until 1837. *Mandeville, p. 165.*

Following are the Pastors, with the dates of their coming to Flushing: Rev. Henry Hearden, 1821; Rev. Stephen Dutton, 1823; Rev. William Quim, 1824; Rev. Jacob Mathias, 1826; Rev. Samuel Todd, 1826; Rev. Israel Scott, 1828; Rev. Jeremiah Miller, 1829; Rev. Israel Scott, 1831; Rev. Edward C. Africanus, 1850; Rev. Japheth P. Campbell, 1853; Rev. William H. Ross, 1854; Rev. J. R. V.

To the "Flushing Female Association" is to be awarded the honor of having established the first free school in Flushing. This Association, organized Feb. 12, 1814, was composed of a number of public-spirited women, most if not all of whom were members of the Society of Friends, who banded together to further the interests of education. Each member paid $2.00 a year into the treasury. Contributions soon began to come in from the outside, to assist the Association in its work.[5] The school was opened April 6, 1814, in a dwelling in Liberty street, near the site of the building now owned by the Association. For a few months the 1814

Thomas, 1855; Rev. George Wier, 1856; Rev. James M. Williams, 1857; Rev. Leonard Paterson, 1858; Rev. William Moore, 1860; Rev. Geo. W. Johnson, 1862; Rev. D. Dorrell, 1864; Rev. William H. Ross, 1866; Rev. Edward B. Davis, 1867; Rev. Henderson Davis, 1868; Rev. Abraham C. Crippen, 1871; Rev. Benjamin Lynch, 1872; Rev. Chas. H. Green, 1874; Rev. Jas. M. Williams, D. D., 1875; Rev. E. T. Thomas, 1876; Rev. John Frisby, 1877; Rev. Edw. B. Davis, 1878; Rev. T. C. Franklin, 1879; Rev. J. G. Mobray, 1880; Rev. William F. Townsend, 1882; Rev. Chas. N. Gibbons, 1885; Rev. T. B. Reed, 1888; Rev. Israel Derricks, 1890; Rev. Jas. J. Moore, 1891; Rev. William Heath, 1893; Rev. Peter E. Mills, 1894; Rev. Jas. W. Fishburne, 1897; Rev. William H. Bryant, 1898.

5 The following bequests were received: Thomas Tom, $250; Thomas Lawrence, $100; Matthew Franklin, £150, "the interest to be applied to the use of finding poor negro children books, and also toward paying their schooling, them that their parents did belong among the people called Quakers"; Nathaniel Smith, $500; James Byrd, $200. Charles and Scott Hicks furnished wood for the school for eleven years. *Mandeville, p. 128.*

members of the Association served in turn as teachers. The pupils, white and black, were admitted free of charge, except in the cases of a few whose parents were able and wil-
1815 ling to pay. Mary McMannus was engaged as the first teacher, at a salary of $15 per quarter, and with an allowance of $26, per quarter, for her board. The income of the Association, for the first year, was $570.51.[6]

1817 This charitable work in behalf of the negro population of Flushing, was soon followed by a more comprehensive act in their behalf by the State of New York. On March 31, 1817, an act was passed, freeing all slaves who had been born after July 4, 1797, so soon as they should reach the age of twenty-eight, for males, and twenty-five for females. Every child born in slavery after the passage of the act, should be set free on reaching the age of twenty-one. The slaves in Flushing had always, as a rule, been kindly treated. The Quakers had been working for nearly a hundred years for the abolition of slavery. Their sympathy for the slaves and their interest in the negroes' education and general well-being were widely known. Flushing became the rendezvous of freedmen, who hoped to secure the blessings of freedom without its responsibilities. A very undesirable element was thus added to the population of the

---

6 *Treasurer's Book of the Flushing Female Association.*

village. These negroes became so numerous, so aggressive, so lawless, that the peace and quiet of the community were greatly disturbed. They filled the streets at night; they held out-of-door dances and barbecues, which generally degenerated into drunken brawls. Town ordinances and the mild influence of the Quakers were without avail. The 1825
apprentices and other young men of the village took matters into their own hands. They formed a sort of vigilance committee and attacked with volleys of rotten eggs, these noisy gatherings which made sleep impossible. A few attacks of this sort had the effect of breaking up the gatherings, or at least of transferring the orgies from the public square to the shanties on Crow Hill and Liberty street.[7]

Some ten years or more after the Rev. Mr. Griffin began 1822
his ministrations among African Methodists, a group of white people organized a Methodist Church. They worshipped for a time in a private house adjoining Garretson's seed store, in Liberty street. Their first Pastor was the Rev. Samuel Cockrance. Their church was built in 1822. It stood on the south side of Lincoln street, about midway between Main and Union streets.[8]

---

7 *Mandeville*, p. 67. *History of Queens County*, p. 91.

8 A new church was built, in 1843, on the east side of Main street, just north of Washington. In 1875, the church was removed to its present site in Amity street. In 1834 the

The first post-office in the town was located at the Alley. It was in this year moved to the village. This change met with much opposition, even on the part of people living in the village. While the postoffice was at the Alley, they said, the mail was left at the Flushing hotel which was open at all hours. The post-office, they feared, would be open only at certain hours, and would not furnish the accommodation then enjoyed.[9]

Methodist Church in Flushing was separated from the circuit and became a station with a resident Pastor. Following are the names of the resident Pastors, with the dates of their coming to Flushing: Rev. Alexander Hulin, 1834; Rev. David Plumb, 1835; Rev. John L. Gilder, 1836; Rev. William Thatcher, 1837: Rev. Daniel Wright, 1839; Rev. George Brown, 1840: Rev. Elbert Osborn, 1841; Rev. John J. Matthias, 1842; Rev. Benjamin Griffin, 1843; Rev. David Osborn, 1845; Rev. John W. B. Wood, 1847; Rev. John B. Merwin, 1848; Rev. Samuel W. Law, 1850; Rev. Abraham S. Francis, 1851; Rev. Ira Abbott, 1852; Rev. William F. Collins, 1854; Rev. Thomas H. Burch, 1856; Rev. J. L. Peck, 1858; Rev. R. H. Hatfield, 1860; Rev. Horace Cooke, 1864; Rev. G. R. Crooks, 1866; Rev. G. Taylor, 1869; Rev. W. H. Simonson, 1872; Rev. George Stillman, 1875; Rev. Levi P. Perry, 1877; Rev. Alvine C. Bowdish, 1879; Rev. Robert W. Jones, 1880; Rev. C. C. Lasby, 1883; Rev. Thomas S. Poulson, 1886; Rev. Harvey E. Burnes, 1889; Rev. John W. Maynard, 1891; Rev. George L. Thompson, 1893; Rev. Theodore S. Henderson, 1896; Rev. A. H. Wyatt, 1898.

9 *Mandeville, p. 73.*

The first Postmaster was Curtis Peck, who kept the office in the Pavilion. Then followed in office: William Peck, Dr. Joseph Bloodgood, Dr. Asa Spalding, Francis Bloodgood, Charles W. Cox.

The year that brought the post-office to the village was also marked by the experiment of running a small steamboat between New York and Flushing. In the following year, a boat built expressly for the route began regular daily trips. She was the Linnaeus, commanded by Capt. Jonathan Peck.[10] 1823

St. Michael's Roman Catholic Church had its beginning in 1826. There were then but twelve members of that Church in Flushing. They invited the Rev. Father Farnham, of Brooklyn, to visit Flushing and minister to their spiritual needs. He came and celebrated the first Mass in October of this year, in a building in Main street. Some time after this, in 1835, a house in Liberty street was purchased, and fitted up for public worship. The Rev. Michael Curran and the Rev. Felix Larkin, of Astoria, held service here once a month. This building was twice enlarged, and answered the needs of the congregation for a number of years. 1826

This year was also an important one for Flushing's educational interests. In the fall of this year, the Rev. William A. Muhlenberg became the Rector of St. George's

10 The Linnaeus ran for ten years. She was followed by the Flushing, Capt. Curtis Peck; the Statesman, Capt. Elijah Peck; the Star, Capt. Elijah Peck; the Washington Irving, Capt. Stephen Leonard; the Island Star, Capt. Silas Reynolds; the Enoch Dean, Capt. William Reynolds. *Mandeville, p. 72.*

Church.[11] He took rooms in the Pavilion hotel. One day at dinner he overheard some gentlemen discussing the subject of building a boys' school in Flushing. He joined in the conversation and quite without premeditation said that if they would put up a suitable building, he would undertake the management of the school. He thought little more about the subject, and was surprised to receive a visit from the gentlemen that evening. They came to accept his proposition. The Flushing Institute was incorporated, the corner-stone was laid, Aug. 11, 1827, and the school began
1828 its first session in the spring of the following year. The Institute was a success from the start. Mr. Muhlenberg was unusually happy in his management of boys and had the faculty of soon winning their confidence and respect.[12]

---

11 Some of our well-known hymns—such as "Like Noah's weary dove," "Saviour who Thy flock art feeding," and probably "Shout the glad tidings"—were written by Mr. Muhlenberg, during the first few months of his residence in Flushing. *Muhlenberg's Life, p. 83.*

12 "In their griefs, who so tender and sympathizing as he! One of the younger boys, son of Francis S. Key, author of the 'Star Spangled Banner,' was under Mr. Muhlenberg's care when his father died. Tidings of the event came late in the day, with a request for the boy to be sent home the next morning. 'Never, if you can help it, tell bad news at night,' was a life-long maxim with Mr. Muhlenberg, and the little fellow was allowed to retire undisturbed with the rest, while the devoted school-father attended himself to the arrangements necessary for an early morning start."

"He could exercise a little muscular Christianity at need. One of the students attempted a practical joke upon

He pursued the policy of trusting the boys and placing them on their honor. It is said that he always wore rather heavy and creaking boots, that he might not appear at any time to steal upon the boys unawares.

At this stage of our history we must refer to the split that occurred in the Friends' Meeting. It is not within the scope of this work to discuss the causes that led to it. Suffice it to say that at the yearly meeting, in 1829, certain 1829
members of the meeting separated themselves from the others and established the "Orthodox" Meeting. The old Meeting-house was retained by that portion of the society which was henceforth known as the "Hicksites." At a monthly meeting held in Flushing, 7th day, 3rd month, 1829, the committee that had been appointed to collect the names of all the members belonging to the meeting, i. e. the Hicksite meeting, reported that there were seven men, sixteen women, and eleven minors, in all thirty-four, "who have attached themselves to the society that separated

---

himself, by walking into his chamber at midnight, in the regulation, long, white bed gown, as a somnambulist. Mr. Muhlenberg instantly penetrated the disguise, and springing out of bed grappled the youth tightly and drew him to the wash-stand, where stood a large ewer full of water, the whole contents of which he discharged upon his head. The discomfited lad slank away as he could. He had anticipated great fun in telling his comrades the next morning how finely he had scared the Rector." *Muhlenberg's Life, pp 105. 122.*

during the yearly meeting." Two men and one woman were undecided to which meeting they would attach themselves. Twenty-seven men, forty-two women, forty-two minors, in all one hundred and eleven remained "attached to this monthly meeting."[13] The Orthodox Quakers built a Meeting-house just east of the old Meeting-house. The Orthodox meeting is now extinct; the Hicksite meeting is very small.

1835 The Institute continued to flourish, but Dr. Muhlenberg —he received his degree about this time—was of a restless disposition, and was always planning something new. He now entertained visions of a thoroughly equipped college. To realize these, he bought one hundred seventy-five acres
1836 of land at Strattonport and on Oct. 15, 1836, laid the corner-stone of what was designed to be an extensive structure, to cost about $50,000. But the building never rose above the basement story. The panic of 1837 deprived him of the assistance of friends on whom he had relied. A wooden building was put up, in which the Grammar School
1838 was opened in 1837. Temporary buildings were erected for the College, and St. Paul's College was opened, with a full corps of professors, in 1838. The school at the Flushing Institute was now moved to College Point, as that locality was thereafter called.

---

13 *Records of the Monthly Meetings.*

The same home-like sympathy between Rector and pupils, that marked the school life of the Institute was maintained at St. Paul's College. The Doctor wrote hymns and carols, composed music for them and led the pupils in singing. The well-known Christmas carol, "Carol, brothers, carol," was composed at this time.[14]

The college flourished until 1844, when Dr. Muhlenberg moved to New York to become Rector of the Church of the Holy Communion.

14 The following statistics of the college were reported, Jan. 13, 1840: "Number of students, 105; volumes in Libraries, 7,000; value of property, $70,000; annual cost of salaries of professors and instructors, $9,000."

Muhlenberg's Life, p. 141.

CHAPTER XVIII

MODERN FLUSHING

We are now approaching the end of our story, and shall
1837 hereafter confine ourselves to the Village of Flushing. The Village was incorporated, April 15, 1837. The Gazetteer of the State of New York, published the year before, describes Flushing as a village of about one hundred and forty dwellings, "some of which are neat and several magnificent." There were then in Flushing: one Episcopal Church; two Methodist Churches, "one for white and the other for colored worshippers;" two Quaker Meetings: "the Flushing Institute: a respectable Seminary for ladies[1]; six extensive stores: three hotels: one tide grist-mill; the extensive and celebrated garden and nursery of Messrs. Prince, known as the Linnean Garden." Two sloops belonged to the village; a steamboat ran twice a day to New York; stages ran to Brooklyn. The Gazetteer adds: "The facility of conveyance, the attractiveness of the Linnean Garden,

1 Kept by Joshua Kimber, who had succeeded Lindley Murray Moore in 1827. Mr. Kimber's school occupied the house that still stands just west of the old Meeting-house.

the delightful voyage, whether by land or water, make this a favorite place of resort to citizens of New York."[2]

The village boundary line began at the creek, just beyond the bridge on the College Point causeway, and ran east, crossing Whitestone avenue about three hundred feet beyond Bayside avenue—just including the Osgood property. At a point near the junction of Bayside avenue and Parsons avenue, the line turned south, and ran to the corner of Sanford avenue and Long Lane (now S. Parsons avenue). From this corner, which marked the farthest limits of the village in that direction, the line ran west to the creek, forming an acute angle with Sanford Avenue, and crossing Jamaica avenue just south of the Jaggar homestead (now Captain Hinman's). Sanford avenue was not open below Jamaica avenue. Bowne avenue was the street farthest east. Long Lane began at the village limits, and ran south. Jaggar avenue was a private lane leading from Main street to the Jaggar house; Lincoln street was then called Liberty street; Amity street was not opened, neither was Locust street east of Main.[3] A tide mill, kept by William Hamilton, stood at

---

2 *Gazetteer of the State of New York*, p. 635.

3 North Prince street was not opened until 1841. It was first called Linnean street. Furman says: "In the month of July, 1841, eleven human skeletons were unearthed, in excavating the ground to run a road through the Linnean Garden. . . The place where they were found has been for

the bridge on the College Point causeway. There were no houses northeast of the Park, except a few which stood in large country places, such as those of Walter Farrington and Samuel B. Parsons, on Broadway, and Silas Hicks, Henry Mitchell and Howard Osgood, on Whitestone avenue. On the west side of Main street, the Redwood property extended from the L. I. Railway Station to Amity street. On the east side, the Wright property was on the corner of Madison street; next came the Institute; then the Leggett property and the Garretson property. The lower part of Main street was more thickly settled, but even there the houses stood apart from each other, with gardens between. The Pavilion, once a famous hotel, stood on the corner of Bridge street and Lawrence avenue, where the old electric power house now stands. The Town Hall stood where the fountain now stands, facing on Main street;[4] the school house was on the lot now occupied by the Empire Hose Company's building, in Lincoln street. The population of the village was less than two thousand.

---

fifty years used as a horticultural nursery. They were within a circle of thirty feet, their heads all lay to the east, and some nails and musket balls were found with them." *Long Island Antiquities, p. 98.*

4 The old Town Hall was removed to Bridge street after the erection of the new Town Hall, in 1864, and has since been used as a shop. It is now occupied by Joseph Crooker.

Soon after Dr. Muhlenberg had moved his school to College Point, a girls' school was established at the Flushing Institute, and the name of the building was changed to St. Ann's Hall. The Rev. Dr. Frederick Schroeder was the Principal of this new school. Among other attractions, St. Ann's Hall was provided with "a gymnasium, with a great variety of alluring calesthenic exercises, a hippodrome for horsemanship, nine hundred feet in circumference, and archery grounds extending the whole length of the garden and the hippodrome." 1839

St. Thomas's Hall—a school for boys—was built this same year. It stood where St. Joseph's Academy now stands. The Rev. Francis L. Hawks, D. D., was the Principal and Proprietor. He was assisted by fourteen instructors. The school had accommodations for one hundred and twenty pupils. The chapel was spoken of as "one of the most beautiful in the country."

Flushing was busy at this time not only with educational matters; religious affairs also claimed the attention of the people. A new Church, the Protestant Reformed Dutch Church was organized, with seven members. Services were held, after the organization, in the school house in Church street, the Rev. William R. Gordon, of Manhasset, officiating. Mr. Gordon was afterwards settled here as the 1842 first Pastor of the Church. Two years later, the congregation built a very attractive stone church, on the corner of Washington and S. Prince streets, at a cost of $12,000.[5]

This year witnessed the beginning of Flushing journalism. To Charles R. Lincoln is due the credit of beginning this important work. The first periodical printed in Flushing was the Monthly Journal of the Institute, issued by the Institute during Dr. Muhlenberg's time, but this had no connection with subsequent journalism in Flushing. Mr. Lincoln came to Flushing, in 1840, to publish the Repository, edited by the students of St. Thomas's Hall, and The Church Record, edited by the Rev. Dr. Hawks in the interest of the Episcopal Church. The Repository was published about a year and a half. The Church Record continued about six months longer. Then Mr. Lincoln established the Flushing Journal. The first number appeared in October, 1842. This was a specimen number. Its regular weekly issue, did not appear until March of the fow-

5 The corner stone was laid, Aug. 16, 1843. There were present on this occasion and taking part in the service the Rev. Drs. De Witte and Brownlee, of New York, and the Rev. Dr. Garretson of Newtown. Mr. Gordon's successors in the Pastorate of the Church were: Rev. G. H. Mandeville, 1851; Rev. William W. Holloway, 1859: Rev. E. S. Fairchild, 1865; Rev. O. E. Cobb, D.D., 1872: Rev. James Demarest, D.D., 1890; Rev. Rockwell H. Potter, 1898. The new Reformed Church, at the corner of Amity street and Bowne avenue, was built in 1892.

lowing year. The Journal was the only newspaper in Flushing until 1852, when George W. Ralph, started the Public Voice. The Public Voice continued about a year and a half. In 1855, Walter R. Burling, a compositor on the Journal, established the Long Island Times as a weekly. Thomas H. Todd, who afterwards established the Long Island Star (of Long Island City), and Eugene Lincoln, the founder of the Glen Cove Gazette, were also compositors on the Journal at this time. Burling issued the first daily in Flushing in 1865, when the Flushing Daily Times appeared. The two papers continued without further change, the Journal as a weekly and the Times with a slight change of name as a daily and weekly, until the death of Mr. Lincoln in 1869.[6] After Mr. Lincoln's death, the Journal was continued by his estate under the editorship of Joseph E. Lawrence, at one time editor of the Golden Era of San Francisco. In 1870 the Journal was purchased by E. B. Hinsdale, and William H. Gibson became the editor. Five years later, C. W. Smith purchased the Journal. In 1878

6 Charles Richmond Lincoln, was born in Dorchester, Mass., in 1806. He learned his trade as printer in New York. Here he began the publication of a daily paper called The Star. A fire destroyed his printing office shortly after the commencement of this enterprise. In 1836, he went to Greece with the Rev. Dr. Hill to act as printer to the Episcopal mission established in Athens. After his return from Greece he came to Flushing.

the Times became the property of the Rev. E. S. Fairchild, who edited it for about a year, when Walter R. Burling again became editor and proprietor. In 1879, Mr. Smith, proprietor of the Journal issued the first number of the Evening Journal. Thus Flushing had two dailies. The next change came in 1881, when the Long Island Times Publishing Company purchased the Times and engaged George R. Crowley as editor. About a year later the Times became the property of L. E. Quigg. Robert Wilson, the foreman of the Times, severed his connection with the paper at the time of its sale, and in 1883 established the Long Island News. Mr. Quigg was editor of the Times until 1886, when the paper was purchased by C. W. Smith of the Journal. Mr. Smith published both the Journal, and the Times until the following year, when he suspended the Daily Times and sold the Weekly Times to James H. Easton. Three years later, in 1890, the Journal was sold to J. H. Ridenour, the present editor and proprietor. In 1897, Mr. Easton sold the Long Island Times to the Flushing Publishing Company, C. W. Smith returned to Flushing to become its editor, and the daily edition was revived. The Journal has within the last few years established a well-equipped job printing department, and has turned out some fine specimens of book making.

Dr. Hawk's school had a short life. After four years, it was closed because of financial difficulties. The property 1843
was purchased by Gerardus B. Docherty, L L. D., and Dr. Carmichael. Dr. Carmichael withdrew after a year.[7] In
1845, Ezra Fairchild, who had conducted a boys' school in 1845
New Jersey since 1816, made arrangements with Dr. Docherty to take possession of St. Thomas's Hall, and bring his school from New Jersey to Flushing. Mr. Fairchild and his school came to Flushing, but Dr. Docherty, for some unknown reason, did not carry out his agreement concerning the surrender of St. Thomas's Hall. The school was forced to take refuge in the Pavilion. Here it was established for a year. Mr. Fairchild then took from
Dr. Schroeder his unexpired lease of St. Ann's Hall. Later 1846
the property was purchased, and the old name of Flushing Institute was restored. The school and the name remain to-day. Under Mr. Fairchild and under his son, E. A. Fairchild, the present proprietor,[8] Flushing Institute has

---

7 Dr. Docherty continued until 1848, when the Rev. William H. Gilder purchased the property and opened the Flushing Female College. *Mandeville, p. 126.*

8 The relationship between Master and pupils, at the Institute, is well illustrated by the following unique announcement of the opening of the fall term, which appeared in the New York dailies, Aug. 10, 1868: "Dear Boys—Trouble begins Sept. 15. E. A. Fairchild." This advertisement was copied far and wide. Harpers Monthly

had a long and useful career. There are Institute boys all over the United States and in most of the Central and South American countries.[9]

The same year that brought the Fairchilds to Flushing to re-establish the Institute, saw the opening of Sanford Hall, as a private asylum. Sanford Hall had been erected in 1836 by the Hon. Nathan Sanford, as a private resi-

---

reprinted it, with the note: "Is there extant a boy—be he boy of fifty or boy of ten—who will not appreciate the grim humor of the following advertisement." Mrs. Spofford, in the Galaxy, commented on it.

9 Many prominent men in these southern countries made their acquaintance with the English language at the Institute. Their initial efforts, preserved by the Principal, furnish some rare specimens of composition. Here is an essay on Divine Providence. "God has observing the order more maravillous and exact in life and death of man; both are measure and regular of best way: and nothing is more evident than the wisdle of God in the poblation of world. In a number give of years, die a proportional number of lives of all ages. By thirty fifeth and thirty sixth, persons lives die one every one year: but the proportion of birth is great. For tenth year in the same space and time and between the same number of individuals are birth twelve. In the fierst year about third children die generally one: in the fifeth one of every twenty fifeth: and so forth decrease the number of death till the age twenty fifeth, to another time begin increase. How evident is the care of the divina providence extend upon his creature till the same moment in which enter in the world, she watch and protect withou any distinction between the poor and rich, the great and small. The life is in extreme uncertain allthou by the strong of the physical constitution some individual there are none subject to sickness, they can however strong he may safe by a contagion of one epidemic."

dence.[10] It is said to have cost nearly $130,000. Mr. Sanford died soon after its completion. In 1844 it was bought by Dr. James Macdonald and his brother Gen. Allan Macdonald. In the following year they moved their institution for the treatment of nervous diseases from New York, and established themselves in Sanford Hall.[11]

Contemporary with the interest in education, was the development of agricultural interests. The Queens County Agricultural Society was organized in 1841, with Effingham 1846
Lawrence as its first President. The fifth Fair of the Society was held in Flushing. "The American Institute, of New York, held a plowing and spading match. There was a band of music from Governor's Island. The performers and delegates rode through the village in a wagon tastefully decorated, and drawn by thirty-six yoke of oxen. The exhibition-tent was decked with flowers from Flushing's far-famed

10 Sanford was elected U. S. Senator, 1815; in 1823, he succeeded Jas. Kent as Chancellor of the State of New York: in 1826, he was again elected U. S. Senator. He died in Flushing, Oct. 17, 1838.

11 Dr. McDonald died, in 1849. "His funeral took place on May 8th. . . The shops in the village were closed, and it was a day of sincere and general mourning. . . Thus passed away from the earth, one of God's noblest men, beloved in life and lamented in death by all who knew him." *Mandeville, p. 138.*

Dr. Barstow was resident Physician of Sanford Hall for forty-one years He moved to New York in 1895.

nurseries. Dr. Gardener gave the address in the Reformed Church."

1848 The Board of Education was organized under an act of Legislature, in 1848. The first Board consisted of Effingham W. Lawrence, Edward E. Mitchell, Samuel B. Parsons, William H. Fairweather, and Thomas Leggett, Jr. But the history of Flushing's public schools goes back at least to 1843. In that year we find a Board of Trustees comprised of John W. Lawrence, John Wilcomb, William W. Valk, M. D., and Samuel Willet, Clerk, in charge of school district No. 5, which comprised the whole of the village and some additional territory. About this time, 1843, a new school-house was erected at a cost of $950. This school-house stood at the corner of Garden and Church streets, on what is now part of the lawn in the rear of Henry A. Bogert's house. Some time before 1844, the school established by the Flushing Female Association had received assistance from public funds. In that year this help was withdrawn, and the money was devoted to the school directly under the care of the trustees. Now came a critical period in the history of our public schools. To the wisdom and perseverance of Samuel B. Parsons and Thomas Leggett, Jr., Flushing is indebted for the impetus given at that time to the interests of education. A larger and better school-house and better provisions for education were needed. But it was difficult to overcome the indifference of the people and their unwillingness to submit to a slight increase in the tax rate. Many stormy meetings were held. Finally, at a public meeting held Dec. 26, 1847, "it was resolved, by a vote of thirty-seven to five, to raise three thousand dollars by tax, and to authorize the Trustees to sell the old building, to contract for a new one on the plan of the New York public schools, and to propose a suitable site." In the next year (1848) many meetings were again held, and much discussion ensued concerning a site for the new school. The Legislature authorized "the Board to raise $6,500 by tax or mortgage for the erection of a building, limiting the annual assessment to one-fifth of one per cent. on all taxable property in the District." The lot on Union street was purchased, and the school-house was built which was torn down in 1897. The school opened in November, with seven teachers and three hundred and eighty-one pupils. Thomas F. Harrison was the first Principal. From that time to the present there has been a constant growth in the size and efficiency of the schools.

The Village of Flushing did not grow rapidly at this 1851
period of its history. In 1851 it had a population of about

2,000– not many more than it had at the time of its incorporation. It, however, still maintained its reputation as a desirable place residence. Barbour's Historical Collections, published this year, speaks thus of our village: "Its various attractions, with great facility of communication with New York, have induced many wealthy citizens to locate in its immediate neighborhood. Some of the private residences are among the most imposing and splendid edifices in the State. The Village of Flushing contains a number of flourishing literary institutions for both sexes. This place is also distinguished for its excellent nurseries of fruit and other trees."[12]

The year 1851 witnessed the establishment of another Church in Flushing, i. e. the First Congregational Church. The Council that was convened to accomplish its organization met in the school-house in Church street, July 1st. The Rev. D. C. Lansing, D. D., was chosen Moderator and William C. Gilman, Scribe. Among those present and taking part in the proceedings were the Rev. Dr. R. S. Storrs and the Rev. Dr. Henry Ward Beecher. The organization effected consisted of eighteen members, three of whom were received on profession of faith, eleven by letters from the

12 *Historical Collections, p. 291 et sq.*

Reformed Church of Flushing, four by letters from other places. The first Pastor was the Rev. Charles O. Reynolds. The first Church-building of the society was dedicated, Jan. 29, 1852. It stood on the east side of Union street, south of the corner of Washington street.[13]

On September 29th, of this year, the County Fair was again held in Flushing. "The delegation from the American Institute and invited guests rode from the steamboat wharf to the Fair grounds in a wagon drawn by fifty-six yoke of fine oxen, with music, under the escort of Bragg's horse guards and the Hamilton Rifles. . . There was a plowing match and a fine display of flowers and fruits. The horses . . . were of truer form and points than those at the State Fair."

Before another County Fair was held in Flushing a rail- 1854
road had been constructed between Hunter's Point and Flushing. It began operations in 1854. The Flushing station was the present Main street station—then at the

13 The present Congregational Church was built in 1856. The old building was then moved to the rear of the new Church, and was used for a Sunday school. There it stood until a few years ago. Following is the list of Pastors of the Congregational Church: Rev. Charles O. Reynolds, 1851; Rev. S. Bourne, 1854: Rev. Henry T. Staats, 1860; Rev. Henry H. McFarland, 1863: Rev. Martin L. Williston, 1870; Rev. Albert C. Reed, 1873: Rev. James O. Averill, 1879; Rev. John Abbot French, D. D., 1881. Dr. French was not a stranger in Flushing when he was installed as Pastor. He had some years before, from 1866 to 1868, served the Church as "Stated Supply."

outer edge of the village. It was at first intended to run the road to Williamsburg, but this route was afterwards
1855 abandoned.[14] The effect of the railroad on the attendance at the next Fair, which was held in September, 1855, was very perceptible. The ten o'clock train brought nearly four hundred people. E. A. Lawrence, the Supervisor of the Town, met the guests, and made a speech of welcome, which was responded to by George W. Clinton, the orator of the day. They all then proceeded to the Fair grounds on Sanford avenue and Union street. The New York Times, in its account of the Fair, said: "There was one other production, however, which eclipsed everything else, both in number and beauty of the specimens—a production which, though by no means indigenous to Queens County, is nevertheless brought to a perfection there that one but seldom sees so general elsewhere. We mean, of course, the lovely women. Such a collection of elegant, well-bred, handsome, intelligent-looking, fascinating young ladies was surely never seen before."

1857 In 1857 the village limits were extended by removing the southern boundary, which formerly crossed Jamaica

14 The first Board of Directors: Wm. Smart, David S. Williams, Samuel B. Parsons, James Strong, Aaron C. Underhill, James W. Allen, Isaac Peck, John D. Locke, Jonathan Crane, Thomas Leggett, Jr., William H. Schermerhorn, George W. Quimby, D. S. Duncombe.

avenue, just south of Sanford avenue, to Hillside avenue—then called Ireland avenue. There was little, if any change made at this time in the other boundary lines.

The next Fair in Flushing was held Sept. 22, 1858. The invited guests, in a carriage drawn by fifty-six oxen, accompanied by "Sheldon's splendid band," drove through the principal streets. Fully seven thousand persons attended this Fair. The Fair was held on a ten-acre lot, belonging to Thomas Legett, Jr.,[15] which was enclosed by a high board fence. "Simon R. Bowne exhibited twenty of his fine horses: and E. A. Lawrence, a fat ox weighing 2500 pounds. Gabriel Winter contributed a floral temple. . . The pick-pockets reaped a harvest in a small way." In 1866, the Town of Hempstead gave to the Agricultural Society, for a nominal sum, the ground at Mineola where the County Fairs have since been held. 1858

The year 1854 saw the completion of the present St. George's Church[16] and the beginning of St. Michael's. 1854

15 Back of the Town Hall, between Farrington street and Congress avenue.

16 This is the third Church built by St. George's parish. The second, now used for a Sunday school, was built in 1821. Grace Church, Whitestone, was part of St. George's parish until 1858, when it became an independent parish. St. Paul's Chapel, College Point, was built in 1860. All Saint's, Bayside, was built in 1892, and the district was set apart as a separate parish. Following are the Rectors of

The former was consecrated, June 1st., by the Rt. Rev. Jonathan M. Wainwright, Provisional Bishop of New York. It cost $33,000. The corner stone of St. Michael's Church was laid June 24th. The Church was far enough advanced towards completion to admit of its being used for public worship on Christmas Day. It was not finished until two years later, when it was dedicated by the Rt. Rev. Dr. Loughlin, Bishop of Brooklyn.[17]

Within the same year the First Baptist Church of Flushing was organized, with the Rev. Howard Osgood as its Pastor. There were, at the time of the organization,

---

St. George's Church and the dates of their induction: Rev. William Urquhart, 1704: Rev. Thomas Poyer, 1710: Rev. Thomas Colgan, 1733: Rev. Samuel Seabury, 1757; Rev. Joshua Bloomer, 1769: Rev. William Hammell, 1790; Rev. Elijah D. Rattoone, 1797; Rev. Abram L. Clarke, 1803; Rev. Barzillai Buckley, 1809: Rev. John V. E. Thorne, 1820; Rev. William A. Muhlenberg, 1826: Rev. William H. Lewis, 1829: Rev. J. Murray Forbes, 1833; Rev. Samuel R. Johnson, 1834: Rev. Robert B. VanKleeck, 1835: Rev. Frederick J. Goodwin, 1837: Rev. George Burcker, 1844; Rev. J. Carpenter Smith, 1847: Rev. H. D. Waller, 1898.

17 The lot on which St. Michael's Church stands was purchased in 1841. A wooden building was erected in the same year, and used until the present Church was built, in 1854. St. Michael's parochial school was organized in 1851. The first school-house stood between the Church and rectory. In 1854, it was moved across the street. In 1880 the present school-house was built. The resident Pastors of St. Michael's Church are as follows: Rev. Dennis Wheeler, 1848; Rev. John McMahon, 1851: Rev. James O'Beirne, 1853; Rev. Henry O'Loughlin, 1873: Rev. John McKenna, 1877; Rev. Eugene J. Donnelly, 1892.

nine members. The first Church-building of this society was erected in the following year. It stood in Washington street, between Union street and Bowne avenue. In 1872, this building was moved to the corner of Jamaica avenue and Jaggar avenue, where it still stands, and is now used for a Public Library. The present Baptist Church, at the corner of Sanford avenue and Union street, was built in 1890. In the same year, the Park Branch of the Baptist Church was built. It is a neat chapel standing in Bowne avenue, Hitchcock Park.[18]

The school property which had been known as St. 1860
Thomas's Hall, and later as the Flushing Female College, was purchased, in 1860, by the Rev. James O'Beirne for the Sisters of St. Joseph. This has since been the Mother House of the order. St. Joseph's Academy—a school for girls—was established by the Sisters, and has been in successful operation ever since. Its commanding location, its fine buildings and beautifully-kept grounds, make St.

18 Following are the Baptist ministers who succeeded the Rev. Howard Osgood: Rev. Frederick Graves; Rev. John Bray; Rev. C. W. Nichols; Rev. John Higgs; Rev. D. Meason; Rev. Harvey Alley; Rev. R. T. Middleditch, D.D.; Rev. L. F. Moore, 1875; Rev. A. S. Burrows, 1881; Rev. William Morrison, 1886; Rev. D. Powell Chockley, 1892; Rev. Charles E. Knowles, 1894.

Joseph's Academy one of the very attractive features of the village.[19]

1861 When the war of Rebellion broke out, it found in Flushing a well-organized company, ready to answer the call for troops.[20] The Flushing Guard was organized, about 1839, as Light Infantry, and was attached to the 93rd Regiment, N. Y. S. M. At its first parade, in 1840, it had twenty-six uniformed men. In 1843, the company was changed to Artillery; in 1845, it was again changed to Light Horse Artillery, and was attached to Storm's famous First Brigade. At that time it was commanded by Capt. William A. Mitchell, and was attached to Col. Hamilton's Regiment. The Battery offered its services at the outbreak of the Mexican war, but they were not accepted. In 1848, the Battery had won a reputation throughout the State, in Light Horse evolutions. Its drill called together many celebrated tacticians. It became known as the "Incomparable" and was called "Bragg's Battery," in honor of the hero of Buena Vista.

---

19 The central portion of the Academy was built in 1868; the west wing, in 1872; the Chapel, in 1879. The school has about 130 pupils.

20 Another military organization in Flushing was the Hamilton Rifles, organized 1849. They made up Company A, in the 15th Regiment, N. Y. S. M. The 15th Regiment was made up of Queens County men and was commanded by Col. Charles A. Hamilton. *Mandeville, p. 82.*

At the outbreak of the war, the Battery was commanded by Capt. Thomas L. Robinson, and was attached to the 15th Regiment, N. Y. S. M. When the call came for troops, in 1861, the regiment failed to offer its services. A committee of Flushing's citizens, therefore, proposed to the officers of the Battery that, if the Battery would enlist, the committee would equip the soldiers with all things needed. Permission having been received from Washington, the officers began recruiting to fill the ranks; and the Flushing Battery was ready to march to Washington, Dec. 2, 1861, with five commissioned officers and one hundred and fifty men.[21] This was the only company organized in the county. Other volunteers joined companies and regiments elsewhere. Flushing furnished in all about two hundred and fifty volunteers during the war.

The Flushing Battery returned to the village, June 7, 1864, and was received with great enthusiasm. The company 1864

21 The officers were: Capt. Thos. L. Robinson; First Lieuts. Jacob Roemer and William Hamilton; Second Lieuts. Henry J. Standish and William C. Rawolle. Captain Robinson was dismissed from service, March 4, 1862; Lieutenant Roemer, was promoted Captain and commanded the Battery (known as Battery L.) throughout the war. He was commissioned Bvt. Maj. Dec. 2, 1864. Lieutenant Standish resigned, in 1862. The following officers also served in the Battery at different times during the war: First Lieuts. Moses E. Brush, Thomas Heasley; Second Lieuts. William Cooper, J. Van Nostrand, Chas. R. Lincoln, Alonzo Garretson, J. J. Johnson, William E. Balkie, George H. Durfee. *Major Roemer's Reminiscences.*

marched down Main street to the Flushing Hotel, where a bountiful feast had been prepared for officers and men. On June 21st., the company was mustered out of service.[22]

Flushing's first railroad ran through Winfield to Penny
1869 Bridge, leaving Woodside to the north. From Penny Bridge the road followed Newtown Creek to Hunter's Point. Conrad Poppenhusen and associates laid out a road

---

22 "The reception, given to the Battery by the citizens of Flushing, was an overwhelming one, and, doubtless, there are many still living in the village who will remember that joyful day. I can yet see the crowds filling the street, and cheering at the top of their voices as the brave boys of the 34th New York Battery entered the village. . . . I know we marched down Main street to the hotel, where a splendid dinner was waiting for us, but how I reached the place I hardly know. Conducted by Mr. C. R. Lincoln, who took me by the arm, we marched through what seemed to me a sea of faces on either side, while the assembled multitude shouted, hurrahed, and showered us with flowers. We finally reached the hotel and were put in charge of my beloved pastor, the Rev. Dr. J. Carpenter Smith. He led me to the head of the table in the dining room, and then, in behalf of the citizens of Flushing, bade my command and myself partake of what they had provided for Flushing's heroes.

Near the close of the banquet, the following brief resume of the Battery's doings was given: 'This Battery has taken part in 57 different engagements, has marched 18,758 miles, and thrown from its guns during this time over 56 tons of iron. The whole number of enlisted men that have belonged to it during its four years' career is 271, of whom 19 yielded up their lives in the service of their beloved country, and 47 have been discharged for disabilities incurred in the field, through wounds or disease.'"

Roemer's Reminiscences, pp. 302 et sq.

from Hunter's Point through Woodside, and thence directly to Bridge street. Before this road was built, the Poppenhusens purchased the old road east of Winfield. They then built the road from Hunter's Point through Woodside to Winfield, and also the College Point and Whitestone branch. This was in 1869. Later they completed their original line by running a road from Woodside directly to Bridge street. This road left Corona, Newtown, and Winfield some distance to the south. Thus the trains from Main street and the trains from Bridge street ran on two distant roads from Flushing to Woodside. This combination of roads, now under the control of the Poppenhusens, was known as the Flushing and North Shore Railroad.

In 1872 the Central Railroad of Long Island was built. This was commonly known as the Stewart road. It 1872
was run in harmony with North Shore road, branching off from that road just below Lawrence avenue, and running through Garden City and Hempstead to Babylon. The Poppenhusens were becoming a very influential element in railroad interests on Long Island. They came into competition with the Long Island Railroad on the South Side. By way of retaliation, Oliver Charlick, President of the Long Island R. R., built a road parallel to the North Shore road from Woodside to Flushing. This road was opened in 1873. The

1873 old station still stands on Jaggar avenue, just south of Bradford avenue. The Charlick road, or the White Line as it was called, put down the price of an excursion ticket to Long Island City to fifteen cents. The North Shore road was compelled to do the same thing in the following spring. Two years later, in April, 1875, Oliver Charlick lost the Presidency of the Long Island R. R. The Poppenhusens had been buying stock in this road wherever they could find any for sale. In 1876 they were found to be in full control; Conrad Poppenhusen was elected President of the Long Island R. R.; the fare on both the Charlick road and the North Shore road was advanced; and on April 17th of the same year, all trains were discontinued on the Charlick road. The Central, or Stewart road never paid, and was abandoned in 1878. The Woodside branch was abandoned about the same time. This, in brief, is the history of Flushing's railroads.

1870 In 1870, the subject of supplying the village with a water system began to be agitated. Two years later, the Trustees were authorized to proceed with the work. The question of a site for the pumping-house and of the source of water supply caused much discussion. Douglass Pond, Kissena Lake, and Spring Lane were proposed. The Trustees were equally divided between Douglass Pond and Kissena Lake. The State Legislature was asked to change the number of Trustees from six to seven, that the question might be settled. This change was made, and Douglass Pond was selected.

The system was completed and put into operation, Dec. 1874
3, 1874. The event was the occasion of a great celebration. Houses were decorated; a procession marched through the streets; a dinner was served at the Flushing Hotel; and a public meeting, with speeches, was held in the Town Hall in the evening. The water in the pond did not prove to be satisfactory. Wells were dug which have since supplied the village with an abundance of pure water. In 1886, mains were laid to Willets Point. The stand-pipe was erected in 1897.

In 1883 the area of the village was considerably en- 1883
larged. The community had grown beyond the old limits. The boundary lines at that time established were those in force when the village became a part of New York City. An intelligent notion of the extent of the village will best be gained by stating where these boundary lines crossed the principal thoroughfares leading out of the village. On Whitestone avenue the village extended to the limits of Whitestone village, just beyond the residence of J. F. B. Mitchell; the union of Broadway and Sanford avenue marked the limits of the village toward the east; the line running south included the corner of the Flushing Cemetery near the entrance; the southern line crossed Jamaica ave-

nue at the bridge over the outlet of Kissena Lake; the western line followed the creek.

In the winter of this same year, 1883, the Art Class of Flushing was organized with seven members, for the purpose of aiding in the establishment of a hospital.[23] The by-laws of the Art Class limited the membership to twenty-five. This number was soon reached, and constituted the class for years. Sales of fine needle-work were held by the class, in New York and Flushing, just before Christmas and Easter. In this way the class earned, and paid to the trustees of the Hospital about $300 a year, for many years.[24]
1884 Early in the year following the organization of the Art Class, i. e. on February 4, 1884, the Flushing Hospital and Dispensary was incorporated. Soon after the incorporation of the Hospital, on April 3rd, the trustees elected a Board of Lady Managers.[25] This board for three years did

---

23 The original members of the Art Class were: Miss Marie Bramwell, President; Mrs. Eugene T. Lynch, Secretary; Mrs. R. S. Bowne, Mrs. John Gihon, Miss Constance V. Bramwell, Mrs. E. M. Travers, Mrs. E. F. Thompson.

24 The class was disbanded in 1896, having contributed to the Hospital about $4000.

25 The first board was composed of Mrs. J. L. Hicks, Mrs. E. T. Lynch, Mrs. R. S. Bowne, Mrs. Abram Bell, Mrs. W. B. Worrall, Mrs. A. K. P. Dennett, Miss F. Burdett. Mrs. Hicks was for years First Directress. Of the Lady Managers, Mrs. Hicks, Mrs. Bowne and Mrs. Lynch afterwards became Trustees of the Hospital, and served many years.

the work of the Hospital. The managers visited the sick poor in their homes, supplied them with medical attendance, with medicines and nourishing food, and when necessary with the care of a nurse. Cases that could not be properly treated at home were sent to hospitals in New York and Brooklyn. During the winter of 1884-85, the Board of Lady Managers rented a house at No. 41 Congress avenue, and established there a temporary hospital. The work gradually widened, and the interest in it increased until 1887, when the Hospital at the corner of Forest and South Parsons avenues was built. The ground was given by John Henderson, who also loaned the Trustees $3000 toward building the Hospital. When Mr. Henderson died, in 1890, he directed that this debt be cancelled, but his estate was not able to pay all of his bequests, and his Executor has declined to release the Hospital. Soon after the erection of the Hospital, in February 1888, the Trustees elected as their successors members of the Board of Lady Managers. From that date until 1895 the Trustees of the Hospital were women. In the latter year men were again elected, including all the members of the medical board. Since then the hospital has been entirely under the care of male Trustees. In addition to the Art Class, the Hospital has had the assistance of the Green Twigs—a society of young ladies.

Besides helping the Hospital in other ways, this last-named organization has given the Hospital an ambulance, surgical instruments and case, and furniture for certain rooms.

The work of the Hospital has grown from year to year.[26] The training-school for nurses was started in 1890; the Babies' Ward, the gift of Charles H. Senff, was built in 1893, at a cost of $4000. Since 1895, the Hospital has received an annual appropriation from the town. This source of revenue was lost when Flushing became a part of New York City. In 1897, Charles H. Senff gave the Hospital $10,000 for a new surgical ward, and F. Augustus Schermerhorn gave $4000 for a new kitchen and laundry. In this same year a legacy of $500 was received from the estate of Anton Roesingh, and one of $2500 from the estate of Hannah Willets.

The Flushing Hospital is the only institution of its kind in Queens County outside of Long Island City. It has from the start received the cordial support of the physicians of the town, and has thus been enabled to do a good and

---

26 In 1894, the Hospital treated 257 indoor patients at an expense of $7800; in 1895, 242 patients, expense $8700; in 1896, 273 patients, expense $11,000; in 1897, 393 patients, expense $12,555. The property of the Hospital, in 1897, was estimated to be worth $25,000.

much needed work. It is an institution of which Flushing may well be proud.

To attempt to give a detailed account of all of Flushing's institutions would carry us beyond the scope of the present work.[27] We must content ourselves, therefore, with a brief survey of the village as it is to-day, and so bring our

27. The Athletic Club has a gymnasium on Jaggar Avenue, and Golf Links on Whitestone avenue. The Niantic Club House stands at the corner of Sanford and Parsons avenues. The Young Men's Christian Association, organized in 1895, occupies a house in Locust street. The Good Citizenship League, a woman's club, was organized and incorporated in 1891. The United Workers, organized in 1893, is a society for the improvement of the condition of the poor. Connected with this organization are the Woman's Exchange and the Day Nursery. The United Workers was the outgrowth of the work of the Good Citizenship League. The Business Men's Protective Association began its work in 1893. Its object is to cooperate in the collection of bills and in determining the financial standing of customers. The Association has shown its public spirit in encouraging public improvements. The officers are: George Pople, President; John J. Trapp, Secretary and Attorney; D. H. Van De Water, Treasurer.

In addition to the older schools of Flushing, whose history we have followed, should be mentioned the Flushing Seminary and Kyle's Military Institute. The former is a school for girls. Hans Schuler, B. D., Ph. D., is the Principal. Dr. Schuler purchased the school kept by Mrs. Masters, in 1888, and organized the Flushing Seminary. Mrs. Masters' predecessor was Miss S. O. Hoffman, who established the school in 1874. Miss Hoffman's school was at first for day scholars only. In 1876 a limited number of boarders were received. Kyle's Military Institute, a boarding school for boys, Paul Kyle, Principal, was first established in College Point. It came to Flushing in 1892, and

history to a close. The Village of Flushing has always been a place of residence. Those institutions have been fostered that would render the village attractive to persons seeking homes; manufacture has not been encouraged.[28] The village streets are macadamized, well-shaded with fine trees of many varieties, lighted by gas and electricity, and swept and sprinkled at public expense.[29] The side-walks are paved with stone flagging. A complete system of sewers extends throughout the village. The steam and electric cars make frequent trips between Flushing and the city. These conveniences and improvements have made Flushing

---

located in its present building at the corner of State and Farrington streets.

Flushing has two banks—the Flushing Bank and the Queens County Savings Bank.

In addition to the Churches referred to in the foregoing pages, Flushing has a German Lutheran Church, incorporated in 1893, the Rev. Dr. R. Mekler, Pastor; and a Baptist Church for colored people—the Ebenezer Baptist Church. The Church building of the Lutheran society was built in 1894.

The 17th Separate Company of the N. Y. S. M. was organized in 1876. The Armory, located in Amity street, between Main and Union streets, was built in 1894.

28. The principal manufacturing establishments in Flushing are—the machine shops of J. L. Bogert, the Sash and Blind Works of C. W. Copp, the De Bevoise Waist Co., Heinrich Franck Sohne & Co. Coffee Addition Works, the Harway Dye-wood Co., B. & W. B. Smith's Glass Works.

29. This at least was the condition of Flushing in the year 1897.

an attractive home for business and professional men of New York. Here they find pleasant homes amid rural surroundings, within easy reach of their places of business. A number of artists have been attracted to Flushing by its quiet beauty. The annual exhibition of their work is one of the pleasant events in the village life.

It is interesting to note how many of the improvements and conveniences that are to-day enjoyed by the inhabitants of Flushing were unknown ten years ago. In this respect, however, our village is not different from many other communities, so rapid has been the development of those things which add to the comforts of life.

Among the older institutions of Flushing that have not been already described, are the Fire Department, the Gas Works, and the Public Library. The earliest legislation on the subject of our Fire Department was a law, passed March 24, 1809, entitled: "An Act for extinguishing fires in the Village of Flushing, in Queens County." This law created a Board of Trustees, to consist of not less than three or more than five members, who were to constitute "The Fire Company of the Village of Flushing." These Trustees were to be elected annually, by 'certain persons . . . who have associated for the purpose of purchasing a fire-engine, and such other inhabitants as may be proprietors of the said engine, when purchased for the use of the said village." The Trustees were authorized "to appoint a sufficient number of firemen (willing to accept) not exceeding eighteen, to have the care, management, working, and using the said fire-engine." The first Captain of the Fire Company seems to have been a man named Stansbury. He was succeeded by Treadwell Sands, who served twenty years. The engine-house stood on Main street, where Van Siclen and Townsend's green grocery now stands. Before the purchase of the fire-engine, the only means of fighting a fire was by pouring on water from buckets which were passed along a line of men extending from the nearest pump to the fire. The present Fire Department was organized in 1854.[30] Public cisterns, located in different parts of the village, supplied the water. When the present water system was established, in 1874, fire-engines gave place to hose-carriages, and the cisterns were filled up or covered over.[31]

The Gas Company was incorporated Oct. 16, 1855, with a capital of $20,000, and the exclusive right of supplying

---

30. *Mandeville, p. 80.*

31. Officers of the Fire Department, 1897: James H. McCormick, Chief Engineer; John Carrahar, First Assistant; George Townsend, Second Assistant; Geo. W. Worth, Treasurer. Names of the various companies: Empire Hose Co. No. 1, Rescue Hook and Ladder Co., Young America Hose Co., No. 2; Mutual Engine Co., No. 1; Flushing Hose Co., No. 3; Murray Hill Hose Co., No. 4.

gas to the village for twenty years. Gas was turned on in January, of the following year. Five years later the Company reported two and a half miles of pipe, one hundred metres, eighteen street lamps, and a monthly consumption of 100,000 cubic feet of gas. In 1868, new works were built with a greater capacity.[32]

The Flushing Library Association owes its origin to Edw. L. Murray, L. Bradford Prince,[33] Joseph K. Murray, F. A. Potts, and other public spirited men. It was organized in 1858, and incorporated in the following year. The first officers of the Library were: E. A. Fairchild, President; L. B. Prince, Secretary; J. Milnor Peck, Treasurer.

The library was at first open only to members of the Association, who paid an annual fee of one dollar. In 1884 it became a free library. To-day it has 7,000 books, and an annual circulation of 19,608. The library, when first organized, was located in a room at the northeast corner of Bridge and Prince streets; then it was moved to a room over

---

32. *Mandeville, p. 79. History of Queens County, p. 109.* The first officers of the Gas Company were: James R. Lowerre, President; Gilbert Hicks, Treasurer; Charles A. Willets, Secretary.

33. L. Bradford Prince was born in Flushing, in 1840. He was elected a member of the Assembly five years in succession, 1870-1875; a member of the Senate in 1875; appointed naval officer of New York, 1878; Chief Justice of Mexico, 1879; Governor of New Mexico, 1889.

the drug store at 51 Main street; then to the southwest room in the Town Hall. Later we find it in the Savings Bank building, in a building on the north side of Amity street, east of Main street, and in the store room at 129 Main street. In 1891, the present building was purchased from the Baptist Church.[34]

But the past ten years have brought to the village a greater number of improvements than any previous period of five times the length.[35] Ten years ago the streets were not macadamized. They were not sprinkled, except in certain localities where individuals, by private subscription, sought to protect themselves from dust. There was no means of protection against the discomforts of mud. The streets were poorly lighted by an insufficient number of gas lamps. There

---

34. The present officers of the Library are: President, William Elliman; Secretary, Walter L. Bogert.

35. The names of the Trustees who have served within this period should be recorded. They are: E. V. W. Rossiter, James T. Chapman, James A. Renwick, John H. Wilson, Nicholas Mehlen, Samuel Berrien, Francis F. Keeler, M. J. Quirk, Patrick R. Brogan, Ernest Mitchell, Frederick P. Morris, John D. Hashagen, John Hepburn, James F. Connor, James A. Macdonald, John W. Crawford. E. V. W. Rossiter was President of the Village for six years. He declined the nomination for re-election, in December, 1894. Henry Clement served as Treasurer of the Village for twenty-five years. He resigned in January, 1891. Mr. Clement died Sep. 8, 1895. Clinton B. Smith was Clerk of the Board of Trustees from 1889 to 1898. Edward E. Sprague was for many years Corporation Counsel.

were no electric lights; there were no electric fire signals.[36] Cows were allowed to run at large. When the Village Trustees passed an ordinance, in 1890, forbidding cattle to run loose on the streets, the measure met with no little opposition. A liberty-loving correspondent of the Evening Journal asked: "Whether the craze for the removal of fences is to be indulged in at the expense of our personal liberty?" The ordinance was enforced, the President of the Village personally assisting in its enforcement. The result has been that fences, being no longer necessary, have been gradually removed, to the great improvement of the appearance of the streets. Within the past ten years, the free delivery of the mail has been established, two electric roads have been built,[37] the steam road has completed the change from a

36. The electric fire signals were established in 1893; the electric street lights in 1896.

37. The Flushing and College Point Electric Road was incorporated in 1887; the track was laid in 1888; the first car was run on Thanksgiving day, 1889. The motive power was a storage battery. This system was found to be impracticable. In 1890 the Trustees gave consent to use overhead wires. Early in 1891 cars began to make regular trips. In 1894 the road passed into the hands of a Receiver. In 1895 the electric road from Long Island City was built to Flushing. The company operating this road purchased the Flushing and College Point road. The system is now known as the New York and Queens Co. Railroad. In 1896 the Brooklyn Heights Electric Railroad was built to Flushing. The first through cars were run on October 24th, of that year.

single to a double track. Ten years ago Murray Hill, now covered with block after block of pleasant homes, was a nursery; Ingleside and Bowne Park were farms.

The greatest advantage that Flushing has enjoyed over many other localities, an advantage that has made these many improvements possible, has been an honest government. Party politics have not entered into the election of Village Trustees. Voters have never been notified of the party affiliations of candidates. Very few, if any, of the Trustees have sought office from other motives than a desire to serve the public interests. In their efforts to improve the village and to protect it from threatened evils, the Trustees have been ably supported and assisted by the Flushing Village Association.[38]

The subject of better streets began to be agitated in
1890 1890. The Village Association at once took up the subject, and secured the consent of a sufficient number of tax-payers to empower the Trustees to issue bonds to pay for the contemplated improvement. From that time, the work went steadily on until the close of the year 1897, when, with few exceptions, all of the streets were macadamized and in perfect order.

---

38. The Flushing Village Association was organized in 1886.

In 1894 a great danger threatened the community. The Flushing Jockey Club, organized and backed by a number of pool-room men of New York, leased the Flushing race-track, and inaugurated a season of races. The great evil of this institution was, that it was established to "make foreign books," i. e. the races run on the Flushing track were of secondary importance, and were simply an excuse for opening booths where bets were placed on races all over the country. This brought to Flushing a great crowd of disreputable characters, and threatened to destroy the peace and quiet, and to corrupt the morals of the community. The Trustees passed an ordinance making the practice unlawful. The Village Association called a mass meeting to protest against the evil. The Association appointed a committee to co-operate with the Trustees, and authorized the committee to draw upon the treasurer of the Association for any money in his possession that might be needed to carry out its work. Certain "book-makers" were arrested on warrants sworn out by John D. Hashagen and Ernest Mitchell, Village Trustees. The defendants were brought before County Judge Garretson, and convicted of violating the Ives law, the very law under which they claimed protection. An application was made to Supreme Judge Bartlett for a stay of proceedings, on a writ of certiorari. 1894

This was denied, and the fines were paid. Being thus deprived of the privilege of making books on foreign tracks, the Jockey Club began to lose money. After its one season, it did not return to Flushing.

The Village Association did not content itself with merely opposing the Flushing Jockey Club. The State Constitutional Convention was in session at Albany during that summer. A committee of the Village Association consisting of Joseph K. Murray, Foster Crowell, James T. Franklin, L. M. Franklin, G. Webster Peck, sent a petition to the convention begging that the article of the Constitution which prohibited lotteries might be so amended as to include a prohibition of pool-selling and all forms of gambling. The amendment was adopted by the Constitutional Convention, and ratified later by popular vote.

At the November election, 1894, the question whether Flushing should be consolidated with New York City, was submitted to the people. Flushing voted against the proposition — 1,407 to 1,144. In spite of this vote, the work preparatory to the extension of the limits of New York City, so as to include the town of Flushing, went steadily on.
1896 Flushing opposed this measure at every stage of its progress. While the bill was before the Senate's Committee on Cities, March, 1896, a delegation from the Village Association con-

sisting of John W. Weed, Foster Crowell, Albert S. Thayer, William Bunting, Jr., George W. Hillman, Jr., G. Webster Peck, appeared before the committee to protest against the proposed legislation. Mr. Weed was the spokesman for the committee. Later, a memorial, addressed to Governor Morton and the State Legislature, and signed by more than seven hundred residents of Flushing and Jamaica, protesting against the measure, was forwarded to Albany. But the bill was passed, signed by the Governor, and sent to the Mayors of New York, Brooklyn and Long Island City. The Village Trustees and the Village Association appointed committees to appear before the Mayors and show why the measure should be vetoed.[39] The Mayor of New York and the Mayor of Brooklyn vetoed the bill; but it was re-passed by the Legislature, signed by the Governor, and became a law, in April.

The Village Association did not, however, relax its efforts in behalf of Flushing. Consolidation was inevitable; the next question was to secure as favorable provision for Flushing as possible. The work of framing a charter

39. The committee from the Village Trustees was: James A. Macdonald, Ernest Mitchell, James A. Renwick, John Hepburn. Frederick Storm, Assemblyman, assisted the committees from Flushing, in various ways, during the fight against consolidation.

for the enlarged city was placed in the hands of a commission.[40] The Village Association appointed a committee to look after the interests of Flushing, while this work was going on. The committee consisted of Foster Crowell, Albert S. Thayer, John W. Weed, James A. Macdonald, and William Bunting, Jr. The proposed charter was published in December, 1896. The Charter Commission offered to grant public audiences, for twelve days in January, on questions connected with the charter. The Village Association's
1897 committee asked to be heard on the following subjects: (1) "The basis of representation, and the method of choosing representatives in the municipal assembly, to be chosen from the more sparsely inhabited boroughs, especially Queens; (2) Provision for direct means of public inter-communication between portions of the city separated by water." The Commission granted a hearing on the first question, January 6th, and on the second question, three days later. John W. Weed spoke for the committee. The original draft of the charter gave the Borough of Queens two councilmen out of thirty-five, and three aldermen out of one hundred and one. These councilmen and aldermen were to be chosen from the Borough at large. The commit-

40. Judge Harrison S. Moore, a resident of the Town of Flushing, (his home is at Little Neck) was a member of the Charter Commission.

tee sought to secure for Queens a larger representation in the municipal assembly, and a provision that the representatives be chosen from sections of the Borough rather than from the Borough at large. As the result of the first hearing, the charter was amended so as to provide that there be one alderman for each assembly district: and three councilmen, instead of four, for each Senatorial district except Richmond and Queens, which should each have two. The charter was further amended so as to provide that in Queens one councilman should be chosen from Long Island City and Newtown, and one from Flushing, Jamaica, and Hempstead. Thus the efforts of the Association Committee secured for the Borough of Queens a larger representation in the municipal assembly, and for the old towns of the county something approaching local representation.

The committee appeared before the Commission, January 9th, on the subject of inter-communication between different portions of the city, with the result of securing a change in the charter allowing the city to construct, own, maintain and operate a department of public docks and ferries.

The Board of Education, represented before the Charter Commission by Joseph Fitch and John Holley Clark, also secured a change in the charter giving the Borough of

Queens two assistant superintendents, in addition to the one superintendent as originally provided.

Though the Village Association had been able to effect several important changes in the city charter, still the document was far from being all that was desired. As a last effort, therefore, the Association's committee addressed a communication to Governor Black, in April, 1897, stating many objectionable features in the charter, and requesting him to veto it. The charter received the Governor's approval, and on the first of January, 1898, the Town of Flushing became a part of New York City.

The Village Association, in addition to the service above referred to, did much to defeat the scheme for connecting Newtown Creek and Flushing Bay by a ship canal. An exhaustive report on the subject was submitted to the Secretary of War, who, in making an unfavorable report to Congress, used many of the arguments originally advanced by the Village Association.

1895 While Flushing was beginning this struggle for existence, the town passed the 250th anniversary of its settlement.

It is to be regretted that the year was allowed to pass without due commemoration. The Society of Friends, however, arranged and carried out in the same year, viz., on

May 29, 1895, a celebration of the 200th anniversary of the building of their Meeting-house. For this enterprise they are to be commended, but if their own records are to be relied on, their gathering was one year too late to celebrate the 200th anniversary of the opening of their first Meeting-house, and at least twenty-two years too early to celebrate the bi-centennial of the present Meeting-house. However, on the day above named nearly two thousand Quakers and their friends assembled in Flushing, from New York, New Jersey, Pennsylvania, Maryland, Ohio and Indiana. Old friends exchanged greetings, places of interest were visited, speeches were made.[41]

On the First Sunday in November, 1897, the Rev. J. Carpenter Smith, S. T. D., completed his fiftieth year as Rector of St. George's Church. The anniversary was appropriately celebrated by his congregation; and the older residents of the village, of every creed, joined in presenting their congratulations. 1897

Within the limits of the Town of Flushing are also the villages of College Point, Whitestone, Bayside, Douglaston

41. Programme of the public meeting: Historical Sketch, James Wood; Position of Woman in the Society of Friends, paper by Marianna W. Chapman; What the Society of Friends has Accomplished for the World, paper by Aaron M. Powell; poem by Mary S. Kimber.

and Little Neck. College Point, before it was taken into the city, was an incorporated village; so was Whitestone. College Point is a manufacturing place; its population is mainly German. It has a fine water front and many beautiful homes. The development of College Point's business interests was mainly due to the enterprise of Conrad Poppenhusen, who settled there, in 1854, and erected a large factory for the manufacture of hard-rubber goods. The Poppenhusen family were instrumental in extending the railroad to College Point. The village has good schools, churches of various denominations, a fine water system, and many social and charitable organizations. The first means of communication between Flushing and College Point, across the meadows, was a plank walk, built by Dr. Muhlenberg. The causeway was built in 1855. The trains of the Long Island Railroad and the electric cars now furnish frequent communication between Flushing and College Point.

Further east on the North Shore is Whitestone. It has a fine water-front, many pleasant homes, good schools and churches.

Still further east is Willets Point, a Government Post. This point of land, at the narrows which are generally regarded as the dividing line been the East river and Long

Island Sound, was fomerly a part of the Willets farm. In 1861, it was purchased by the United States, and fortified as a military post. It later became the headquarters of the Engineer corps of the army.

Beyond Willets Point is Little Neck Bay, in early times known as Matthew Garretson's Bay. On the western side of the Bay is situated the village of Bayside, with its many large and comfortable country places; on the other side are the villages of Douglaston and Little Neck.

On the first of January, 1898, the town of Flushing, with all its villages, became a part of New York City.

THE END.

APPENDIX

APPENDIX.

I

THE CHARTER, OCTOBER 10, 1645.[1]

Know all men, whom these presents may any wayes concerne, That We *William Kieft*, Esqr. Governr Genll of the Province called *New Netherlands*, wth ye Councill of State there established, wth ye Virtue of a Commission under the hand and Seale of the High and Mighty-Lords, the Estates Genll of the *United Belgick Provinces*, His Highness, *Frederick Hendrick*, Prince of Orange, and the Right Honoble Lords, the Lords Bewint Hebbers, of the West India Company, Have given and graunted, And by virtue of these p'nts, do give, graunt and confirm unto *Thomas ffarington*, *John Townsend*, *Thomas Stiles*, *Thomas Saull*, *John Marston*, *Robert ffield*, *Thomas Applegate*, *Thomas Beddard*, *Laurence Dutch*, *John Laurence*, *William Laurence*, *William Thorne*, *Henry Sautell*, *William Pigeon*, *Micheall Milliard*, *Robert ffirman*, *John Hicks*, *Edward Hart*, their heires, Excors Admtrs Assignes, Successors or Associates, or any they shall joyne in Associacon with them, a certaine quantity or parcell of Land, with all the Havens, Harbors Rivers, Creekes, Woodland, Marshes, there unto belonging, and being upon the Northside of *Long Island*, to begin at ye westward part thereof, at the Mouth of a Creeke upon the East River, now commonly called and knowne by the name of *fflushing Creeke*, and so to run Eastward, as farr as *Mathew Garretsons Bay*; Together wth a Neck

---

1 *Laws and Ordinances of New Netherland. New York Deed Book, II, 178.*

of Land commonly called *Tues Neck*, being bounded on the Westward part thereof, with the Land graunted to *Mr. Francis Doughty* and *Associates*, and to the Eastward part thereof, with the Land graunted to ye Plantacon and Towne of *Hempsteed*, and so to rune in two direct lines, unto the South of ye Island, that there may be the same Latitude in breadth, on the South side, as on the Northside, for them and their Patentees, Actually, really, and perpetually to enjoy, and Possesse, as their owne free Land of Inheritance, for them and the said Patentees, their Associates, heires, Successors and Assignes to Improve and Manure at their own best advantage according to their discretion. Always Provided ye said Patentees or Associates, shall settle such a competent Number of ffamilyes, wthin the space of two yeare, after the date hereof, as the Governor Genll of this Province, for the time being, or any hee shall appoint, shall think convenient, may be accommodated, within the said Limitts;

Alwayes Provided the first Settlers, to be sufficiently accommodated, excepting for and to the use of the above said Right Honoble the Lords Bewint Hebbers, a certain Parcell of Land, within the Towne of *fflushing*, for their own use;

ffurther giving and graunting, And by virtue of these pr sents, We do give and Graunt, unto the said Patentees, their Associates, Heires, Executors Admtors Successors and Assignes, upon the said Land to build a Towne, or Townes, wth such necessary ffortifications, as to them shall seeme Expedient; and to have and Enjoy the Liberty of Conscience, according to the Custome and manner of *Holland*, without molestacon or disturbance, from any Magistrate or Magistrates, or any other Ecclesiasticall Minister, that may extend Jurisdiccon over them, with Power likewise, for them the said Patentees, their Associates and Successors to Nominate, Elect, and Choose, a certain Officer over them, who may beare the name or Title, of Scout or Constable, Wee do hereby give graunt and Confirme, as large and ample Power and Authority, as, is usually given to the Scout of any Village in *Holland*, or Constable in *England*, for the apprehencon of any Malefactor, or any that shall go about to disturbe tho Publique Peace and tranquility of the said Towne of ffushing, And him or them to bring before the Governor Genll of this Province, for the time being, and there to make Proces agst such delinquents;

ffurther giving and graunting, And by virtue of these Pr nts, we do give and graunt unto the said Patentees, their Associates and Successors to have and enjoy the free Liberty of Hawking, Hunting, ffishing, ffowling within their abovesd Limitts, And to use and Exercise all manner of Trade and Commerce, according as ye Inhabitts of this Province may or can by virtue of any Priviledge or Graunt made unto them, indueing all and singular the said Patentees, their Associates and Successors wth all and singular the immunityes of the Province, as if they were Natives of the *United Belgick Provinces*;

Alwayes Provided, the said Patentees, their Associates and Successors shall reverendly respect the above named High and Mighty Lords for their superior Lords and Patrons, so long as they shall continue within the Jurisdiction of this Province, and at ye expiracon of ten yeares to begin from the day of the date hereof, to pay or cause to bee paid to an Officer, thereunto deputed by the Governor Genll of this Province, for the time being, the tenth part of the Revenue, that shall arise by the Ground manured, by Plough or Howe, in case it be demanded, to be paid to ye sd Officer, in the ffield, before it bee Housed, Gardens, or Orchards, not exceeding one Holland Acre, being excepted; And in case any of ye sd Patentees, their Associates, Heires, Executors Admtors Successors and Assignes shall onely improve their Stocks, in Grassing or Breeding of Cattle, Then the Party so doing, shall at the expiracon of the ten yeares aforesaid, Pay or cause to be paid, such reasonable Satisfaction in Butter or Cheese, as other Townes shall do in like Cases;

Likewise enjoyning the said Patentees, their Associates, Successors and so forth, in the dating of all Publick Instrumts to use the New Stile, together with the Weights and Measures of this place.

In Witnesse whereof, we have here unto sett our hand and Seale of this Province, dated this tenth day of October, 1645, stilo novo, in the *ffort Amsterdam.*

Memorandum, before the Ensealing hereof, It was Agreed, and Ordered by the Governor, the Land should rune North and South, but as farr as the Hills.

Willem Kieft

Ter Ordinnantie, &C.

Cornelius Van Tienhoven, *Secrets.*

II

SIGNERS OF THE "REMONSTRANCE

OF THE INHABITANTS OF FLUSHING. L. I., AGAINST THE LAW AGAINST QUAKERS."[2]

[Dec. 27, 1657.]

Edward Heart Clericus.

Tobias Feake
The Marke of William Noble
William Thorne, seignior
The marke of William Thorne Junior
Edward Tarne(?)
John Storer
Nathaniel Hefferd
Beniamin Hubbard
The marke of William Pigion
The marke of George Clere
Elias Doughtie
Antonie Feild
Richard Stocton
Edward Griffine
Nathaniell Tue
Nicholas Blackford
The marke of Micah Tue
The marke of Philipp Ud
Edward ffarington
Robert ffield, senior
Robert field, junior
Nick Colas Parsell
Michael Milner
Henry Townsend

---

2 *Historical Documents XIV*, 403.

George Wright
John Foard
Henry Samtell
Edward Heart
John Mastine
John Townsend

III

AN EXACT LIST

OF ALL Ye INHABITANTS NAMES Wthin Ye TOWNE OFF FFLUSHING AND P'CINCTS OF OLD AND YOUNG FFREEMEN AND SERUANTS WHITE & BLACKE &C, 1698.[3]

9 { Coll: Tho Willett and Mtrs
Alena his wife
Elbert }
Cornelius } Sones
Abraham }
John }
Alena } Daughters
Elizabeth }
John Clement: Servt
Negros ffrancis }
Jeffrey Hary Jack } 7
and Dick Mary }

9 { Justice Tho: Hukes and
Mrs Mary his wife
Isaac: Benjamin—Charles } Sones
Wm Stephen Charely }
Mary; daught
Negros: Will Cuffee } 6
Sherry ffreegeft and Jane }
Majr. Wm Lawrense
and Deborah his wife
William Richard
Obadiah Damell
11 Samuel John
Adam Debo: Sarah
Negros James Tom } 6
Lew Bess 2 child }

---

3 *Documentary History of New York, I, 432.*

Richard Cornell
and Sarah his wife
Sone Richard
Sarah
6 Elizabeth Daug
and Mary
Negros Tom
Lewi Toby 6
Sarah and Dina
John Esmond and
5 Elizab: his wife
John and Mary
Wm Jewell serut
Samll: Thorne and
Susana his wife
Benjamin
8 Samuel and Sone
Nathan
Jane Kesia
and Deborah Da:
Negros Coffe
Dina Kate 5
Charles Tony
James Clement
and Sarah his wife
Thomas
Jacob
12 Joseph and two Sones
Samll and
Nathan
Mary
Hannah
Margarett Daug
Bridgett
Negros Toby

Dutch Inhabitants

Cornelius Barnion
and Anna his wife
Johannis sone

Alke Anna }
7 Elizabeth and } Da:
Arante }
Negros Antony }
Jack Corose } 6
Mary Isabella }
Martin Wiltsee and
Maria his wife
6 Cornelius Hendrick
Johannis and Margarett
Elbert Arinson and
Cataline his wife
5 Rem and Elbert sones
Anneke—negro Dick'r
Garratt Hanson and
Janneke his wife
Hance Rem Jan } 6
10 Peter Danll Jores }
Janake Cattaline Dau
Negro Jeffrey 1
Lorus Haff
Canuerte his wife
Jewrin Peter } Sones
11 Johannis and Jacob }
Stinchee Maria }
Tuntee Margaretta } Dau
Sauta }
Edec: Van Skyagg and
Ebell his wife
7 Cornelius ffrancis
and Arian
Elizabeth Rebecca
Poulas Amarman
3 and Abiena his wife
Abena: Daughter
Bam Bloome and
4 ffammily his wife
Garratt, Johannis
Eliz Bloodgood
5 Wm and Elizabeth
one negro Will

Dirick Poules
and Sarah his wife
8 Peter Thynis
Rich'd: Wm Jon
Charles Sarah
one negro Tom
2 John Bloodgood
and Mary his wife
2 Powell Hoff and
Rachell his wife
2 John Jores and
Maria his wife
Derick Brewer and
3 his wife Hannah
1 child

French Inhabits

John: Genung
3 and Margreta his wife:
John: sone
negros 2
ffrancis Burto and
Mary his wife
5 John ffrancis
Abigal: Daug
Sarah Doughty
4 Benjamin } Sones
William }
Sarah Seruant
Negros: Okee and Mary
2 Mary Perkins
Abigale Daug
Bess: Robin Maria } 3
Hanes }
2 Ann Noble
Abigale Serut
Negros: Jack Jan 2
3 Mary Bowne
Annis Ruth; Daugh
Negros: James and } 2
Nell }

Arther powell and
4 Margrett his wife
Richard Arther sones
John Hinchman
and Sarah his wife
7 John James
Mercy Mary and
Sarah
Negroo Hetchtor 1
Richard Chew and
ffrances his wife
7 Rich'd Henry Tho
Hannah Charely
Mary Elizabeth
Thomas Runley and
4 Mary his wife
Thomas sone
Hannah
ffrancis Doughty
and Mary his wife
8 Elias palmer
ffrancis Obadiah
Sarah Charely Mary
Negros Vester Rose 2
John Talman and
Mary his wife
7 John James peter
Mary Elizabeth
Charles Tom
Sarah 2 ch 5
John Thorne Senr and
5 Mary his wife
Hannah and Sarah Wm
Negros Alex wo: 2
William ffowler Carp
and Mary his wife
8 William John
Joseph Benj
Mary Rebeca
Negro Jack 1
John Thorne Jun'r

6 Katherin his wife
John Mary
Eliz: Deborah
Henry Taylor and
5 Mary Sarah his wife
Sarah phebe
Negro Tonny 1
Edward Greffin ju
4 Deborah his wife
Edward Mary
2 William Owen and
Mary his wife
2 Hugh Cowperthawt
Mary Southick
Negro Anthony—1
2 Henry ffranklin
and Sarah his wife
1 negro
3 Patience Cornelius
Elias: Mary—
Tho: ffarrington
and Abigale his wife
Thomas Robert
Benjamin—
8 Elizab: Bridgett
Abigale
Negros—Mingo } 2
Winnee }
Harman Kinge
6 and Mary his wife
John Joseph
Benj. ffrancis
Toby 1
William ffowler wea
3 and Judith his wife
William sone
Thomas Willett
3 and Sarah his wife
Sarah—Daughter
Negro Lay—1
Thomas Hinchman

4 and Meriam his wife
Thomas and Sarah—
2 George Langley and
Rebeca his wife
Mary and Sampson—2
Matt ffarington
5 and Hannah his wife
Matthew Sarah and
Edward
John Manton
ffrances John
5 Cornelius
Deborah Ebell—
Thomas Yeates
and Mary his wife
6 Mary ye mother
Wm Benj Jane
Elias Doughty
Elizabeth his wife
5 Elias Eliz: Thomas
Negro: Jack—1
Charles Doughty-
and Elizabeth his wife
6 John Charles—
Sarah Elizabeth
1 negro black boy 1
John Harrington
and Elzbth his wife
John Edward Matthew
13 Thomas Sam'll Robert
Mercy Margrett
Dorythy Anna—
Elizabeth
Sam'll Bowne
and Mary his wife
6 Samll Thomas
Ellmer Hannah
Negros Simon
Nany mingo 3
Joseph palmer
6 and Sarah his wife

Dani'll Esther
Ric'h pricilla
Tho: Hedger and
Elizabeth his wife
Eliakim Thomas
11 Mary Hannah—
Jane Sarah Deborah
Elizabeth
Joseph Thorne and
Mary his wife—
Joseph William
11 Thomas John—
Benjamin Abraham
Hannah Mary Susan
1 Negro Tom:—1
Sam'll Haight and
Sarah his wife—
10 Nicholas Jonathan
David John Sarah Mary
Hannah phebe—
and 1 negro 1
Thomas fford and
3 Sarah his wife—
Thomas Child
2 Esther fford
William
Negro Anthony—1
John Embree and
6 Sarah his wife
Robert John Samll
Sarah
Hatham'll Roe and
3 Elizab'th his wife
David
Charles Morgan
and Elizabeth his wife
7 Charles James Thomas
Sarah Ephraim Sophy
Negros: peter James
John Cornelius and
Mary his wife—

10 John Dani'll Sam'll
Joseph Deborah
Mary phebe Sarah
Negro: Zambo: 1
Jona Wright Senr
and Sarah his wife
9 Sam'll Richard Charles
Job: Mary Hannah
John
Henry Wright and
4 Mary his wife
Hannah Sarah
Jona: Wright Ju
4 and Wine his wife
Jonathan Elizabeth
Dauid Wright and
4 Hannah his wife
Dauid phebe
Joseph Lawrense
and Mary his wife
4 Richard Thomas
1 Negro Jack—1
2 John Hopper Peintr
and Christopher
2 John Hopper Jun
and Margarett his wife
John Harrison
and Elizabeth his wife
7 William Edward
Henry Eliz Ann
Negros Hechtor }
Kate } 2
Margery Smith
3 Judeth Hannah
Samuel Tatem and
Elizabeth his wife
6 Sam'll Eliza patience
Mary negro—1
Benj Havileind and
5 Abigaile his wife
Adam Benj John

Abigalo Bethia
William·Benger and
5 his wife Elizabeth
John Jacob Eliz
John Jeauiland and
3 Sarah his wife
John
Thomas Wildee
and Elizabeth his wife
8 Edward Rich'd
Tho Obadiah
Isaaih Eliz'bth
Edward Greffein Se
3 and Mary his wife
Deborah
Negro; Jack:—1
John Rodman
and Mary his wife
9 John Samuell—
Joseph William
Thomas An Eiliz:
Negros—11
John Lawrence and
his wife Elizab'th
7 William Richard
Eliz: Mary Deborah
Negros James Rose
Bess Robin Moll—5
Benj ffeild and
Hannah his wife
6 Benj John Antho
Sam'll
Negros Jo: Betty—2
John Greffin and
Elizabeth his wife
5 John Benj Isaac
Joseph Elizab'th
Rich'd Greffin and
5 Susan his wife
Sam'll Sarah Rich'd
Dauid Roe Mary

3 his wife
Mary: Negro Sam 1
Rebecca Clery
4 Athelena Rebecca
phebe Negro: 1
Philip Odall and
his wife Mary
7 Philip Mary
John Elizab'th
Deborah
Joseph Hedger
and Hannah his
7 wife—Joseph
Margrett
Uriah Sarah
Hannah
Antnody Badgley
5 Elizab'th his wife
Anthony George—
phebe: 1 Negro 1
Dan'll Patrick and
4 Dinah his wife
Sarah James ffeke
One Negro 1
John Ryder and his
wife, John Robert
6 Hettie Wintie
One negro 1
2 Dennis Holdrone
Sarah his wife
Josiah Genning
3 and Martha his wife
one child
Edee Wilday
3 Rebecca and Mary
ffreemen—men
Tho: Lawrense
James Clement Ju'r
John Clement
John Huker
Jacob Cornell

Thomas ffeild
Joseph ffeild
Derick Areson
John Areson
John Yeates
John Man
James ffeke
Robert Snelhen
Tho: Steuens
John Dewildoe
Abraham Rich
Robert Hinchman
Inhabitants 530
Negros 113

According to ye best of our Knowledges

Jonathan Wright
James Clement

[*Endorsed.*] a trew Lest as it is returned to us by the above constable and Clerk the Last of august 1698.

Tho. Hicks
Danl'l White
John Smith
Edward White
Samuel Mowett
John Tredwell
William Hallett

IV

AN ACCOUNT

OF EACH INHABITANT OF FFLUSHINGS PROUISIONS AS FFOLLOWET.[4]

[A. D. 1711.]

	Bacon lb.	Wheat bush.	Indian bushels	Cheese	Butter
Jus. William Bloodgood....	120	13	30	180	
Jus. David Wright..........	55	10	6	18	
Benj: ffield....................	160	130	20	240	
James Clement Junr.........	20		6	12	
John Rodman..............	90	80		210	
Mary Talman...............	40	18		127	
ffrancis Doughty...........	40		20	100	
Thomas Rushmore..........	50			15	
Thomas Weekes............	198	190	48	300	
Margret Powell.............	30				
Joseph Hedges.............	15	5		15	
Joseph Van Cliff...........	130	10	1	54	
Joseph Rodman............	150	60	20	100	
Phillip Udall...............	18	25	2	24	
Obadiah Lawrence.........	40	6	10	60	
Samll Haight Junr.........	36	6		70	
Jewrin Ryder...............	12	4	5	16	
Tho Hinchman.............	6	6	5		

4 *Copy of Document in New York State Library, LV, 129.*

	Bacon lb.	Wheat bush.	Indian bushels	Cheese	Butter
Matthew ffarington	74	110	20	186	
Sarah ffranklin	45	13	3	230	
Thomas ffield	40	100	2	70	
John Marston	80	35	25	28	
Jon Bloodgood	13		1		
Jacob Doughty	70	70	8	75	
Stephen Ryder	17	10	20	35	
Samuell Talem	65	40		64	
John Baldwin	45				10
John Mann	27	4		12	
Richard Dachy	40		5	24	
Anthony Badgley	23	6	1		
Eliakim Hedges	86	80	2	24	
Benj: Thorne	25	20	3	42	4
Samll Thorne	90	75	2	75	3
John Essmond	10	30			
Jacob Heaviland	12				
Benj Heaviland	10	15		34	
John Hickes	25	30		10	
John Van Wyck	95	6	12	170	
Charles Hickes	40	22	2	36	
Thomas Hickes	60	20		150	
Hugh Cowperthwt	96	1		81	
Wm Doughty	45	6			
Sarah Doughty	30	4			
Henry Wright	70			20	
John Yeats	48				
John ffarington	45			98	
Elias Cornelius	30	2			
Samll Bowne	170	15	15	60	
Mary Bowne	45	9	9	15	4
Thomas fford	38	6			

	Bacon lb.	Wheat bush.	Indian bushels	Cheese	Butter
Samuell Haight	45	40	12	125	
Joseph Thorne	125	20	10	140	
ffrancis Burto	6	1			
John Hopper	15				
Christopher Hopper	20	2		45	
Stephen fford	30	4		36	
John Genunge	90	5	6	65	
John Embree	85	80	2	65	
Sarah Wright	22		1		
Charles Wright	20				
Richard Greffin	75			24	
Maj. Wm Lawrence	220	200	50	200	
Joseph Lawrence	90	5	1	130	
Edward Greffin	18	18	2	18	
Nathaniell Roe	140	140	3	90	
John Greffin	28	4	3	72	
Elizeth Wilday	40				
Wm Lawrence Junior	50	4	1	32	
John Lawrence	40	10	2	30	
Thomas Parmitter	70				
Henry Taylor	43	3		30	
Jonathan Wright	48	40	2	30	
John Ryder	40	8		25	3
William ffowler	120	10		84	
Joseph Thorne	140	20	20	128	
John Taylor	24				
William Thorne	185	140	5	115	
Mary Thorne	84	9	2		
John Washborne		3	1	8	
Richd Cornell	23	6	5	322	
Richd Cornell Junr	5		4	36	
Jacob Cornell	83	8		60	

	Bacon lb.	Wheat bush.	Indian bushels	Cheese	Butter
Samll Thorne Junr.........	40	7	3	80	10
Nicholas Haight...........	12	3		9	
Charls Doughty............	50	6	3	48	
James Jackson.............	50	20	6		
Elias Doughty.............	57	8	2		
Peter Stringam............	12				
Peter Haff................	15	2	2		
Thomas Clement............	20	2			
John Burto................	8	2		80	
Cornels Hoglant...........	38			20	16
Barn Bloome...............	30	14		25	
Dirck Brinker.............	68	20	2	80	35
Tho Acreson...............	15				11
Peter Mefor...............	35	50	7		
Lawre Haff................	46	6	6		
Joseph Palmer.............	18		4		
Anthony Glean.............	50	6			
Wm Burling...............	55	30	3		
Tho Rattonne..............	30				
Jon Lowcie................	6		3		
Tho Willett Junr..........	90	7	20	75	
Coll Tho Willett..........	250	80	25	156	
Samll Ketcham.............	25	1			
Tho Chambers..............		6		12	
Jerim Genung..............	50		1	40	
John Clement..............	28	1		20	
John Vanleiw..............	50	5	2		
James Clement.............	90	4	2	50	
Joseph Thorne.............	13				
Danill Lawrence...........		12			
John Serls................	12				

Endorsed, "Accot of Provisions in ffushing, July 1711."

V

A LIST

OF THE OFFICERS AND SOULDIERS BELONGING TO THE COMPANY OF JONATHAN WRIGHT, CAPTN.[5]

[A. D. 1715.]

Willm Thorne, Lieutenant	Anthony Badgeley } Serjants
John Tallman, Ensign	Tunis Covert } Serjants
John Taylor } Corporals	
James Lewis, Junr } Corporals	Thom Gleane, Drummer.
Johanus Van Wick	Wilm Burling
Nathl Roe	Steven ffoard
Steven Ryder	Thom: Clement
Christopher Hopper	John Baalding
Samll Clemment	Benjamin ffield
Joseph Lawrence	John Embree
Joseph Hedges	John Hix
Thom: Rattoone	ffrancis Doughty Junr
Wm Hix	Steven Hix
Elikiam Hedges	Thom: Hix
James Talman	Joseph ffield

5 This is to certify that the above, with the copy on sheet No. 1 is a correct copy, and of the whole thereof, of a document on page 59 of a manuscript volume, in the custody of the Regents of the University of the State of New York in the State Library, entitled New York Colonial Manuscripts, vol. 60.

George Rogers Howell,
Archivist.

Cornelius Maston
John Bloodgood
Samll Embree
Thom: Eacason
John Washbon
Ram Oderyonson
Samll Bowne Junr
John ffarington
John Griffen
Richard Griffen
Charles Doughty
Elias Doughty Senr
Thom: ffoard Senr
John Esmund Senr
Joseph Thorne, Bay Side
Thom ffield
James Clement
John Yeats
Nicholas Haight
John Ryder
ffrancis Yeats
Thom: Bowne
Willm Smith
Jacob Griffen
Thom: Carle
Adam Lawrence
Samll Stringam
Thom: Stringam
John Doughty
Samll ffield
Thom: Hedges
Benjmn ffowler
Harculus Ryder
Richd Willdey
Isaiah Willdey
Thom: Willdey
John Coe
Richd Lawrence
Abraham Gray
Samll Griffen
Richd Lawrence of ye Neck
Thom: Lawrence
David Roe
Thomas Thorne
John Bowne
Thom: ffarington, Bay Side
Thom: ffarington of ye Towne
Samll ffarington
James Cromell
Elias Doughty
Danll Lawrence
Samll Lawrence
Cornelius Van Wick
Garret Bloome
Thom: Jaxson
Uria Hedges
Thom: Hinchman Junr

VI

SUFFERINGS OF THE FRIENDS

IN FLUSHING DURING THE REVOLUTIONARY WAR.[6]

Taken from Daniel Bowne, for refusing military service,
by Captain Hoogland's warrant, a silver watch, worth £7, 1776
and a looking glass, worth £3.

29th of 8th month. Taken from John Bowne, by the Major of the Light Horse, for the use of the army, 21 old sheep, at 13 shillings each, and 15 lambs, at 11 shillings each; and 9th of 9th month, taken by Captain Moxome, 31 bushels of oats, at 3 shillings per bushel.

Distresses made upon the goods of Ebenezer Beaman, by order of the militia officers: A dictionary, worth 12 shillings; two large pewter basins, 16 shillings; diaper table-cloth, and pewter funnel, 28 shillings; looking-glass, £3; an iron-shod cart and tackling, £14; a horse, £18, 14 s.

Taken from John Lawrence by the militia Sergeant, for not appearing under arms, a warming-pan, to the value of £1.

Taken from Ann Field, by order of Captain Hoogland, 1777
being to serve military purposes, a watch worth £8; 2½
bushels of wheat, £1. 10 s.; a horse, £25.

Taken from John Bowne, for not appearing with the militia, a fat hog, £5.

---

6 *Onderdonk's Documents and Letters, Second Series, p. 59.*

1778 Taken from John Bowne, by Captain Hoogland, for not appearing under arms when required by the militia officers, household goods, worth £2. 3s. 6d.

1780 Taken from John Farrington, a gun, worth £2; a table, £3; 2 hogs, £8. 10 s.

April 3. Isaac Underhill and Thomas Willett, being desired by the British commanding officers at Flushing to view the damages, or quantities of timber cut off a certain tract of timber-land, consisting of about 35 acres, belonging to John Bowne, conclude that there has been taken 5 standard cords for the use of His Majesty's troops.

David Colden certifies the above appraisers to be men of fair character, and well qualified to make the estimate.

1781 Jacob Lawrence, with three others, took from Ebenezer Beaman, a riding saddle, worth £5.

Three turkeys, worth 50 shillings, taken from Ann Field, on a demand of 24 shillings for guarding the fort at Whitestone.

Taken from John Bowne, on demand of 39 shillings, to defray the charge of guarding the fort at Whitestone, a pair of boots, £2. 8 s.

12th of 2d month. Jacob Lawrence, Sergeant, with others, took away from James Bowne, 11 fowls, worth £3, on a demand of 39 shillings for guarding the fort.

24th of 2d month. David Rowland, Sergeant, came to Isaac Underhill's, and demanded £4 for money advanced for a horse to go to the King's service, and for expenses in guarding the fort, etc., and on his refusing to pay it, went into his mill and took 8 bushels of Indian corn, worth £4.

3d month. There came to John Farrington's house, David Rowland, a Sergeant under Captain Hoogland, for a demand of £3. 8s., took away a piece of linen, worth £3. 6 s, being levied by way of tax, as was said, to defray the expense of guarding the fort at Whitestone.

Taken at sundry times, from John Burling, jr., for fines, by order of Captain Hoogland, to answer militia purposes: A pewter dish, worth 8 shillings; 6 pewtor plates, 12 shillings; a pair of tongs, 12 shillings; a tablecloth, £1. 10s.; 7 pewter plates, 14 shillings; a copper sauce-pan, 8 shillings; a pair of andirons, £2; 6 silver tea spoons, £1. 10s.

Taken by Philip Husted, 2½ bushels of corn and bag, to defray the expense of guarding the fort at Whitestone, £1. 10s.

Jacob Lawrence took, on demand of 27 shillings, an overcoat and a dunghill fowl, worth 50 shillings.

Taken from Willet Bowne, at sundry times, by order of Captain Hoogland, being fines to answer military purposes, a geography, worth 14 shillings; 6 pewter plates, 12 shillings; 2 bushels of wheat and the bag, £2; 9 bushels of corn, £3. 12s.; a watch, £8; 2 bushels of corn and the bag, £1. 4 s.

4th of 3d month. Then came Moses Fowler, and demanded of Phebe Cornell £4. On her refusal to pay, he searched her closet and found money to the value of £3. 18s., being levied by way of tax, as was said, for defraying the expense of guarding the fort at Whitestone.

29th of 6th. month. Philip Husted, Sergeant, and Jacob Lawrence with him, demanded 25 shillings of Solomon Underhill, for guarding the fort, and took wheat to that value. 1782

Taken from John Farrington goods worth £3. 11 s. 4 d.

Total amount of distraints of Friends in Flushing, from 1776 to 1782, was £194. 11s. 10d. [7].

---

7 The Friends who escaped oppression by the military authority suffered at the hands of their co-religionists:

"1776. Samuel Cowperthwait assisted at the fortification in New York, and is not principaled against defensive warfare. He is disowned." "Jonah Hallet is disowned for bearing arms."

VII

ADDITIONAL NOTES

Relating to the History of Flushing.

"As for freedom and pleasure to hackl, hunt, fish and fowle, theare is great varietie, and all daynties of fruits that Ittaley or the Gardens of Spaine affordeth, may be had out of those ritch grounds, for it is as hott as Spaine ore Italley and as full of pleasure and comforte." *The Commodities of the Island Called Maniti ore Long Isle which is in the Continent of Virginia. for sale at the Sign of the Two Storks. no date.*

1647, Thomas Robertsen deeds a house and plantation, in Flushing, to George Wolsey.

1648, Jan. 17. Order issued by Council to John Tonsen and others of Flushing, to appear before the Council, and show cause why they refuse to contribute to the support of a minister, and oppose the nomination of a sheriff. Inhabitants ordered to proceed to a nomination of such an officer. *Calendar I, 116.*

1649, Aug. 14. Anneke van Beyern, widow of the late Daniel Patrick, now the wife of Tobias Fecx, of Flushing, L. I., gives power of attorney to Adriaen van der Donck, who is about to depart for Fatherland, to investigate the state of her affairs there, and collect whatever may be coming to her. *Calendar I, 48.*

1652, March 11. Mark Menloff is compelled to confess the guilt of stealing and killing a hog. March 25. Maria de Truy, wife of Jan Peeck, testified that she had heard certain

Indians speak about the above. March 25. Menloff and his whole family banished. *Calendar I 125 et sq.*

1654. Goodman Harck's wife complains against Richard Pontum, who is suspected of having burnt her barn. *Calendar , 141.*

1655, June 1. Divorce granted to John Hicks from his wife Harwood Long. *Calendar I, 149.*

1658, Nov. 14. Widow of William Harck is ordered to render an account, to Robt. Terry, John Tonson, William Palmer and John Coo, for certain cattle belonging to Thos. Farrington, a minor. *Calendar I, 202.*

1661, Oct. 20. Jacob Kip complains that Jno. de Sweet has taken his canoe. *Calendar I, 230.*

1662, Jan. 12. Roelof Jansen, collector of excise, brings suit against Samuel Edsal for buying liquor from Manhattans, without a permit. Judgment for the defendant. *Calendar I, 233.*

1662, July 2. Complaint is entered against William Bentfield for exporting liquor from Flushing to New England, without paying duty. *Calendar I, 239.*

1677, Oct. 9. Governor Andros employs John Thompson of Seatalcott "to goe to Flushing and other parts upon Long Island, to search for sea coal mines, of which he had probable information."

1676, "We are informed that a person belonging to Flushing, that formerly made a profession of truth has been taken with the Ranters, and that of late has signified that he sees the evil of his outrunnings, yet doth not frequent the assembly of the Lord's people, so Francis Cooley and John Adams are desired to speak to the party. *Manuscript History, p. 109.*

1680. Town of Flushing is charged " To hew & cryes," £1. 1s.

1680, Feb. 20. Little Neck at this date is called Cornbury. *Calendar II, 85.*

1682, Feb. 16. Christian Dean and Thos. Robinson give information that the magistrates of Flushing do not prevent wheat being shipped in Cornbury Bay. *Calendar II, 98.*

· 1690, Oct. 30. Commissions issued to Samuel Edsall, Thomas Williams and Hendrick Ten Eyck, or to one of them, to command a sloop, with volunteers, and proceed to Flushing Bay and secure the persons and papers of suspected rebels. *Calendar II, 199.*

1692, Sep. 10. "Jno Bowne, Hew Coperthwait and Jno Rodman having spake, in behalf of ffriends with miles ffoster; about their dissatisfaction with him in his sarving George Keith boockes to ye greef of ffriends. *Minutes of Meetings.*

[Keith attacked the Quakers, charging them with heresy. His books therefore appear to have been on the Quakers' *Index Expergatorius.*]

1702, Sep. 28. Flushing meeting of Friends sends an address to Lord Cornbury, "setting forth ye Late Sufferings of friends, haveing their votes being Refused and their Goods Distrained on, for Building a Dwelling house for the Nonconformist Preacher in Newtown and elsewhere." *Minutes of Meetings.*

[It was reported at the next Quarterly meeting that the Governor had restored the goods which had been taken from Friends.]

1703, May 20. John Embree, inhabitant and freeholder of the town of Flushing, petitioned for an injunction against William Lawrence, restraining him from trespassing on his land. *Calendar II, 313.*

1703, Aug. 2. William Lawrence complains that John Embree has trespassed on his estate, called Tews Neck. *Calendar II, 315.*

1704, April 4. Thos. Worden, of New York, pipe maker, asks for license to dig clay on Island of Nassau, between high and low water mark. Referred to Justices of Queens County, to report whether the locality be within the bounds of the patent of Flushing. *Calendar II, 323.*

1711. Great scarcity of provisions on Long Island. vide appendix IV.

1715, Aug. 12. Anthony Gleane of Flushing, blacksmith, asks for letters of administration on the estate of Jas. Bettersby, school master of the same place. *Calendar II, 427.*

1719, May 28. Thos. Hinchman of Flushing gave affidavit that he had heard Justice Whitehead say, that it was as lawful to play cards as it was to read the Bible. *Calendar II, 440.*

1726, June 17. Patent granted to Charles and Francis Doughty and others, to establish a ferry between the east side of William Thorne's Neck and the west side of Deborah Lawrence's Neck, on the mainland. *Calendar, II, 495.*

1736, March 3. "Last Thursday night, about 10 or 11 o'clock, the house of Benjamin Lawrence, of Flushing, was burnt to the ground and nothing of his goods saved. The man and woman were abroad about their affairs, and at that time, the man, coming home, saw the house all in a flame, and ran in and pulled his four small children out of their bed, and threw them naked upon the snow, and attempted to fetch out some of his goods, but the fire was so far advanced, that he could not get the least rag to cover them from the piercing cold of that night, but all was burnt. *N. Y. Gazette, March 3, 1736, (Onderdonk.)*

"The same day, Thos. Willet had occasion to drive his cattle over a creek, on the ice, which breaking in, he lost eight cows."

1736, Sept. 27. "On the 6th inst., the house, ware-house and all the goods and merchandizes of Mr. John Foster, at Flushing, at midnight, were consumed to ashes, and little or nothing saved, but his books, papers and the Scriptoir which they were in."

1751, March 13. Edmond Annely advertises his pottery at Whitestone—"he having set up the potter's business by means of a German family that he bought, who are supposed by their work to be the most ingenious that ever arrived in America."

1859. "It was reported at this meeting that Benjamin Thorne has hired a man to go in the Army to War in his Son's Stead, also, that John Rodman has hired a man to go in his Rum."

A few months later: "It appears to this meeting, by the persons appointed to speak to Benjamin Thorne, as also his owne mouth that he still continews unwilling to condemn his Miss conduct in Hireing a man to goe to War in his Son's Stead, or to give Friends Satisfaction for the Same, it is the Judgment of the Meeting that we can have no younity with such Practices, nor with him untill hee both condemn and leave the same."

The report concerning Rodman: "Hireing a Man in his Roome for the Expedition was not unadvised, but the result of Mature consideration, and if the like occasion offered, he should doe it again." *Minutes of Friends' Meetings (Flint, 182.)*

1786, Oct. 12. " Died at Moorfields, Flushing, on Sunday evening, aged 34, Mrs. Gertrude Onderdonk, the amiable consort of Lambert Moore, Esq., formerly comptroller of His Majesty's customs. The funeral sermon was preached by his nephew, the Rev. T. L. Moore, the Episcopal Minister of S. Hempstead."

"Died at Flushing, Sunday, se'nnight, Gerard G. Beekman, Esq., aged seventy-seven, a citizen of New York, whose hospitality and good old wine endeared him to many friends. He had retired from business, to pass the remainder of his life in quiet and enjoy those rational amusements which the delightful plains of Long Island afforded him." *New York Journal, Sept. 5, 1796.*

1878, May 7, Judge Murray Hoffman died at his residence in Flushing. He was buried in St. Mark's Churchyard, New York City, May 10th. Judge Hoffman was born in New York City, Sept. 29, 1791; he graduated from Columbia College, 1809; was admitted to the Bar; was Assistant Vice-Chancellor, 1839-43; elected Judge of the Superior Court, in 1853, and held the position of judge until 1861. Among his published works are: Offices and Duties of Masters in Chancery (1824); Treatise on the Practice of the Court of Chancery (3 vols., 1840-43); Treatise on the Corporation of New York as Owners of Property, and Compilation of the Laws relating ot the City of New York, Vice-Chancery's Reports (1839-40); Treatise on the Law of the Protestant Episcopal Church in the United States (1850); Ecclesiastical Law in the State of New York (1868); The Ritual Law of the Church, etc. (1872).

Judge Hoffman took a lively interest in the affairs of his Church, and was often a member of her conventions. He was a man who "will long be remembered in the annals of the Bar of this country as a distinguished member of the profession, and whose memory will be kept green in the hearts of Churchmen for the contributions he has from time to time made to its canonical literature"—*(New York Times.)* His funeral was attended by a large number of distinguished men—bishops and clergymen, judges and lawyers.

1885, October 23. "Morris Franklin, President of the New York Life Insurance Company, died at his home in Flushing, yesterday. He had been ill several weeks with a severe cold. He was born, Oct. 20, 1801, on Broadway, near Leonard street, this city. Morris Franklin was educated by Goold Brown, studied law with Benjamin Clark, and was admitted to practice almost upon reaching his majority. His interest in politics was always great, and he was an enthusiastic Whig. When the Board of Aldermen was composed of leading men of the city, he was one of its directing members, representing what was then the Seventh Ward. For two years he was its President. He was elected an Assemblyman, serving three terms, and was in 1842 sent to the State Senate. Later, he became the Whig candidate for Mayor, but the day before the election the result of the contest was so doubtful that he yielded to the advice of his friends, and permitted a Whig coalition with the Know-Nothings, James Harper being elected. Mr. Franklin was a member of the Volunteer Fire Department, and for many years its foreman. During the great fire of 1835, he held a hose in Wall street all night. Just forty years ago, the Nautilus Life Insurance Company was bought out by a newly organized corporation, calling itself the New York Life Insuarance Company, and Mr. Franklin abandoning the practice of law became its first President. This office he retained till his death. Mr. Franklin was a Director of the Central National Bank and of the Empire City Fire Insurance Co., and a Trustee of the House of Refuge. He moved to Flushing in 1863, and has held the offices of Trustee and President [of the village] several times."—(*New York Tribune.*) Mr. Franklin was also a Warden of St. George's Church, and took an active interest in all affairs that affected the well-being of Flushing.

1888, December 20, The Hon. John W. Lawrence died at Willow Bank, in Flushing. Mr. Lawrence was born in Flushing in 1800; at the age of sixteen he entered the mercantile house of Hicks, Jenkins & Co.; at the age of twenty-one he became a partner in the firm of Howland & Lawrence in the shipping and commission business. Mr. Lawrence was for fifteen years President of the Queens County Savings Bank, for some years President of the Seventh Ward Bank of New York, for a third of a century President of the Lawrence Cement Company, and for some time he held a similar position in the Rosedale Cement Company. For fifteen years he was President of the village of Flushing and for many years Warden of St. George's Church. In 1840, he was elected a member of the Assembly; in 1845 he was elected a member of Congress. He declined to accept a renomination for Congress. He also declined the nomination for the office of Lieutenant Governor of the State.

1894, August 14, James Strong, S. T. D., LL.D,, D.D., was buried in Flushing cemetery. Dr. Strong was born in New York City, Aug. 14, 1822; graduated at Wesleyan University, Middletown, Conn., 1844; teacher of ancient languages in Troy Conference Academy, West Poultney, Vt., 1844-46; professor of Biblical literature and acting

President of Troy University, 1858-61; then professor of exegetical theology in Drew Theological Seminary, Madison, N. J. Dr. Strong was also one of the company of Bible revisers. He was the author of Harmony and Exposition of the Gospels (1852); Harmony in Greek (1854); Scripture History, etc. (1878); Irenics, (1883); one of the editors of Lange's Commentaries and of McClintock and Strong's Cyclopaedia of Biblical, Theological and Ecclesiastical Literature. Dr. Strong resided in Flushing some time between 1846 and 1858, and proved himself a public-spirited citizen. He did much for the interests of public education in the crisis of 1848; he was one of the first Directors of the Flushing's first railroad, in 1854; and assisted in establishing the Flushing Cemetery where he was buried.

1894, December 3, Benjamin W. Downing died. Mr. Downing was born at Glen Head, L. I., in 1835. He began life as a school teacher. He later studied law, and opened an office in Flushing. In 1864, he was elected District Attorney of Queens County. He held the office of District Attorney for many years, and secured the conviction of a number of notable criminals. He was removed from office by Governor Cleveland for receiving money from the relatives of a murdered man to assist in the prosecution of the murderer. Mr. Downing protested that none of this money remained in his hands, but was at once paid to detectives. Mr. Downing was twice a candidate for the office of County Judge, but was both times defeated. During Mr. Downing's residencce in Flushing he was closely identified with local interests; he served as Trustee of the Village for several terms and was at one time President of the Board; he was a member of the Board of Education for about twenty years and at one time President of that body; he was largely interested in Flushing real estate. Mr. Downing removed from Flushing in 1882.

Population of the Town and Village of Flushing:

Year.	Village.	Town.
1790		1,607
1800		1,818
1810		2,230
1814		2,271
1830		2,820
1840		4,124
1850	about 2,000	5,376
1860		10,188
1870	6,223	14,650
1880	6,683	15,906
1890	8,436	19,803

VIII

THE TREES OF FLUSHING[8]

Flushing has long been noted for the great number, rare beauty and unusual variety of its trees. The nurseries have given Flushing this advantage. The Huguenots began horticulture here in the seventeenth century. As late as 1839, there were still fruit trees standing, of the varieties introduced by the French. William Prince began his nursery, in 1737. It increased in size, until, in 1860, the gardens and nursery of W. R. Prince & Co. comprised 113 acres. The Bloodgood nursery was established in 1798, by James Bloodgood. The Commercial Garden and Nursery, of Parsons & Co., were established in 1838. The Kissena Nurseries are the successors of the Parsons nurseries. These are the oldest and most extensive of Flushings nurseries. Until 1840, Flushing had practically the monopoly of this industry.

Flushing can boast of one hundred and forty genera of trees, with from three to twenty species to each genus. Thus there are about two thousand varieties of trees standing within the limits of the town.

Of specimen trees, i. e. as nearly perfect examples of their kinds as possible, we have many. Of Tulip trees we may mention two magnificent specimens, in the grounds of Robt. B. Parsons. These trees are seventy-five feet high,

---

8 Condensed from a Lecture delivered, by Dr. J. W. Barstow, before the Good Citizenship League, in 1893.

and more than three feet in diameter at the base. Without doubt, they are the finest Tulip trees on Long Island. A fine specimen of the European Linden is to be found in the grounds of Jos. K. Murray. It is a perfect cone, a beautiful object to the eye, and a striking feature of the landscape. In the adjoining nurseries of Keene & Foulk is a Cut-leaf, Drooping Birch of exceptional size and beauty—probably the finest specimen of its kind in the United States. There are many varieties of Beeches in Flushing. There are some native Beeches still standing on the hillside across the Creek and in the rear of the old Remsen place, but the greater number of our Beeches came from England and Norway. The finest specimen of the English Beech stands in the S. B. Parsons property on Broadway. A noteworthy specimen of the Cut-leaf Beech stands not far from it. In the same enclosure is a choice specimen of the Drooping Beech. But the largest and most perfect specimen of the Drooping Beech is in the grounds of Mrs. Jackson, in Washington Place. Some years ago, Sir Joseph Hooker, Director of Kew Gardens, pronounced this tree the finest of its kind in the world. Another perfect specimen, though smaller, is in the grounds of Jas. W. Renwick. Maples, in all their many varieties, constitute the larger part of Flushing's shade trees. Of these, six varieties are native. Of imported Maples, the Japanese Maples are the most conspicuous. Though dwarfed in size, the exquisite shapes and colors of their leaves have made the Japanese Maples a valuable and popular group. They were first introduced by the Parsons Bros., in 1854. Until about fifteen years ago Flushing could boast of English Elms, second only to those on the Boston Commons. Since the appearance of the Elm Beetle, the English Elms have all but disappeared from Long Island. There are still some good specimens of the

American Elm in the village. We have certain trees, interesting because of their rarity. A beautiful row of the Southern Cypress stands in Broadway, in front of the S. B. Parsons place. They were planted by Mr. Parsons about fifty years ago. Especial attention is drawn to the double row of the Chinese Taxodium on Parsons Avenue, just south of Broadway. These trees were planted by Robt. B. Parsons about fifty years ago. There is no such group of these rare trees in the United States. Two magnificent specimens of the Cedar of Lebanon are among our most prized trees. One of these stands in the door-yard of the Prince House, on Bridge street and Lawrence Avenue, and the other is within the limits of the old Bloodgood Nursery, on Bayside Avenue, opposite the Wickham place. These trees are nearly a hundred years old.

Of nut trees, besides our native Chestnut, Walnut and Hickories, we have the Spanish and Japanese Chestnuts, the Butternut, Madeiranut, Pecan, Bitter Almond, and English Filbert. Nearly all of these produce their fruit yearly.

To our native Dogwood are to be added other flowering trees of rare and beautiful varieties, e. g. the exquisite Japanese flowering Apple, Peach and Cherry. But among the flowering trees, the chief glory belongs to the Magnolias, of which we have five native varieties and others chiefly Japanese and Chinese.

Our evergreens—in great and bewildering variety—come from all parts of the world, from Maine, from Oregon, from the Colorado Canons, from the slopes of the Himalayas. They cannot be matched by any similar collection on earth.

Two specimens of Primaeval Oaks still stand, one in State street and one in the Hicks place, on Whitestone Avenue. They belong to the same group as the old Fox

Oaks. The old Oak that, until two years ago, stood in the middle of Parsons Avenue, was estimated by the late Prof. Asa Gray, in 1872, to be about six hundred forty years old.

IX

TITLES OF BOOKS

QUOTED, OR REFERRED TO, IN THIS HISTORY.

[The many other books "consulted" do not appear in this list.]

History of the State of New York, John R. Brodhead 2 vols., New York, 1859, 1871.

History of New Netherland, E. B. O'Callaghan, 2 vols., New York.

Documents Relative to the Colonial History of the State of New York, E. B. O'Callagan, Editor, 14 vols., Albany 1856-1883.

Representation of New Netherland, Adriaen Von der Donck, 1650. Translated by Henry C. Murphy, 1849.

History of Long Island, Benjamin F. Thompson, 2 vols., 1843.

Laws and Ordinances of New Netherland, Albany.

Massachusetts Historical Collections, 41 vols., Boston, 1806-1871.

Documentary History of New York, E. B. O'Callaghan, 4 vols., New York, 1850.

The Annals of Newtown, James Riker, Jr., New York, 1852.

New England History, Chas. W. Elliott, 2 vols, New York, 1857.

History of New England, J. G. Palfrey, 5 vols., Boston, 1858.

Newes from America, John Underhill, London, 1638.

Flushing Past and Present, Rev. G. Henry Mandeville, Flushing, 1860.

Early Long Island, Martha Bockee Flint, New York, 1896.

A Brief Description of New York, Daniel Denton, London, 1670.

Journal of George Fox, Philadelphia, 1832.

Long Island Antiquities, Gabriel Furman.

Register of New Netherland, E. B. O'Callaghan, Albany, 1865.

Quakers on Long Island and in New York, Henry Onderdonk Jr.

Quakers of Hempstead, Henry Onderdonk Jr.

New York. The Planting and Growth of the Empire State, Ellis H. Roberts, Boston and New York, 1887.

Men, Women and Manners in Colonial Times, Sidney George Fisher, Philadelphia, 1898.

A Journal of Travel from New Hampshire to Caratuck, on the Continent of North America, George Keith, London, 1702.

History of St. George's Parish, Flushing, J. Carpenter Smith, Flushing, 1897.

Antiquities of the Parish Church, Jamaica, including Newtown and Flushing, H. Onderdonk, Jr., Jamaica, 1880.

The Friends' Library, 6 vols., Philadelphia, 1839.

History of New York During the Revolutionary War, 2 vols., Thomas Jones, New York, 1879.

Genealogical Notes of the Colden Family, E. P. Purple, New York, 1873.

Biographies of Francis Lewis and Morgan Lewis, Julia Delafield, 2 vols., New York, 1877.

The American Revolution, John Fiske, 2 vols., New York, 1896.

American Archives, 9 vols., Washington, 1837-1851.

The Empire State, B. Lossing, New York.

Journals of the Provincial Congress, 2 vols., Albany, 1842.

History of Queens County, New York, 1882.

Queens County in Olden Times, H. Onderdonk, Jr., Jamaica, 1865.

Documents and Letters to Illustrate Revolutionary Incidents of Queens County, H. Onderdonk, Jr., New York, 1846. Second Series, Hempstead, 1884.

Gazetteer of the State of New York, Thos. G. Gordon, Philadelphia, 1836.

Calendar of Historical Manuscripts, 4 vols., Albany, 1865-1868.

Orderly Book of the Maryland Loyalists Regiment Kept by Capt. Caleb Jones, Brooklyn, 1891.

Letters of the Brunswick and Hessian Officers During the American Revolution, Albany, 1891.

B. F. Steven's Facsimiles of Manuscripts in European Archives Relating to America, 25 vols., London.

A History of the People of the United States, John Bach McMasters, 5 vols., (5th unpublished), New York, 1892-1895.

History of the City of New York, Mrs. Martha J. Lamb and Mrs. Burton Harrison, 3 vols., New York.

Diary of George Washington, Richmond, 1861.

Life and Work of William Augustus Muhlenberg, Anne Ayres, New York, 1881.

Reminiscences of the War of the Rebellion, Bvt. Maj. Jacob Roemer, L. A. Furney, Editor, Flushing, 1897.

Manuscript History of the Society of Friends in Queens County, H. Onderdonk, Jr. In the Archives of the Westbury Meeting.

Minutes of Friends' Meetings, Previous to 1805, In the Archives of the Sixteenth street Meeting House, N. Y.

Minutes of Friends' Meetings, since 1805, In the Archives of the Westbury Meeting.

Historical Collections of the State of New York, J. W. Barber, New York, 1851.

INDEX

This Index contains references to the notes and the Appendix, as well as to the History.

C

G

H

S

T

U

V

W

www.ingramcontent.com/pod-product-compliance
Lightning Source LLC
Chambersburg PA
CBHW021038030726
47496CB00006B/1599
9783337369187